Cherished By You

Steph Nuss

STEPH NUSS

CHERISHED BY YOU

Copyright 2015 by Steph Nuss

All rights reserved.

This book is a work of fiction. Any references to historical events, real people, or real locales are used fictitiously. Other names, characters, places, and incidents are the product of the author's imagination, and any resemblance to actual events or locales or persons, living or dead, is entirely coincidental.

STEPH NUSS

Prologue

Tessa

"Tess? Tessa?"

The memories from the sex dream I had the night before flashed through my mind. I shook them away and focused on my brother, Treylor, who sat across from me at the dining room table. "Yeah? What's up?"

He laughed, shoveling cereal onto his spoon. "Did you hear anything I just said?"

"Nothing before my name," I confessed with a smile.

Dropping the spoon back into his bowl, the smile on his face fell as his expression turned serious. Whatever he'd been talking about was important, and I instantly felt bad for spacing out over breakfast.

"Well, I'm listening now," I prompted, taking a sip of my orange juice.

Trey leaned his elbows on the table and sighed. "I've been thinking about moving out."

The silence that flooded the room was palpable. I honestly wasn't expecting those words to come out of his mouth. Trey was only five years younger than me, and currently a sophomore in college. He had a part-time job and attended NYU full-time. I practically raised him since I was a little girl because our parents were rarely sober, and here he sat telling me he wanted to move out. Breakfast churned in my belly as I placed my cup back on the table.

"Josh has been wanting to move out of his parents' place for a while now," he continued. "But he can't afford a place on his own, so he asked me if I'd be interested. And honestly, Tess, I am."

I nodded silently. I knew this day would come, so I couldn't understand why it was such a shock to me now. We were both adults, and every kid eventually wanted to leave the nest. It wasn't the crappy, drugged-out nest our parents built; it was the home I made for us at the meager age of eighteen when I gained full responsibility for a thirteen-year-old after losing both our parents. My boss at the diner where I worked got us into this rent-controlled apartment in Chinatown, while the rest of the building paid a pretty penny to call this place home.

And now Trey didn't want to live here anymore.

It was heartbreaking for me.

Especially since we lived so close to campus for him.

"Would you please say something?" he asked with a hint of humor. "You're starting to freak me out."

I smiled weakly. "Has Josh found a place yet?"

"No, he didn't want to start looking until he found a roommate," he explained.

"I see." I nodded again, feeling as if I'd been blindsided by all of this. How long had Trey been thinking about moving out? Did he really not like living here, or did he just want his independence like Josh? None of that really mattered given the fact that he wasn't a minor anymore. He was free to do whatever he wanted, and he definitely wasn't asking for my permission. I just hated the thought of him leaving, not for my sake but for his. He had everything going for him right now. He was doing well in school and had a great job as building security for the Madison Square Garden Company. Elly's dad helped him get the job last year. It paid well, but apartments in the city weren't cheap.

"Tessa," he stated, giving me his adorable boy smirk. "You know how much I love and appreciate everything you've done for me."

"I know," I said, rolling my eyes.

"I just think this could be perfect for us because you've never been on your own either. I mean, you could host girls' nights or bring a guy home and not have to worry about freaking out your little bro while you guys go at it."

"Treylor!"

Laughing, he shrugged his shoulders. "I'm just saying, I think this would be good for you, too. Not just me. I've loved living with you, but you know I'll be fine living on my own. You've taught me how to cook, how to do my laundry, how to respect my neighbors and protect myself. And with this place being so cheap, you wouldn't even have to get a roommate if you didn't want to."

I nodded understandingly. For years, I'd put my life on hold to worry about Trey's, and he knew it. I never complained because I loved taking care of him and teaching him things and making sure his homework was done. Our parents never gave two fucks about those fundamentals. They only cared about themselves and their substance abuse.

I loved being an older sister, which was why I suggested, "Why don't you guys take this place and I'll move out?"

"Tessa—"

"Just hear me out," I stated, as I gathered our dishes. "You can walk to school and work from here, and it's affordable for both you and Josh because it's under rent control. It's a great neighborhood and, honestly, I'd feel better knowing that you're living in a safe neighborhood rather than some hole-in-the-wall dump because it's all you two can afford while going to school full-time and only working part-time."

"So, I'll go to school part—"

"No, Treylor," I snapped, glaring back at him. "You're getting a college degree. I'm not going to let you throw away your education just for some independence!"

"Okay, okay," he said, leaning back in his chair. "So, you'd move out? Where would you live? I don't want you in some dump, either."

"I'll find something nice."

"And who are you going to live with?" he asked. "I don't want you living with some nut job off of Craigslist. There are serial killers on there, you know."

He watched one Lifetime docudrama with me, and now he was terrified of Craigslist. "I'm sure I can find some inexpensive place to live on my own."

"I know I just suggested it, but I don't really like the idea of you living alone," he stated.

Smiling, I started rinsing the dishes and loading them into the dishwasher. "I think I can handle it. I *am* the one who taught you how to throw a punch."

He laughed out loud, stood up from his seat and walked into the kitchen. Leaning against the counter, he smiled down at me, which reminded me just how grown-up he was now that I had to look up to meet his eyes. "You're the best sister in the world, you know that?"

I playfully punched his hard stomach and smiled. "And don't you forget it!"

Chapter One

Tessa

I spent the morning at work searching online for apartments, which caused a ball of anxiety to tighten in my stomach as reality smacked me in the face. I knew living in the city was expensive, but I didn't think it was *that* expensive. I'd found studio apartments, where the bathroom and kitchen were practically in the same room, and I still couldn't afford them. I was one second away from a cry fest when Justin Jameson and Carter Jennings walked into Elly's psych clinic for lunch. Just the sight of Justin in his professor ensemble brightened my day. He paired brown loafers with khaki pants that hung from his lean hips. The navy blue sweater vest over his light-blue plaid button-down highlighted his wiry frame and made his hazel-blue eyes pop against his tan skin. His long, sandy blond hair was pulled back into a low ponytail, his normal work style. To some, his appearance probably wasn't sexy in the slightest, but it was one of my favorites.

Ever since Carter had moved back to the city last year, he and Justin spent most of their lunch breaks at Elly's clinic. It wasn't too far away from NYU, where they both taught. Now that Carter and Elly were married and expecting their first child together, not a day went by that he missed having lunch with her.

"Hey, Tessa," Carter said, placing their bags on the table in the lobby.

"Hey, guys," I said, smiling politely. I was in no mood to have lunch with anyone, even my friends, so I decided to forgo the sandwich I'd packed and continue apartment hunting. "Elly's last patient just left, so she should be out in a minute."

"Okay," Carter said, taking a seat. He started unpacking the lunch he'd brought, a smile proudly stamped across his face. Justin sat across from him, doctoring his sandwich with dressing.

Elly soon appeared in the lobby, rocking an adorable black dress that slightly hid her baby bump. "Hey, guys!"

"Hey, babe," Carter said, as Justin offered her a silent nod.

She immediately greeted Carter with a kiss and plopped down in the seat next to him. "What'd you bring us today?" she asked, rubbing her belly.

"A turkey sub without mayo this time," he replied.

"Oh good, because Baby Jennings is not a fan of mayonnaise," she said with a cringe as she unwrapped the paper. "Did you get the vinegar and oil and oregano?"

Carter laughed. "Of course."

"I love you," she said, offering him another kiss. She turned her attention toward me and smiled. "Tessa, are you going to eat with us?"

I sighed and shook my head. "Nah, I'm not really hungry."

"How are you not hungry?" Elly asked, before taking a bite of her sub.

Well, I wasn't eating for two, and the reality check of apartment hunting had completely stolen my appetite.

"What are you looking up on there?" Carter asked, nodding toward my computer.

Leaning back in my chair, I gazed over at my friends and confessed. "Trey wants to move out and get a place with a friend, but I told him they could have my place and I would find something. So, I'm apartment hunting now."

"Are you having any luck?" Elly asked.

"Not really," I said gravely. "Even the crappier places I've found are on the higher end of my budget. I had no idea how expensive apartments were now. Living under rent control will do that to a person."

"You know, I could give you a raise," Elly said, smiling genuinely. "But you'll probably just say you don't need one, so why don't you move in with us for the time being?"

"No, I don't deserve a raise, and I couldn't do that to you guys. You just got married a few months ago, and you have a baby on the way. Thanks for the offer, but I just can't."

"Okay," Elly said, rolling her eyes. "But the offer still stands. You're always welcome."

"I know," I said, turning my attention back to my computer screen. I decided to widen my search to other boroughs, so I began looking there while they ate in comfortable silence.

"What about Paige?" Elly asked. "She has a spare bedroom at her place."

"You lived with Paige back in college," I stated. "You really think she wants a roommate now? She couldn't wait to find her own place once you guys graduated."

"True," she said.

"Speaking of Paige," Carter said. "Where is she? She usually has lunch with us."

Paige had texted me earlier, saying she had a lunch meeting for work. Elly and I shared a glance, and then she turned to Carter and sighed. "She had a work lunch she had to attend today, and she'll probably have them until the baby arrives. She's avoiding me now that she knows I'm pregnant."

"Are you serious?" Carter asked, brows furrowed.

"Carter," Elly warned, shaking her head.

"Whatever," he stated, taking a bite of his sub. "She needs to get over whatever issues she has with babies. Everyone loves babies."

"Some people prefer a child-free lifestyle," she continued. "We've talked about this."

"I know, but she's one of our friends," he argued. "All I'm saying is that she shouldn't feel the need to avoid us for nine months."

Elly smiled at him and then playfully took a bite of her sandwich and asked with a mouthful, "Can we please drop this so I can go back to enjoying my lunch?"

"Yes," he laughed, placing a chaste kiss on her cheek. "Fuel up, babe."

I laughed as I scrolled through the apartment listings. I'd been spoiled for too long, and now I was paying for it. I worked full-time as Elly's receptionist, and I still couldn't afford any of these places. I couldn't imagine what dump Trey and Josh would've ended up finding on their measly part-time paychecks.

"Move in with me."

Turning my head back toward the table, I looked up in shock and found Justin staring back at me. "W-what?"

"I said, you can move in with me."

I couldn't possibly live with Justin Jameson, especially not after the sex dream I had starring him the night before. I had the world's biggest crush on him, and it'd somehow moved into wet dream territory. How the hell was I supposed to live with him?

"I can't," I said shyly, shaking my head. "I-um-I don't know if I can aff—"

"I have an extra bedroom," he explained. "I've never had a roommate before, but I think we could make it work. Plus, I think I speak for everyone when I say I can't let one of my friends live in a box just because it's in her budget."

Great. Now, I'm his charity case.

"Thanks, but I don't think I can afford even half your rent."

Justin lived in a nice condo near Washington Square. The building had a doorman and included amenities like a spa and housecleaners. It also had a five-star restaurant and a lounge in the lobby. I probably couldn't even afford a third of the rent at a place like his.

"You wouldn't have to worry about rent," he stated, his smile widening. "I bought the condo years ago, so it's mine now."

Of course, he had it paid off already. Justin came from ridiculously smart, rich parents who authored science textbooks now. Apparently, they'd been genius scientists back when he was younger, but they'd since retired to write. He never talked about them and we'd never met them. All I knew was that they passed all of their intelligence on to him, which led to Justin entering college at the age of fourteen. Now, after acquiring several doctorate degrees in various fields, he was 30-years-old and already tenured at NYU.

I didn't even graduate high school.

"I can't just live with you for free," I said, feeling my cheeks heat with embarrassment.

"Why not?" he asked earnestly.

Carter and Elly quietly watched us as if they were watching a tennis match, back and forth, with considerable interest.

"I-I don't know," I stuttered, nervously playing with the buttons on my keyboard. "I would feel like I owe you, and I don't want to be some charity case."

Justin sat back in his seat and gave me a smirk. "You're no one's charity case. You're my friend."

My heart sank at the mention of our friendship. Sadly, *friends* were all we'd ever be.

Get over it already, Tess.

"If it makes you feel better, we can split the utilities or groceries or whatever," he said, before popping a chip in his mouth.

I watched as he chewed, smiling back at me, and the knot of anxiety that had settled in my stomach quickly crawled up into my throat. His sweetness was one of the things I loved most about him. He would do anything to help anyone. He didn't have a mean bone in his body. But God, it would be impossible to live with him, feeling the way I did about him.

Justin was a man of habit: he wasn't too keen on change. So, the fact that he even offered me his guest bedroom was a huge step for him, especially since he'd never had a roommate. We were opposites in almost every way. He came from money and intelligence; I came from parents who abused drugs and alcohol. He had several academic degrees; I only had my GED. Where he was the silent observer of our group of friends, I was our social butterfly, always chatting away and eager to go out and have fun.

For years now, I'd believed he deserved a woman more like himself, but my beliefs couldn't deter my feelings for him. He had no idea how I felt about him, and I chalked it up to his obliviousness to women and the effect he had on us.

"I think this is perfect!" Elly cheered. She gazed over at me excitedly, and I sent daggers her way. She knew how I felt. She knew he favored consistency. Yet, she was encouraging this living arrangement.

"What do you say, Tessa?" Carter asked with a smile.

The three of them stared at me, silently begging for my answer. Justin looked slightly amused, as if he couldn't figure out why I even had to think about it. Carter appeared as eager as his wife, which made me question what he knew about my feelings toward Justin. Elly's gaze never waived, pleading with me to agree.

So, I did.

"Okay," I replied, nodding stiffly.

"Yay!" Elly squealed, clapping her hands. "When can she move in, Justin?"

He laughed, smiling back at me. "As soon as you want. The room is already furnished, but you're welcome to change anything and make it your own."

You're welcome to change anything. Who was this guy and where did Dr. I-Hate-Change go?

"Thanks," I offered. "I really appreciate it."

"Maybe we can help you move in this weekend?" Elly suggested.

"No," Carter rebuked, shaking his head at her. "You will not be helping with anything. You can just sit back and relax with our baby."

"I'm pregnant, Carter; I'm not debilitated!"

"I know," he said, sliding his hand over her bump. "I just don't want anything to happen to either one of you. You can just order us around while we move Tessa in. How does that sound?"

"Perfect!"

"Great," Justin muttered, unenthusiastically. "Just what we want—a woman ordering us around."

"Don't act like you don't like it, Jameson," Carter teased, wrapping his arm around Elly's shoulders and pulling her closer. He placed a kiss on her temple and then stood from his seat. "We should be getting back to work."

Elly pulled him back down for a longer kiss and then swatted him on the butt. "Okay, I'll see you later. Love you."

"Love you," he said, smiling down at her.

Justin cleaned up the table, discarded their trash, and then came over to my desk and leaned up against it. "So, are we moving you in this weekend then?"

I sighed. "Yeah, I think the sooner, the better. You know teenagers. They want their independence. The sooner I'm out, the quicker Josh can move in."

"I understand," he laughed.

Gazing into his beautiful, bright blue eyes, I smiled. "Thanks again for offering me your spare room. I probably would've ended up in a box in the Bronx again."

"You deserve much more than that," he replied. Then he pushed away from my desk and walked toward the door with Carter. "See you later, roomie!"

Laughing, I waved at them as they exited Elly's clinic. "Bye, guys!"

Once they were gone, Elly rushed over to my desk and perched on the edge, wearing a huge grin and laughing. "This is probably the best thing that could've ever happened to you!"

"No, it's not," I muttered, rolling my eyes. "How am I supposed to live with him, Elly? I've been in love with him for years, and he doesn't even know it! He completely ignores any of my advances or flirting."

"Justin's introverted," she explained. "I think once you move in with him, you'll see a totally different side of each other, and I mean that in a good way. He's really quiet when we're all together, but one-on-one, I think he'll open up to you. He may act like he's oblivious, but no guy can live with a woman he's not related to and not think about having sex with her."

"Oh my God, I never even thought about all the crap he's going to learn about me. Like my period schedule. Am I supposed to keep my tampons in his bathroom or hide them in my bedroom? See, nothing in his place will be mine!

Everything is *his* because it's *his* place that *he* bought! Do you understand what I'm saying?"

"Yes," she sighed, rolling her eyes. "And I think you're freaking out over nothing! Justin is an adult. He knows you have a period. Leave your tampons wherever you want. It's not like he's going to have the nerve to tell you to put them somewhere else."

When I just stared at her, she continued. "I about choked on my food when he said you could move in. This is progress for him, Tessa! He's never had a roommate before, so he wouldn't have offered if he didn't want you there."

"You know, I'm really starting to hate this positive, no worries side of you," I mumbled, shaking my head.

"Hakuna matata!" she cheered with a little shake of her hips, causing us both to break out in laughter.

Chapter Two

Tessa

I spent the rest of the week packing all of my clothes and personal belongings. Since Justin's spare room was fully furnished, I was leaving behind my bedroom set for Josh. So, I really didn't have much to move. Trey was keeping all of the living room furniture and kitchenware that we'd acquired over the years, and with all of my knickknacks already tucked away in a suitcase, the apartment was starting to look like a bachelor pad.

I prayed that the boys would take care of the place.

Stepping out of my room, I found Trey in the kitchen cooking my favorite: chicken quesadillas. Earlier, we had gone grocery shopping together one last time because I couldn't leave without knowing the shelves and fridge were fully stocked. He'd offered to cook dinner because it was my last night in the apartment.

"So you all packed and ready?" he asked, leaning against the counter.

"Yes, you're ready to get rid of me, aren't you?" I teased, taking a sip of my strawberry margarita.

"That's not it, and you know it," he laughed.

"Promise me you guys won't trash this place. That you'll keep it in good condition and won't throw a bunch of parties or do college stuff."

"College stuff," he smirked. "I promise, Tess. There's no way I won't take care of the home you built for us."

I took a seat at the dining table and relaxed. "Thank you."

"So," he started, turning his back to me as he focused on flipping a quesadilla, "this guy you're moving in with is a friend?"

"Yes, just a friend," I said, smiling. "He teaches at NYU."

He glanced over his shoulder at me. "What's he teach?"

"Psychology."

"Really? I'm taking General Psych this semester." He grabbed two plates, slid a quesadilla onto each, and carried them over to the table. "What'd you say his last name was again?"

"Jameson," I said, rolling my eyes. "Justin Jameson."

Laughing, he sat across from me and took the pitcher of margarita mix and filled his glass. "You're friends with Dr. Jameson? How did I not know this?"

"Probably because you don't pay attention."

"Whatever," he replied. "And you're going to live with him?"

"Yes," I said with a frown. "What's your deal? Why the twenty questions?"

"I just think it's funny how I've never heard you talk about this friend, Justin, and now you're moving in with him."

He took a bite out of his food and smirked. "You know, you don't have to hide your boyfriends anymore, right? I'm not a kid."

Tossing a chip at him, I hit him in the face and laughed. "He's not my boyfriend. He's seriously just a friend!"

"Your face just turned the color of these margaritas!" he exclaimed, pointing at me. "You like him!"

"Shut up!" I stated sharply. "You're ruining my last night in this place!"

"Oh, whatever, I bet you can't wait to move in with Dr. Jameson," he teased.

Shaking my head, I sneered. "Don't call him that."

"What else am I supposed to call my teacher? What do you call him? Dr. Hot Pants?"

I stopped mid-bite and dropped my fork. "He's your teacher? Seriously?"

"Yeah, every Monday, Wednesday, and Friday," he answered.

I downed the rest of my drink and poured another as Trey watched me from across the table, holding back whatever joke was sitting on the tip of his tongue.

"You're not helping me move tomorrow," I said.

His brows furrowed as he leaned back in his chair. "The hell I'm not. I don't care that he's my teacher. It's not like I'm going to ask you to sleep with him to boost my grade or anything like that."

"Treylor!"

"What? Psychology isn't my best subject, sue me!" he exclaimed, and then shoveled a forkful of food into his mouth.

"I would never do that."

"And I would never ask you to," he said, rolling his eyes. "I was joking. I mean, I'm not a fan of Psych, but it's a required class I have to take."

I nodded, and then we both went back to eating in silence. The TV was on in the background, but all I could focus on was the fact that Justin was Trey's teacher. As if it wasn't enough that I had feelings for him, the world had to go and make him my brother's professor.

"You know, the only reason I want to come tomorrow is so I can see your new place, meet your roommate, and make sure you're going to be safe. I've never actually talked to the guy before, but I swear I won't say anything about you having the hots for him."

My chair scraped across the floor as I stood from my seat and smiled over at him. "Fine. You can come. But I do not have the hots for him."

"I know," he droned dramatically. "You've told me three times. Shut up about him already!"

Laughing, I grabbed my plate and walked it over to the sink. "You're such a dick sometimes. I'm so glad I'm moving out!"

"Oh, I'm sure you are!" he laughed, wiggling his eyebrows suggestively. His laughter escalated as I walked out of the room, shaking my head. "You walked right into that one, Tess!"

***

It was my last night in my bedroom, and I couldn't sleep. I tossed and turned for most of the night. Hot one minute, cold the next. The sheets were a tangled mess around me as I stared up at the ceiling, tired but too nervous to sleep. All I could think about was Justin.

He'd never given me the impression he didn't want me, but he didn't flirt or come on to me the way other guys did either, which I loved and hated simultaneously. I loved that he wasn't like the guys I'd fallen for before. Those guys were selfish assholes who treated me like crap most of the time, and I'd let them. Justin was a good guy: someone you'd want to spend every minute of every day with because he cherished you undeniably. But I hated how he kept everything to himself. While he quietly observed the rest of the world, he rarely let anyone into his. Just once, I wanted him to let me in, but I feared if I ever told him how I felt, I'd still be denied access to his wonderful mind.

I wasn't sure I could handle such a rejection, which was why I'd spent most of the night telling myself I needed to try to move on. Surely there were other guys in the city just as good as Justin Jameson. I just needed to put myself out there and try to find one. I would never find my happily ever after if I kept pining after Justin.

Grabbing my laptop from the nightstand, I sat up, propping it open. I brought up a search box and typed "online dating sites." This gave me a list of various websites claiming they were the number one site for finding true love. I rolled my eyes as I strolled through the findings. After a while, I shut my laptop in frustration and leaned back against my headboard, blinking back tears.

Online dating, Tessa? Really? This is what it's come to?

Yes.

Ever since Justin Jameson entered our group of friends, I'd stopped looking for a guy. I fell for him almost immediately, with his boyish smile and adorable dimples. His laid-back personality exuded a cool, relaxed presence. He was the total package, in my opinion: sweet and humble, nice and respectable. So, I ignored other guys' advances in hopes that I could eventually grab his attention.

Years later, I still didn't have his attention, and I knew he would never cross the line of friendship/roommate with me now.

Opening my laptop, I clicked on a link and closed my eyes.

You can do this. Online dating is the new thing now; everyone's doing it.

I opened my eyes, took a deep, reassuring breath, and began creating my profile and taking the personality test.

Time to get back in the dating game!

Chapter Three

Justin

"I can't believe you agreed to live with a woman," Cash said, sitting down on the couch in my living room with a beer in his hand.

It was Saturday afternoon, and most of the gang was over at my place, waiting for Tessa and her brother to arrive so we could help move all of her stuff in. Maverick and Harper were at home with their baby girl, Seghen, and Paige had a work function with a client.

I really couldn't believe it either. I'd never had a roommate before who wasn't some sort of family member, but I knew I didn't want Tessa living in some dilapidated hole in Grand Concourse again. Just hearing her talk about growing up there pissed me off.

"Living with a woman isn't so bad," Carter stated proudly, with his arm slung over Elly's shoulder. "They make the place smell good. They're nice to look at."

"They cook," Fletcher added, rubbing Bayler's thigh. They weren't living together yet, but they stayed together enough that he enjoyed the benefits of Bayler's excellent cooking skills.

"Not all of them cook," Carter retorted, nodding his head toward his wife.

"Hey!" Elly exclaimed, smacking him in the stomach. "I'm cooking your baby right now."

The room filled with laughter as I paced over to the window and looked down at the sidewalk. I was nervous because I wasn't sure whether or not Tessa would like living with me. I'd had the place cleaned twice this week in anticipation of her arrival.

"But Tessa loves cooking," Elly continued, smiling up at me. "You can finally stop eating out every night."

I scoffed, glancing over my shoulder at her. "I don't eat out every night."

Bayler laughed. "All you have in your fridge are takeout boxes and condiments."

"And beer!" Carter said, clinking his bottle with Fletcher's.

"Ladies," Fletcher stated, shaking his head at the women. "Jameson has the necessities. Lay off him."

"Tessa is going to freak when she sees the fridge," Elly said, laughing along with Bayler.

I turned to face the gang as anxiety tumbled in my stomach. "What do you mean? Why would she freak out?"

"Because Tessa enjoys cooking," Bayler explained.

"Yeah," Elly said, nodding. "She's used to having a stocked kitchen, especially since she's cooked for her and her brother most of her life."

Now I felt bad about not going grocery shopping. The truth was, I did order takeout often, only because it was easier than attempting to cook a meal. I'd grown up with either a maid cooking for me or my grandma, but no matter how many times Janice Jameson tried to teach me how to cook, the meal never turned out the way she made it.

"You guys can go grocery shopping later," Cash said, running through the television channels. "That way she can pick out whatever the hell she wants."

"Maybe she'll even teach you how to cook," Elly teased, nudging my arm.

"Yeah," Bayler continued, pointing her beer bottle at me. "Every guy should know how to cook. Women love a home-cooked meal they don't have to make themselves."

"I'm not trying to find a woman," I stated, furrowing my brows.

The gang laughed at my candid response, despite the fact that it was true. I'd practically given up on finding a good woman during my college years. The girls I seemed to attract back then only wanted my help passing a class. The only date I'd been on since was a few years ago when my grandma set me up with her neighbor, Elly. The chemistry wasn't there, so we became friends instead, which was perfectly fine with me. She was still in love with Carter, and I'd been a loner most of my life. When Carter moved back to New York, he and Elly started dating, and I gained another friend. Our group of friends continued to grow after that with the addition of Carter's sisters, Harper and Bayler, falling for two of our own, Maverick and Fletcher.

"I call bullshit, Justin," Bayler exclaimed, rolling her eyes. She leaned into Fletcher's side and rested her feet up on the coffee table.

The laughter quickly died down at her blunt retort.

"Excuse me?" I asked, deflecting my surprise.

"All men are predisposed to think with their penises," she explained, entertaining everyone with her words. "I don't care how much of a genius you are; you're still a man, which means that brain of yours down south is focused on sex just like every other man's."

Laughter grew louder around me as I stared her down, the smile spreading wide across my face. We got a kick out of giving each other a hard time, and I enjoyed dishing it out just as much as everyone else. Leaning down next to her ear, I said, "No, Bayler, what I meant was, I don't have to *try* to find a woman."

She nearly spit out her beer as she smacked me on the arm and laughed. "See! Just like every other guy! I knew you had a dick in there somewhere, Jameson."

"Is this the part where I tell you I know how to use it, too?" I asked sarcastically, laughing along with her.

A knock on the door sounded before she could reply, so I walked over to answer it. Opening the door, I found Tessa and a younger guy standing behind her, with three suitcases resting at their sides and a duffle bag slung across his body. She wore an old pair of ripped jeans and a hoodie. Her long brown hair was knotted on top of her head, but it was her light blue-gray eyes smiling back at me that caught my attention the most.

"Hey," I said, grabbing one of the rollers. "Come on in."

"Thanks," she said, crossing the threshold into my apartment.

"Holy shit, this place is nice!" the kid exclaimed, marching in behind her with the rest of her things. For some reason, the guy looked familiar, but I couldn't place where I'd seen him before.

Tessa laughed lightly and rolled her eyes at the guy. "Guys, this is my brother, Trey. Trey, this is everyone."

"Hey, everyone," he said with a wave.

Each of us introduced ourselves. Then Elly and Bayler got up and grabbed Tessa's suitcases as Tessa took the bag from her brother's shoulder.

"Is that all you brought, Tessa?" Fletcher asked, eyeing the luggage skeptically. "Is there more back at your place that we need to go get?"

"No, this is it. I didn't have much," she said with a shrug.

"Oh," he said.

Bayler leaned over his shoulder and rustled his hair. "Don't get any ideas, Haney. You don't even want to know how much shit I have, so don't think about asking me to move in with you."

"Fine," he said, grabbing the back of her neck. He pulled her down to his mouth for a kiss and then let her go. "Let us know if you girls need any help with anything."

"I'm sure we won't," she retorted.

"Elly, remember what we talked about," Carter called from the couch, pointing his beer at her. "No heavy lifting."

She rolled her eyes at him and scoffed. "I'll be fine. Just sit back and enjoy the game."

"Come on," I said, shaking my head at them. "I'll show you guys to the room."

The girls followed me into the hallway, down to the second door on the right. They'd been here many times to hang out, but rarely did they go into any other room besides the living room, kitchen and bathroom.

"This is it," I said, opening the door to my guest bedroom.

Bayler and Elly quickly entered the room, rolling the luggage behind them. Tessa hung back and admired the room from the doorway.

I leaned against the doorjamb and smiled down at her. "Like I said, feel free to change anything you don't like. I want you to feel at home here."

"Thanks, Justin," she said, for the millionth time this week, and I was growing tired of it.

"You're welcome, again," I said, nudging her arm. "You don't have to keep thanking me, you know. I'm happy to have you here."

She blushed, shaking her head. "This room is twice the size of my old one."

"Then I'll leave so you girls can enjoy filling it up with all your stuff."

"Hey, Tessa?"

At the sound of Trey's voice in the hallway, we turned and found him walking our way.

"I want to see this new crib of yours," he said, playfully grabbing her shoulders. "Wow. Is that a king-sized bed? And a sixty-inch flat screen? Screw this, Tess. You can have the apartment back. I'll move in with Dr. Jameson."

Hearing my professional name fall from the kid's mouth made me do a double take.

Was he in one of my lectures?

"Trey, I told you not to call him that," Tessa stressed, shaking her head. She looked up at me, her teeth worrying her bottom lip. "I'm sorry. He's a sophomore at NYU and he's—"

"I'm in your Monday, Wednesday, Friday nine o'clock class," he interjected.

"That's where I've seen you before," I stated with a smile. I hardly remembered any of the students who came to class, mostly because a third of them rarely showed up, but Trey hadn't missed a single lecture since school started. I couldn't forget the faces of students who diligently attended every lecture. "Why don't we grab a beer and let your sister unpack?"

"Okay!" he exclaimed.

"I don't think so!" Tessa sang. She pinched her brother's cheek and smiled at me. "This one's only nineteen. No alcohol."

"Oh, come on, Tess!" he cracked, rolling his eyes. "It's one beer."

"Let the kid have a beer!" Cash yelled from the living room.

"Yeah, Mom!" Fletcher continued, laughing.

"Please!" Carter begged, joining in on the harassment.

She sighed audibly and then pointed at Trey. "One, okay? That's it."

"Gotcha," he said, giving her a salute. "Thanks, sis!"

"Come on," I urged, pushing him back toward the living room.

"I'm sorry," Tessa giggled beside me. "He can be such a shit sometimes."

"Don't worry about it. I can handle Trey and the rat pack." I smiled back at her and nodded toward her room. "Go unpack. I'll get you something to drink, and if you need anything else, just holler."

"Okay, thanks."

When I entered the open main room, I found Trey leaning against the island, checking out the kitchen cabinets, while the rest of the guys sat in the living room watching the game. I joined Trey in the kitchen and grabbed a beer for him and Tessa.

"Here you go," I said, handing it to him.

"Thanks, man" he said, as he popped the top off and took a swig. "Your place is really nice; I know Tessa will like it here. I appreciate you letting her move in with you."

"I'm happy to have her here," I replied, taking a drink of my own beer as I studied him. From the moment he walked through my door, he seemed like an upbeat guy. But now, as I watched him pick at the silver label of the beer bottle, his rootless features gave away his guilt. "You know she loves you. She wouldn't have agreed to move out if she didn't."

"I know," he said with a weak smile. "I just didn't think she'd give me our place. There was no talking her out of it, either. I tried. She's just so stubborn sometimes."

Laughing, I nodded along in agreement. She'd nearly turned down my offer just because I wouldn't let her pay rent. *She's stubborn all right.* "She just wants what's best for you."

"What about what's best for her?" he asked, quizzically.

"What do you mean?" I asked, studying him more closely now. "She'll be safe here, I promise. If that's what you're worried about."

"It's not," he said, shaking his head. "It's just that — never mind. If I told you, she'd probably kill me. She never talks about it, so I'm sure none of her friends know."

His words interested me more than they should. I probably should've just let it go, because if Tessa wanted us to know whatever the hell he was talking about, she would've told us, but she was my roommate now and I had to know what worried him. "Know what?"

He turned his anxious gaze toward the hall for a second and then stared back at me. "I'm only telling you because you're going to be the one living with her now, and I don't know what else to do. She would seriously have my balls if she found out I told you though."

"I won't say anything," I promised.

Taking a deep chug of his beer, he finished it off and set it aside. He spoke in a low, soft tone. "Tessa has these nightmares sometimes. She hasn't had one in a while, but when she does, she just cries uncontrollably in her sleep. I don't know why or what brings it on because she won't talk to me about it, but I just thought you should know because the only way to calm her down is to lay in bed with her and rub her back to let her know she isn't alone. Our mom used to do that whenever one of us couldn't sleep. I'm not saying you have to calm her down. I just wanted you to know so if she ever has one, you can call me."

He handed me a piece of paper with a number on it, and I quickly slipped it into the front pocket of my jeans. "Thanks. I'm glad you told me."

"Told you what?" Tessa asked curiously, walking into the kitchen. She examined our surprised expressions and smiled. "What have you guys been talking about?"

Trey cleared his throat and replied, "I was just telling him that I'm a photography major, you know, so he'd understand that psych isn't my strongest subject and maybe cut me some slack."

I laughed, mentally commending his ability to lie on cue and praying she bought it.

Tessa rolled her eyes. "Justin, don't cut him anything."

"Hey, he already provided alcohol to an underage student," he explained mischievously. "I was seconds away from blackmailing him into upping my C to a B."

"Sure you were," Tessa countered, shaking her head. She smiled over her shoulder at me and asked, "Did you get lost with my drink or is a girl just supposed to help herself around here?"

"You live here now," Trey said, motioning to the fridge. "I think you can help yourself."

Laughing at their sibling banter, I popped the lid off the extra beer in my hand and offered it to her. "Sorry, I got held up by your brother's conniving ways."

"She taught me everything I know," he teased, laughing to himself.

"Don't believe a word he says." She lifted the beer to her lips and tipped it back to quench her thirst.

The grin on my face widened. "I won't."

Without another word, she wandered back out of the kitchen, and Trey and I immediately relaxed.

"Nice cover-up," I praised, giving him a high five.

His smile turned smug. "Been covering up shit around her for years."

"I heard that!" Tessa yelled from the hallway, causing us both to nearly jump out of our skin. "And I will find out what you two were talking about!"

I grabbed another beer for myself and then nodded toward the living room. "Let's just play it safe and watch the game with the guys."

"All right," he laughed.

"But thank you for letting me know," I said quietly, patting him on the shoulder. "I promise she'll be all right here."

"Thanks. I appreciate you saying that."

***

Tessa

When I entered my room again, I found two sets of eyes glaring at me. Elly was sitting on the bed with my laptop in her lap, and Bayler was standing next to her looking equally pissed.

"What the fuck is this shit?" Bayler asked, pointing to the screen.

"Please tell me you aren't seriously considering online dating!" Elly shrieked.

I must've left the site up from last night when I finished making my profile.

Taking another long chug from my beer, I downed at least half of it and then walked over to the bed. I quickly grabbed my laptop out of Elly's hands, closed it and slipped it back inside its sleeve.

"That's none of your business," I snapped, placing it on top of the desk.

"The hell it isn't," Bayler said, taking a seat next to Elly. She stretched her legs out on the gray comforter and crossed her ankles. "Why in God's name would you sign up for online dating? Especially now that you're living with your dream guy."

Rolling my eyes, I plopped down into the chair at the desk and sighed. "I need to try and get over him. I can't even tell you the last time I went out on a date, let alone the last time I got laid by a guy who wasn't battery operated."

"Tessa," Elly said softly, shaking her head. "What's gotten into you lately? You're usually so positive when it comes to relationships, and now you don't even want to give Justin a try?"

"You really think he's going to cross that line with me now?" I asked harshly. "Because I certainly don't. We're friends, and now we're roommates. Justin would never chance burning those bridges, and you know it."

"So, you're throwing out the blueprints for the one bridge you haven't even tried building with him yet?"

"Why are we talking in code?" Bayler asked in a frustrated tone. "The guys are watching football. They're not going to hear a damn thing we're talking about."

"She's right," Elly said, taking a deep breath. "Why are you so quick to give up on him? If I'd given up on Carter years ago, we wouldn't be happily married and expecting a baby right now. You encouraged me to be with him when he moved back. Hell, you started planning our wedding the minute you heard he was back in my life. What happened to that girl?"

"She had a reality check."

"Well, dating other guys isn't going to make your feelings for him go away," Bayler stated, her green eyes piercing me. "Trust me, I gave up on Fletcher, thinking I didn't need him, only to find out that I do. My life is better with him in it. Justin's part of your life just as much as you're part of his, now more than ever. What makes you think that's going to change if you tell him how you feel?"

"Because I'm 'the scrappy one,'" I muttered, kicking one of my empty suitcases. I knew my friends jokingly called me "the scrappy one," but it was true. "I wasn't cut from the same cloth the rest of you were. I didn't grow up in a nice home with wonderful parents who set up trust funds for their children. I didn't graduate high school and go on to follow my dreams. I've scraped through life."

"You haven't had it easy."

Elly would know. We became friends after I finished the counseling program I was ordered to take when I was eighteen.

"Did you see the way Fletcher looked at my three suitcases? Like he couldn't believe that's all I had."

"I think he was just surprised, that's all," Bayler insisted, folding a shirt. "He didn't mean it in a bad way."

"I know he didn't," I said, standing up. I reached for a hanger and went back to filling the closet. "It's just . . . I want to be like the rest of you. I want to be happy, and maybe have the job of my dreams someday. I mean, no offense, Elly, but being my friend's receptionist is not my dream job."

"Jesus, I would hope not," Bayler teased.

Elly laughed. "No offense taken."

"Justin deserves more than the girl who's still scraping through life."

Bayler threw a shirt at me and scoffed. "Oh, come on! We're all scraping through life, just dodging different obstacles. And you know what, I would love to be 'the scrappy one' in this bunch. You can throw a right hook better than some guys I know, and you carry a knife and mace in your purse, and you know how to use them! So, don't give me this bull about how he deserves better than that. He'd be lucky to have an independent woman like you. Next excuse, please."

Elly and I laughed at her response, and I ended up flopping down on top of the bed next to them. Staring up at the ceiling, I smiled and thought about how lucky I truly was to have friends who called me on my bullshit. "I think maybe I just need to get back out there to prove to myself that Justin's it for me, to kiss a few frogs before working up the courage to go after my prince."

"Now you're talking like the girl I know," Elly said proudly.

"Fletcher is going to be pissed when he hears you're trying online dating," Bayler said, giggling softly to herself.

"I know," I groaned, as I turned my gaze to Elly. "And let me guess, Carter will be, too?"

"I swear I didn't tell him about your feelings," she said, holding her hands up in defense. "He figured it out."

"Sure he did," I deadpanned, tossing a shirt at her.

"Well . . ." Bayler stated, "You kind of suck at keeping it a secret. I figured something was up with you and Justin at Carter and Elly's wedding."

"I'm sorry I wasn't trained in the art of secrecy like you Jennings!" I said, ducking from the shoe she tossed at me.

"Wait," Bayler said excitedly, waving around the other shoe. "If we all know, how do we know Justin doesn't not know?"

"Say 'know' one more time," Elly teased, laughing uncontrollably.

"Shut up!" she said, rolling her eyes. "I'm being serious here. He's a smart guy. Surely, he's figured it out by now."

Elly rested her head on Bayler's shoulder and simmered her laughter. "I'm guessing Justin hasn't had the greatest experiences when it comes to women. You know how he went to college at a really young age?"

"Yeah?"

"While the rest of us learned what to do and what not to do during our pubescent high school years, Justin went through all that during college. He was still a minor compared to most of his classmates. Do you remember what teenage boys are like?"

"Ugh, the acne," Bayler shuddered, shaking her head.

"And the smell," I said with a cringe.

"The fumbling hands attempting to diddle our skittles."

I laughed. "The premature ejaculation."

"Exactly," Elly continued. "I don't know the specifics, but I can guess it would've been hard for him to find a girl who wasn't just using him to get an A."

"Yeah," Bayler agreed, her voice lined with skepticism, "but he's not in college anymore."

Elly sighed and deferred the conversation to me. "Bay, I could walk out into the living room completely naked right now, and the only guy, with the exception of my brother, who would attempt to cover me up would be Justin. He's smart and sweet, but it's as if his brain is so full of knowledge it won't allow him to focus on anything else, specifically women. He's completely oblivious to me."

"Well," Bayler huffed arrogantly, "then I think online dating is just the thing you need for him to wake up and smell the pussy."

"Smell the pussy?" Elly repeated in a confused tone. "Do I even want to know where this is going?"

"Yes, my pregnant grasshopper, you do," Bayler said, patting the top of her head. "Justin's going to start hanging around Tessa more often now because they live together. Maybe he sees her in a towel after her shower. Maybe she looks super cute cooking them dinner. Maybe he starts noticing her scent lingering around the apartment. But you know what else he's going to see? He's going to witness her going on all these dates with guys who are not him, and you know what that means? Jealousy. He's going to become jealous, which means he'll have woken up and smelled the pussy."

"That's your suggestion? Make him jealous?" Elly asked in disbelief. "The last thing she needs to do is make him feel more insecure when it comes to women and dating." She turned to me with her brows furrowed, anger radiating from her. "Please tell me this online dating crap isn't just some ploy to get him to notice you."

"It's not, I swear," I said, shaking my head. "I don't want to make him jealous."

"Good." She relaxed back against the headboard and rubbed her forehead. "I'm all for you getting back in the dating game, but do not play dirty, Tessa."

"I would never do that to him," I said solemnly.

"Okay."

We looked over at Bayler, who had her arms crossed over her chest and her lips pressed into an arrogant smile. "What? He's gonna smell the pussy. You just wait."

"Isn't it roses or coffee or something he should be smelling instead?" Elly asked with a cringe, suffering from a bout of pregnancy brain.

I bit back a laugh as Bayler fell over into a fit of giggles. "I think she meant, you know, when a guy goes down on a woman, he gets a whiff of her—"

"Pussy!" Bayler smirked, laughing even harder.

Elly placed her hands over her baby bump and attempted to mask her mortification with a shameless smile. "My baby's first word is going to be 'pussy,' isn't it?"

"Probably," I laughed with a shrug.

She reached for the pillow and smacked Bayler with it. "Now, get up, bitches! These clothes aren't going to unpack themselves!"

***

After all of my things were unpacked and put away, everyone finally left. I jumped in the shower to wash away the sweat and grime of moving. Even though Justin's place was nearly three times the size of mine, he only had one bathroom. We'd have to share, but that didn't bother me since I grew up sharing with Trey. The vanity had his and hers sinks, and Justin had cleared out a few drawers and cabinets for my essentials. He also emptied one side of the shelf in the shower for my bathing items. When I noticed his during my shower, I couldn't stop myself from smelling his shower gel. I'd spent years wondering what kind he used, basking in the scent that lingered around him all the time, and now I knew.

I chastised my curiosity during the remainder of my shower.

Smelling his stuff is not going to help you move on, Tessa! In fact, it's kind of creepy.

Once I was finished, I hurried across the hall to my room, wrapped in a large, fluffy blue towel. I lotioned up and changed into a pair of yoga pants and a sweatshirt that hung off my shoulder. When I opened the door to my room, I heard the shower going again.

Great. Now, he's showering.

My lady box grabbed her mic and hit it a few times to get my attention as images from my sex dream flashed in my mind. Now they were fusing with the fresh, clean scent of his shower gel that my olfactory senses had permanently memorized. I was turned on by the thought of him showering. Naked and alone. Touching himself. Standing in the same place that I'd just been naked.

Stop. It. Right. Now!

Turning my back toward the hall, I wandered around my room aimlessly, trying to rid my thoughts of Justin showering. I tidied up picture frames and other personal items that I'd unpacked earlier. Pretty soon, I found myself admiring my new room, since I really hadn't had the time to do it earlier when everyone else was here. The walls were painted a light gray. The king-sized bed was much too big for me, but the pewter and cream-colored bedding was beautiful and plush, with its stylish pattern of stripes and leaves. The black tufted, upholstered headboard paired stunningly with the black furniture in the room. The dresser, nightstands, and desk all matched, with silver handles and intricate art carved into the dark wood. A gray and white area rug covered the light hardwood floors, adding much-needed warmth to the room.

"Do you like it?"

Turning my head at the sound of his voice, I found Justin standing barefoot in my doorway wearing light gray sweatpants and nothing else. He ran a hand through his shaggy, damp hair as his blue eyes smiled back at me. My eyes traveled down his ripped, lean torso to the delectable V etched into his firm hips. When I caught the outline in his pants, I stifled a groan and tried not to think about him going commando.

"I love it," I replied, gazing around the room. "It's about three times the size of my old room, but I wouldn't change a thing."

He laughed and leaned against the doorjamb, crossing his arms over his chest. "Are you hungry? I thought we could order something in if you're interested."

"Because you don't have anything here to eat, right?" I teased.

"Yes, I'm terrible at shopping for food," he admitted in an annoyed tone.

"That's okay," I giggled, walking toward him. "Because I'm really good at grocery shopping."

Laughing, he led the way into the kitchen, which housed beautiful stainless steel appliances and white cabinets accented by gray soapstone countertops. His kitchen was a dream come true for me. The island added more counter space to cook: something I'd always wished I had more of at my place. I couldn't wait to fill the fridge with food and start cooking in here.

Justin opened a small drawer, pulled out a handful of menus and laid them on the counter. My jaw dropped in shock at the number of choices spread out before me.

"Take your pick," he offered, smiling.

"You have a drawer just for takeout menus?" I asked incredulously.

He hopped up on the counter and proudly stated, "Yep!"

I shook my head at him and shuffled through the menus until I finally found one from a place I'd never tried. "I've never eaten here before."

"Really? This place is great," he said, reaching for his cell phone. "What would you like?"

I leaned against the counter and smiled up at him. It was kind of cute to see him so excited for takeout, even though I wasn't a huge fan of it. "What do you recommend?"

"Hmm, you're not picky, so I'm going to suggest the grilled marinated chicken sandwich. It's amazing."

"Okay," I said eagerly, my stomach rumbling at the thought of food. "What are you going to get?"

"The chipotle chicken wrap," he replied with a smile as he began dialing the restaurant's phone number. While he called in our order, I put the menus back in their drawer and couldn't help noticing the high prices on most of them.

"It should be here in thirty minutes," he said, hopping down from the counter.

"How much was it?" I asked, rounding the island to go fetch my purse.

Justin grabbed my arm and stopped me. "It's your first night here; dinner is on me."

"Thank you," I said, rolling my eyes. "But do you realize how much money you could be saving if you didn't eat out for every meal? Come on."

I led him into the living room and playfully pushed him down on the couch. He'd outfitted the living room with a dark gray recliner and its matching couch and ottoman. Sitting down next to him with my legs curled underneath me, I pulled up the notes app on my phone and started a grocery list for us.

"Okay, I'm making a list of groceries, so you need to tell me if you're allergic to anything specific or if there are certain foods you don't like. Go."

"You're not buying all of the grocer—"

Placing my hand on his mouth, I raised an eyebrow and glared. "I am. If you won't let me pay you rent, I will buy stuff we need. We need food. I cannot live in a place with only condiments and beer."

He laughed against my hand but surrendered. "Fine. I don't have any food allergies, and I'm not picky when it comes to food."

"Okay, are there any specific brands you like better than others?"

"Not really?" he asked, like he wasn't really sure what I meant.

"So, you'll take an off-brand ranch over Hidden Valley?" I offered, wrinkling my nose. "That's just wrong."

Laughing, he flung his arm over the back of the couch, seemingly entertained by my grocery rules. "Hidden Valley, it is."

I tapped it into my phone. "Which I'm surprised you don't already have."

"I'm more of a Dorothy Lynch kind of guy," he said, shrugging his shoulders.

"Yuck!" I exclaimed, shaking my head. "I'll just get a bunch of different stuff tomorrow to make dinners and lunches for us. I refuse to let you eat out every day."

"It's really not that bad," he laughed.

"But it's unhealthy," I stated, giving him a once-over. "Not like that's an issue for you since you have no fat on you whatsoever."

"Everyone has fat on them," he said, eyeing himself. He pushed his stomach out and pinched together a tiny flab of skin from his belly. "Look!"

"That doesn't even count!" I laughed, smacking his abs. "You had to make that happen."

"You're the skinniest person I know," he remarked, taking in my outfit.

"I am not," I said, rolling my eyes. "Anyway, back to the list—"

He grabbed my phone and tossed it on the coffee table. "How about you pick up whatever you want. Really, I'll eat anything."

"I want to get stuff you like."

"Tessa," he said, leaning his head against his arm. "I like everything. My favorite food is homemade; it doesn't matter what it is. You can't really do wrong by that."

"Okay," I said with a nod.

We sat in silence for a while, just watching TV, until he looked over at me and said, "You could've put some of your things out here, you know."

"That's okay." I smiled at him and shook my head. "This is your living room."

His brows furrowed for a second and then turned to face me with a sweet smile lingering on his lips. "This is your place now, too. I need you to understand that. I don't want you tiptoeing around my things or me. I want you to feel at home here."

I gave him a weak smile, but nodded. "It's just going to take some time for me to settle in. I'm not used to having so much space, or such great water pressure in the shower, or a doorman who refuses to call me anything but Miss Wilder."

That last part made him laugh. "George still calls me Mr. Jameson even though I continuously ask him not to."

"I told him three times today to call me Tessa, and he just smiled each time."

"That's George," he said, shaking his head. When his gaze fell back on mine, he continued. "Will you at least think about putting some things out here in the living room?"

"I really don't have anything, Justin," I said, fiddling with the frayed seam of my sweatshirt.

"Liar," he said, poking me in the side. "What about the picture of the New York City skyline? I saw you put it in your closet when I walked by earlier. You could've at least hung it up on the wall in your room."

I stared down at my lap, feeling guilty for not hanging up any of Trey's pictures. He had a real gift for capturing moments, which was why he chose to study photography at NYU. I'd bought him his first professional camera, yet I hadn't hung any of his photos because I didn't want to chance ruining Justin's walls.

"What's wrong?" Justin asked, brushing a damp piece of hair out of my eyes.

Studying his face, I noted the genuine curiosity etched into each of his beautiful features. With his dark blond brows furrowed slightly, his ocean blue eyes calmly waited for my answer. His lips were pressed together in anticipation: his weak grin showing off his boyish dimples. For someone who'd always been so quiet around his friends, he was rather talkative now, which really surprised me. I'd expected ignorance and silence from him, but I'd been welcomed and cared for since the moment I walked into his place. Maybe Elly was right. Maybe we would open up to each other by living together.

"I didn't hang anything because I didn't want to ruin the walls," I admitted shyly.

"Tessa," he said softly, grabbing my hand. He pulled me up off the couch and nodded toward the hall. "Go get the picture."

"Okay," I said eagerly, rushing back to my room. Standing on my tiptoes, I reached up to the top shelf in the closet and grabbed Trey's photos I had framed. There was the New York City skyline photo with the sunset as its backdrop. Trey had taken the second photo at work: a shot of the Knicks playing at Madison Square Garden. I had one photo of Yankee Stadium at dusk, and another one of New Year's in Times Square. Carrying them all out to the living room, I found Justin sitting on his coffee table, studying the walls. One wall was lined with bookshelves brimming with fiction and nonfiction tomes. His parents' textbooks filled the bottom shelf. The other wall housed his entertainment system with his TV anchored to the wall and everything else neatly set up underneath it.

I set the photos on the couch next to him. "We don't have to hang all of these."

He examined each of them closely. "These are amazing, Tessa. Where did you get them?"

"Trey took them," I replied proudly, gazing down at them over his shoulder. "He even helped me pick out the frames for them."

"He's really good," he chuckled to himself. "No wonder he's not into my psych class."

I laughed. "I had no idea he was in your class until the other night."

"I thought he looked familiar when you guys got here today." Justin stood up, taking the skyline photo with him, and placed it against the wall. "He hasn't missed a single lecture this semester."

"Good," I mumbled to myself. "Or else I'd kick his ass."

"I'm sure," he said, smiling back at me. "What do you think about putting it here?"

I nodded. "It'll look great there."

"We could put these New York ones on this wall with the windows, and then the sports ones on either side of the TV. Sound good?"

"Perfect."

We aligned each picture perfectly, and then pressed hanger hooks into the drywall and hung the pictures on the walls. By the time we were finished, a knock at the door signaled the arrival of our food. Justin paid the guy while I admired Trey's pictures. Appreciating his work made me miss him a little bit, and I hadn't even been gone a full day. Reaching for my phone, I took a panoramic picture of the living room and sent it to Trey.

Me: Check out our wall decor!

Trey: Looks great.

"God, this smells amazing," Justin said, setting the bag of food on the coffee table. "I'm starving."

"Me too," I said, taking a seat on the couch.

"You want a beer?" he asked, wandering into the kitchen.

The smell of chicken entered the room, and my stomach growled again. "I'd love one."

He grabbed two of out the fridge, popped the tops off, and handed one to me. With our containers of food in our laps, he lifted his beer bottle in a toast and smiled. "Welcome home, Tessa. I hope you enjoy it here."

With you, how could I not? I thought as I tapped my bottle to his. "Thank you. It's good to be here."

Chapter Four

Justin

It'd been almost a week since Tessa moved in—five days to be exact—and she was already driving me crazy. Not in a bad way where I thought about killing her every time I saw her, but in a way that suffocated me. She, herself, was not smothering, but her actions overwhelmed me. For years, I'd lived alone. I went from living with two people who I wouldn't even really consider parents, since they only thought of me as a post-coital experiment rather than their son, to living with my grandma during my early college years as a teen, and then to my own place by myself. I wasn't used to living with someone. I knew asking her to move in would be a change for me, but I didn't think it would be this drastic.

So, when I got home Thursday night and found Tessa hovered over the stove, stirring something in a pan, I snapped.

"Hey!" she said cheerfully. "Are you hungry? I'm making—"

"I don't care what you're making," I muttered, in an agitated tone that quickly grabbed her attention. I flung my bag onto the back of a barstool, and then grabbed a beer from the fridge, which was now fully stocked and lacking takeout boxes. "This shit has to stop."

She turned off the stove, pulled the skillet of meat off the burner, and faced me with confusion in her eyes. "W-what are you talking about?"

"THIS!" I shouted, pointing to the skillet. "You cook every single night! You make me breakfast. You make me lunches. You pick up my dry cleaning, when I didn't even know I had dry cleaning to pick up! You do my laundry. You—"

"Okay, I get it!" she yelled, crossing her arms over her chest. "I just—"

"I'm not done," I stated harshly, shaking my head. Tipping my beer bottle back, I drank the rest of its contents and then continued more calmly. "Look, I know this is normal for you. You've been taking care of someone your entire life, but I don't need you to take care of me. I know you think you need to do all this crap to earn your stay here because I won't let you pay rent, but you don't, Tessa."

"I'm sorry." She turned her worried gaze down to the floor, and I immediately felt bad for being a dick. "I didn't realize I was bugging you so much."

I placed my empty beer bottle on the countertop and wrapped my arms around her in a hug. "It's not you so much as the things you do."

She nodded against my chest without a word.

"Let's talk," I said, lifting her up onto the countertop. I hopped up onto the counter opposite from her and leaned back against the cabinets. Sadness invaded her features, twisting the dreadful knot in my stomach tighter. "I love your cooking, and

I appreciate everything you do around here. All I'm saying is that you don't have to do it. I don't want you to take care of everything."

"Okay." Again, she nodded and continued avoiding eye contact with me. "I can move out if I'm that much of a bother to you. I know you don't do well with change."

"I don't want you to move out!" I exclaimed, shaking my head. "I just want you to stop doing everything for me! I grew up with a nanny who did everything for me because my parents were too busy running their labs. I used to be part of their experiments until I got older and they grew bored of studying me. That's all I've ever been to them: a post-coital science project. So, they hired a nanny. We also had a chef because they couldn't make their own meals. They hired people to run every aspect of their lives because they were too busy working. Then when I got into college really young, I moved in with my grandma in the city, where she continued doing everything for me. By the time I turned eighteen, I was so sick of people running my life, I moved out and got a place of my own using the money from my savings.

"I know it doesn't sound like a hardship, but I hated growing up like that. I hated having a nanny. I wanted to have dinners with my mom and dad, not some lady who was just getting paid to take care of me. I mean, she was nice and everything, but sometimes I got the feeling that she'd rather be at home with her own kids."

"Justin . . . I'm so sorry."

Shaking my head, I smiled back at her. "You have nothing to be sorry about; it's not your fault. I want you to enjoy living here, and having you do shit for me is not what I had in mind. I love your cooking, but I want to help you cook dinner. I don't want to come home and have my meal already decided for me. That means, some nights I'm going to want to eat out. I've grown used to it, and it's a habit I'm finding really hard to break. I'm also a fan of leftovers, so some nights we don't have to do anything but heat something up. Hell, we don't even have to eat together if you don't want to. I know you probably think I'm crazy for getting so worked up over all this, but I just don't want to go back to the way things were when I was younger. I don't want you doing shit around here because you think you have to. You live here rent-free because you're my friend and I care about you; you owe me nothing for that. Do you understand?"

"Yes," she said softly, nodding. "I understand."

"And the laundry . . . I can do my own laundry."

"I know," she smirked, waving her hand for me to continue. "Continue with your rant."

I smiled at her, and the ball of anxiety that had developed in the pit of my stomach quickly unraveled as I confessed, "I do laundry on Sundays."

Last Sunday, I went into the laundry room and found both hampers completely empty. She'd already washed a load and had another one in the dryer. I had to run ten miles at the gym to calm down.

"What if you're busy on a Sunday?" she quipped, making a jab at my obsessive-compulsive behavior.

"Then I wake up earlier or stay up later to get it done, but Sundays are laundry days."

"So, I can do my laundry on Saturdays?" she asked, a playful smile lighting up her face.

"Yes, just don't touch mine," I replied, hopping down. Still sitting on the counter, she was at eye level with me now. "Are you regretting moving in with me?"

She laughed out loud, but shook her head. "No way. I'm actually surprised it took you this long to snap."

"I'm sorry," I said as I observed her. Her gray eyes sparkled against her fair skin with her soft brown hair framing her oval face. Gone was the sad, distressed look in her eyes, replaced by a playful gleam she wore so well. She was so outgoing and flexible, at times I found myself wishing I were more like her and less like the meticulous neurotic I'd become.

"It's okay," she offered sweetly, patting me on the shoulder. "Next time, just tell me when something's bothering you right away. Don't bottle it all up again. It's not a good look on you."

"Deal." Walking over to the stove, I turned it back on and moved the skillet onto the burner. "Okay, so tell me what we're making here."

"Cheeseburger macaroni," she answered.

"Like Hamburger Helper?"

"Ugh, no." She wrinkled her nose in offense. "This is homemade, not from some box!"

She started to hop down from the counter, but I stopped her. "No, just tell me what to do. Elly and Bayler say I need to learn how to cook."

She smiled and got comfortable, pulling her legs up to sit Indian style. "You do need to learn. So, you'll start by browning the hamburger in the skillet. I've already mixed up my special sauce. It's way better than the box crap."

I did as I was told, breaking the hamburger into little pieces and moving it around the pan with a spatula as it cooked.

"While the meat's cooking, you can go ahead and get out the sauce that's in the fridge and the macaroni from the pantry. Once the hamburger's done, you'll drain it in the colander in the sink, and then stir in the sauce mixture and macaroni. After that, you'll just keep stirring occasionally and cover the skillet with the lid. When the pasta is tender, it's ready to eat."

"All right."

As I grabbed the other ingredients, Tessa changed the subject. "You know, I grew up with parents who weren't really around either. They were too busy doing drugs or getting drunk to worry about taking care of me, so I fended for myself most of the time. When Trey came along, I started taking care of him almost immediately. Even at the age of five I knew Mom and my stepdad weren't able to handle one kid let alone two."

"What about your dad?" I asked.

"He died in a car accident before I was born."

"I'm so sorry, Tessa," I said, shaking my head. "For everything you've had to go through. No kid should have to grow up like that, taking care of everything on their own."

"And no kid should be pawned off on a nanny or a grandparent."

Glancing over my shoulder, I smiled weakly at her, appreciating the fact that she understood. I'd never really talked about my past with anyone before, but her affirmation comforted me. She wasn't pushing me for more, or trying to get me to talk about my feelings. She simply accepted our pasts for what they were, and I admired that about her. I'd always liked Tessa, but right now I felt like kissing her.

I want to kiss you, Tessa Wilder.

Acceptance was all it took for a person to open up, and she'd just broken me.

Chapter Five

Tessa

A few weeks later, I went on my first date with a guy from the Internet. We'd agreed to meet for lunch at a place I'd never heard of before on 46th Street. The minute I walked in, I immediately wanted to leave. It was a vegetarian bar.

A VEGETARIAN BAR.

I preferred meat. Almost anything with a face, really. Even when I ate a salad, I doctored it up with bacon and cheese and drenched it in ranch. I was all for eating healthy, but I wasn't about to go the organic route. Organic was expensive, and it tasted like crap. Hell, humans probably tasted better than the tofu burger I ordered. I should've realized he was a pacifist by his name and occupation: Orion, the conservationist.

I ended up apologizing to him and leaving before the check even arrived. Thankfully, he offered to pay for the whole meal since I barely ate any of mine. However, he did ask for a to-go box so he could take my tofu burger and sweet potato fries home with him.

Ugh, sick!

I ran back to Elly's clinic, rushing over to the table where she, Carter and Justin sat, and fell into the chair next to my roommate.

"Please tell me you packed the leftover tacos from last night," I said, eyeing Justin's lunch bag.

"Lunch didn't go so well?" Elly asked, smiling brightly. She'd teased me all morning about my date going bad, and she smiled victoriously now, as if she'd predicted its demise.

"You could say that again," I stated, rustling through Justin's lunch. I looked up at him regrettably and groaned. "You brought the tacos for lunch and already ate them?"

"Yep," he said, trying to hold back a laugh. "I didn't know I was supposed to bring a backup lunch for you if your date sucked."

"Of course you were," I sighed, jokingly.

Carter laughed. "So, what happened? Where'd he take you?"

"To a vegetarian bar!" I exclaimed, wrinkling my nose in disgust. "Tofu tastes like ass, by the way."

The three of them cracked up as my stomach growled and a headache started pounding behind my temples. I was still starving, and my body wasn't about to let me forget it.

"But you're not even a vegetarian," Elly said, her brows furrowed in confusion. "He had to have known that by looking at your profile. Why would he take you there?"

"Because he's a conservationist who doesn't eat meat," I explained, rolling my eyes. "You know, if we weren't supposed to eat animals, God shouldn't have given us the skills to catch them! We need protein! I can't not eat meat!"

"He probably saw how thin you are and assumed you were a herbivore," Carter stated.

"It was awful," I whined, slouching in my chair. "It wasn't just the fact that he didn't eat meat. It's November, and he had on denim shorts and flip flops."

Elly gasped. "Jean shorts?!"

"Yes, shorts that should only be worn by women in the summertime!" I stated, mentally revisiting his terrible appearance. "Then he had long hair that—"

"Hey," Justin teased, nudging my arm. "I have long hair. What's wrong with long hair?"

"Nothing's wrong with *yours*." I admired his low ponytail, and then reached out and ran my fingers through the soft strands. "You condition yours every day. This guy looked and smelled like he showered maybe once a week."

"Gross," Elly cringed. "That's a little too conservative."

Carter tightened his hold on Elly's shoulders and laughed. "Hey, I'm all for the whole save water, shower together incentive."

"So am I!" I proclaimed. "I'd just prefer to do it on a daily basis."

Justin chuckled softly next to me. "So, are you going to see him again?"

I huffed in annoyance. "No, I just told him I didn't think we were a great match because I loved meat, and he actually agreed, which made me feel better for leaving early. He was nice; I will give him that. But this is New York City. You can get a vegetarian meal at any restaurant that still serves meat. Don't just assume because I'm thin that I'm a salad eater. I have a great metabolism. I can't help that."

The three of them laughed in agreement and began picking up their trash as I headed back to my desk. My stomach ached from hunger, but there was little I could do about it now that I had to go back to work. If I hadn't been so frustrated about the date, I would've grabbed something to eat on the way back to the clinic.

While Carter and Elly talked quietly, Justin leaned against my desk, smiling down at me. "You want me to order you something on my way back to campus and have it delivered?"

"That's okay," I said, shaking my head. This was my own fault for letting a computer choose my date. "Elly has some granola bars in her office. I'll just steal a couple of those."

"I'm sorry the date didn't work out," he offered in a sweet tone.

"Me too," I said with a shrug. "You win some, you lose some."

"Yeah, I guess," he laughed, nodding. "His loss, though."

I felt my cheeks heat under the gaze of his beautiful eyes watching me. "Thanks, Justin."

"Anytime," he said, tapping his fingers on my desk. "Maybe we can order in a bucket of fried chicken tonight, or a big, juicy burger. Whatever you want."

"That sounds perfect," I said, as I rested my chin in my hand and daydreamed about food.

"See you back at home later."

"Later," I said, while my belly wailed, *Feed me!*

Justin

As Carter and I walked back to work in silence, I thought about Tessa and her date. I'd thought she looked more dressed up this morning than usual, but hadn't had the nerve to ask why. Ever since the night I freaked out on her, I'd been noticing things about her. The way she woke up at the same time every morning, even on the weekends, completely befuddled me. She looked like a girl who liked to sleep in, but she proved me wrong. Her peaches-and-cherries scent that wafted through our apartment became my new favorite smell. Whenever I took in a whiff of it, I found myself growing hard. Then there was her clothing. She dressed down when she hung out at home, opting for a tight pair of yoga pants that hugged every inch of her or a pair of old, ripped jeans that hung from her slim hips. She'd wear t-shirts and sweaters she drowned in, hanging off one of her shoulders. I loved seeing her barefoot and bare-shouldered at home with me. But when she went out, she wore dresses and heels and jeans that looked like they were painted on. She was a knockout either way, but this morning, I'd noticed she spent more time on her appearance.

When we got to Elly's clinic and heard Tessa had a lunch date, anxiety ached in my chest until she came back from her date and sat down beside me.

I was still analyzing that ache. She deserved to go on dates. She was a beautiful woman and I would bet most men found her attractive. Any guy would be lucky to have a second of her time. The thing was, even outside of the apartment we shared, I wanted to be that guy spending time with her.

Not some conservationist named Orion who only cared about himself and couldn't properly feed her or even bother to look good for her.

"So," Carter said, interrupting my thoughts. "How's the new living arrangement going?"

"Good," I said with a shrug.

He chuckled beside me. "Care to elaborate?"

I breathed in and quickly sighed. "I like living with her."

"But?" he asked, cocking a brow at me.

"But nothing. She's a good roommate. We get along. My OCD got the best of me last week and I freaked out on her, but we're good now."

He laughed loudly and patted me on the shoulder. "Glad to hear that. What made you upset?"

"She did my laundry on a Saturday," I confessed, shaking my head, preparing myself for the shit he was about to deliver.

He stopped abruptly on the sidewalk and frowned. "But Saturdays aren't laundry days."

I rolled my eyes at his ridiculousness. "Exactly. I'm surprised she didn't pack up her things and leave after my rant."

He continued in step next to me. "We all know you're a bit obsessive about things, Jameson. She knew what she was getting into when she moved in with you. And if there's any one of us who can handle living with you, it's Tessa."

I frowned, confused. "Why do you say that?"

"Because she appreciates everything and hardly ever complains," he replied. "What'd she say after your rant?"

"She just told me to tell her when something bothers me."

"See, she understands your quirks," he explained. "Not everyone would be so tolerant."

"I know." Spotting the bar Carter and I occasionally visited near campus, I nodded toward it. "I think I'll order her a sandwich and fries and have it delivered. She said I didn't need to, but she's a tight-ass when it comes to eating out, and I could hear her stomach rumbling before we left. She shouldn't go the rest of the afternoon without eating something."

"I don't even know why she's trying the whole online dating thing," Carter mused in an annoyed tone.

"I think Tessa just wants what you all have. With the exception of Paige, all of her girlfriends have found their guys."

"Yeah, well she doesn't need to go online to find him. I mean, you heard her, the guy she went to lunch with was a disaster."

"That doesn't mean anything. One in three couples meet online."

"Okay, but would you try it?" he asked.

"God, no," I scoffed, shaking my head. "I hate meeting new people in person. Meeting someone online sounds like a nightmare. The small talk alone would be exhausting."

"I worry about her meeting a catfish. You know, someone pretending to be someone they're not."

"I know what catfishing is," I said, furrowing my brows. "Tessa is smart though. She wouldn't fall for that kind of crap."

"I'd hope not," he said with a shrug. "Anyway, you order her food. I'm going to head to my office. Going to the gym after work?"

"Yeah, I'll be there," I said, opening the bar door.

I walked in and placed my to-go order, giving the waitress the clinic's address. Grabbing a business card from my wallet, I pulled a pen from my shirt pocket and wrote Tessa a note.

***

Tessa

Elly's next patient wasn't due for another thirty minutes, so when I heard the door open, I looked up and found a guy walking into the clinic carrying a bag of food. My mouth watered at the sight.

"I have a to-go order for Tessa Wilder," he stated, placing the white sack on my desk.

"That's me," I said, reaching for my purse. "What do I owe you?"

He shook his head, smiling. "It's been paid for already, tip and everything."

"Of course it has," I mumbled, nodding knowingly. "Thank you."

"You're welcome. Enjoy."

The second he turned to leave, I rummaged through the sack and pulled out a Styrofoam box. Opening it up, I found a crispy chicken sandwich loaded with lettuce, tomato and mayonnaise, along with a pile of crinkle-cut fries with packets of ketchup layered on top of them. Reaching back into the bag, I pulled out the napkins, and that's when I noticed the card at the bottom of the sack.

I grabbed it and smiled at Justin's NYU business card. Turning it over, I saw his scribbles and stifled a giggle as I read: *Here's the meal you should've had for lunch. Preferably with a guy who conditions his hair. Enjoy - J*

"What smells so good out here?" Elly asked, rounding the corner to the lobby. The smile on her face grew wider as she took in the open Styrofoam box. "Food?"

"Yes," I sighed, leaning back in my chair. "I swear, you have the nose of a dog."

"Blame Baby Jennings," she said, patting her belly. "So, he ordered you food?"

Glancing down at the note in my hand, I giggled softly and handed it over to her. "And he wrote me a note."

She read the card and then stole a fry. "And here you thought he couldn't possibly have feelings for you."

"Hey, you had lunch already!" I reprimanded, closing the box to her sticky fingers. "And he doesn't have feelings for me like that. He's just being nice."

"Sure. You keep telling yourself that," she smirked, then stopped and leaned down to sniff the box. "Does that have mayo on it?"

Opening the box, I grabbed the sandwich and took a dramatic bite out of it, responding with a mouthful of food, "Yes, it does!"

She pantomimed a dry heave and shook her head. "I'll be in my office."

"That's right," I laughed, shooing her away. "Let me eat my lunch in peace!"

While I admire my note, I thought as I picked up the card and studied his handwriting.

My afternoon began with one of the worst dates of my life, but Justin had easily turned it around with food and a cute note.

So much for trying to get over him.

Chapter Six

Tessa

As weeks went by, I learned more about Justin. Whenever he was home, he usually had the television on for background noise, even if he wasn't in the living room actually watching it. Money wasn't an issue for him, so leaving shit on when he wasn't using it wasn't a big deal. If it were me, I wouldn't have had the television on unless I was actually watching it. But the minute he walked in the door, he grabbed the remote, clicked it on, and then proceeded to not watch it.

Out of habit, I assumed. I wasn't even sure he knew he did it.

So, when I arrived home from a workout at Jones Jym and found the television off, I did a happy dance to the Selena Gomez song blaring from my headphones as I walked to my room.

Sometimes a girl just needed alone time in her space, where she could get carelessly naked and just be. Maybe jam out and have a private dance party. Maybe take a shower and sing along to the iPod. That's what I needed. I hadn't been able to walk around naked since I moved in with Justin. That was one nice thing about living with Trey. I knew his schedule like the back of my hand. I knew when I had time to myself.

Now that I had some, I was taking advantage of it.

Stripping off my hoodie, I threw it on the floor and kicked off my shoes and socks. Next went the yoga pants and tank. I tucked my iPod into my bra and boogied to another song by Bruno Mars before moving the iPod to my mouth and stripping off my bra and panties.

As the song changed to Liz Phair and she sang about being extraordinary, I pretended my iPod was a mic and lip-synced along with her, feeling free and sexy in my bare skin. I pulled the twist tie out of my hair, letting it fall over my shoulders, and started headbanging to the beat of the drums.

When the song changed and Missy Elliott encouraged me to work it, I took my solo show across the hall. I was still sweaty from my workout, and wanted a shower more than anything right now.

Pushing the bathroom door open, a cloud of steam greeted me, and I immediately stopped dancing as heat engulfed my body. Then I watched Justin step out of the shower, water running down his hard, lean body, like an almighty deity stepping onto his stage.

Fuck, he's hung. Just the sight of his cock in its naked glory made me speechless. I no longer heard the music blaring in my ear buds. I only heard the sound of my heart beating wildly in my chest as I took him in from head to toe.

He tossed his wet hair back out of his face and then ran his fingers through it, crooking his brows at me in amusement.

"Uh, I-uh—" My gaze turned downward again, straight to his magic stick where I couldn't stop staring. "I-I'm-you're—wow."

"Tessa?"

I focused upward at the sound of my name, trying my best not to make eye contact with him as I ripped the headphones out of my ears. "I'm sorry. I didn't know you were home."

"I think we're even," he said, his deep, magnetic voice pulling my gaze back to him. He wrapped a towel around his waist. A surprised grin lingered on his lips while his cool hazel-blue eyes gave me a once-over. "Wouldn't you agree?"

It was then that I remembered I was naked, and quickly covered myself with my arms. "Oh, my, God!"

Running back to my room, I slammed the door shut behind me and leaned against it. Humiliation flooded my system as my heart raced faster. I threw my iPod on the dresser, and took deep breaths to try to calm myself down.

What the fuck just happened? Did I really just see him completely naked? I ogled his tan banana like some crazy female monkey escaped from the zoo, all bright-eyed and eager for it.

It wasn't that I hadn't seen a penis before; I had. But this was Justin Jameson's! The sex dream I'd had about him did not do him justice. He was long, smooth and veiny, with the perfect amount of girth and magnificently groomed.

Just thinking about it made me—

"Tess?"

He knocked on my door, and I prayed the wood floors would swallow me whole. I tied my robe around my waist, exhaling another deep breath before opening the door to him with my head held high. "Yes?"

Standing before me with the towel still knotted at his waist, the boyish grin on his face grew. "Shower's all yours."

"Thanks," I noted, fully composed.

"No problem." He started toward his room, but stopped halfway down the hall and glanced over his shoulder. "Do you mind me asking, what were you doing?"

I crossed my arms over my robe and shrugged nonchalantly. "Just dancing."

"Naked?" he asked curiously, delighting in my discomfort. "In the apartment?"

I sighed, flustered. "Can we please just not talk about it?"

"Sure." His deep, sexy laugh vibrated down the hall and caressed over my skin, causing goose bumps to rise under my robe. He entered his room without another word, and a surge of relief settled over me.

I rubbed away the goose bumps and took a step toward the bathroom.

"I'm sure it was one hell of a show though," he said, poking his head out of his room. His smile fell as his hot gaze ran over me one more time. "It's a shame I missed it."

Laughing lightly, I shook my head. "Well, don't think you're going to get another chance to see it. The show's over."

"Until next time!" he called, closing the door to his room.

"Next time," I scoffed under my breath, berating myself. Note to self: *Next time, make sure the apartment's empty first!*

"I saw his penis," I announced quietly, as I entered downward facing dog.

It was the Saturday after my disastrous naked dance fest, and the girls and I were at our fifth beginner's yoga class at Maverick's gym. Our group of friends had made a bucket list after Elly's cancer scare last year, and one of the items was to learn yoga. Since the guys weren't particularly interested in it, they opted out of joining us, which meant every Saturday morning for the next four weeks was our girl time.

"Did you actually see it?" Bayler asked curiously. "Or did you just see an outline of it again when he went commando in sweats, because that doesn't really count."

"I saw it," I whispered. "All of it."

"Is he hung?" Harper asked.

"He is!" I squealed, earning us a glare from the instructor.

"Wait," Elly said. We stretched up into the standing forward bend pose, and then she continued. "Jesus, mid-pregnancy is really not the time to learn yoga."

"Focus on your breathing," Paige suggested calmly. "It'll make it a little easier."

"Not having this damn bump would make this pose easier."

Bayler hushed them and then smacked my arm. "Back to Justin's penis."

"No," Elly said, shaking her head. "I want to know how you saw it. How'd it happen?"

We exhaled down into upward facing dog as instructed and started our breathing, which usually meant we just continued talking. "Okay, so you know how when you're home alone, you just want to walk around naked sometimes?"

"Definitely." Bayler and Harper nodded in agreement.

"No, who does that?" Elly asked.

"I don't," Paige said, shaking her head. "Are you saying you were walking around your apartment naked?"

"I wasn't exactly walking around," I stated. "I was just dancing in my room to my iPod."

"Naked?" Elly asked, appalled. "Why would you do that? You have a window in your room. Some peeping Tom could've seen you."

"The shades were closed," I explained, rolling my eyes.

"It's liberating," Bayler stated proudly. "Dancing around naked. I get it."

"Exactly," I nodded. "So, I'd just gotten home from a workout, and after some dancing, I decided to take a shower. That's when I realized I wasn't home alone. Justin walked out of the shower just as I walked into the bathroom, so I saw everything. The hammer and nuts. Clear as day."

"Now, *that's* how you do a naked dance party!" Bayler praised, giving me a high five.

"What happened next?" Harper asked eagerly.

"What do you think happened?" We dropped our knees to the mats and pressed our hips back into upward facing dog. "I couldn't stop staring at him, and then I stuttered through an apology, completely forgetting that I was just as naked until he pointed it out. Then I ran back to my room humiliated. I still can't look at him without seeing his penis."

The instructor led us into a warrior one pose as I relived the embarrassment all over again. "It was more embarrassing than when I had a sex dream about him and came in my sleep. Twice."

"That can happen?!" Bayler asked in disbelief. "Wait, when did this dream occur, and why are we just now hearing about it?"

"Yeah, details!" Harper begged.

I sighed. "It happened the night after Seghen was born, and I don't really want to talk about it. It's embarrassing."

"No, it's not," Elly said, in a comforting voice. "It's fairly common for women to have sex dreams."

"And come?" Bayler asked. "Dreams that provide real orgasms? Sign me up. Clearly, my REM cycle sucks because I've never had that happen."

"I have," Harper admitted with a shrug. "I had them a lot when I was pregnant."

"I've been having them, too," Elly said.

Bayler laughed and gave me a nudge. "Were you pregnant in this dream?"

I shuddered, shaking my head. "Not that I remember. I remember that the sex with him was phenomenal; he made me come twice. Then I woke up and realized, you know, that I . . ."

After we switched sides, we moved into warrior two and Paige asked, "So, you had a sex dream about him, now you're living with him, and just a few days ago, you saw his penis?"

"Pretty much," I stated with a nod.

"And you're using online dating to try and get over him?" Bayler asked, shaking her head. "How's that working out for you?"

"If her date with the veg-head is any indication, it's going horrible," Paige teased.

I stepped out of pose, put my hands on my hips and glared at the four of them. "I don't know what else to do! It's not like Justin jumped my bones at the sight of my naked body, like any other guy would."

"Ladies!" the instructor warned, grabbing our attention. "Quiet, please."

The group moved into open triangle. I joined them and focused on my breathing.

"Tessa," Harper whispered. "Maybe he was just surprised and that's why he didn't make a move."

"Maybe," I said with a shrug.

Bayler cleared her throat as we switched sides. "You could always make the move. Guys love confidence."

"I can live with embarrassing myself in front of him," I said, shaking my head, "but I don't know what I would do if he rejected me."

"He brought you lunch after the veg-head failed to properly feed you," Elly said, smiling. "A guy doesn't do that to a girl he'd reject."

"No, a guy does that for a friend," I explained.

"Or maybe he's falling for you and he doesn't even know it!" Harper said optimistically. "Maybe he doesn't really know what to do. This is new territory for him. First, he gets a roommate, and now he's seen you naked. I bet he's had more wet dreams than you."

The four of us laughed at her response and moved into boat pose. We remained quiet for the rest of the lesson as we rolled up into half wheel and then finished by laying on our backs in the corpse pose. After some much-needed girl talk and the calming ambience yoga provided, I was able to end the lesson fully relaxed.

When class was over, we rolled up our mats and left. Harper pulled me aside while the rest of the girls headed toward the gym equipment to start their regular workouts.

"What's up?" I asked her, smiling.

She worried her bottom lip with her teeth and then smiled. "Is your offer to babysit still good? I know Seghen's only four weeks old, but I just want to go out to dinner with Mav. We wouldn't be gone for more than an hour, if that. I'm not even sure I can talk him into leaving her for that long. If I can, would you be interested in watching her?"

"Of course!" I exclaimed, pulling her in for a hug. "My offer is always good to babysit your little princess."

She exhaled and hugged me back tightly. "Thank you. I really appreciate it. I'll let you know what night we decide and we can go from there. Does that work?"

"Sounds perfect," I said, letting her go. "Where is Seghen this morning?"

Harper pointed at the stairs and smiled. "With her dad in his office. I'm headed there now."

"Give her a kiss for me!"

"Will do!" she laughed. "Thanks again, Tessa!"

Chapter Seven

Justin

It was Saturday afternoon, and the guys and I had just won our weekly basketball game against a group of college kids. We'd made shooting hoops at Maverick's gym a ritual right after it'd opened, and had been coming here every week since to shoot around, pickup a game against other members of the gym, or play a game of three-on-two if nobody challenged us.

Resting my hands on my knees, I took deep breaths, feeling more winded than usual after a game.

"You okay there, Jameson?" Carter laughed, patting me on the back.

I nodded, placing my hands on the back of my head. "I think I've gained weight since Tessa moved in."

"Did you gain a vagina, too?" Cashed smirked.

"You know," Fletcher stated, spinning the basketball atop his finger. "You could just work off the weight by having sex with her."

Dropping my arms to my sides, I let out a frustrated sigh and looked at the four of them. "We are not having sex. We're just friends."

"Are you telling us you haven't even thought about it?" Cash asked, smiling widely. "I mean, come on. What's the point of living with a woman if you aren't getting laid on a regular basis?"

"Hey," Maverick said, smacking the back of Cash's head. "I have a little lady who will someday be a woman. Have a little respect, would you?"

"Okay, okay," Cash said, rubbing the spot where Mav hit him. He turned his attention back to me. "But I'm serious. You haven't even thought about having sex with Tessa? She's hot. You'd have to be a saint to live with her and not think about her like that."

"I'm with Cash on this," Fletcher said, nodding. "Are you a saint, Jameson?"

I used to be a saint, I thought. Ever since her lunch date with the conservationist, I'd been having thoughts about taking her out on a date and wondering if she'd enjoy it or not. Then after the shower incident, thoughts of her had turned more sexual. How could they not with a body like hers? I'd seen her in bikinis numerous times, but to see her completely nude was a whole new experience for me, one I couldn't stop replaying over and over again in my head. Her small, perky breasts paired beautifully with her lithe figure. Her hips jutted out slightly against her fair skin, and her arms and legs were slightly toned. Her hair was just long enough to lay over her shoulders, but short enough to not cover her up. I noticed the gap between her thighs and the small brown patch of hair hiding her pussy. Then when she ran from the bathroom, I was rewarded with the faint bounce of her tight ass with each of her steps.

Every time I walked into the apartment, I wondered if I'd get a chance to see her dancing naked. I thought about watching her raw form moving to the music, so carefree and sexy, with every inch of her fully exposed. I'd danced with her enough times at the club to know the way her hips moved and the way she'd grind her body to the beat. Just thinking about her doing those same moves naked was an absolute turn on. Then I'd imagined what her body would look like dancing naked with me in bed. I'd have to take care of such thoughts before falling asleep, which wasn't easy to do when our beds shared a wall. Every time I jerked off, I worried about her hearing me. Those anxious thoughts would turn sinful again as I thought about her joining me.

"Justin?" Cash said, waving his hand in front of my face.

"Yeah?" I asked, shaking away those mental pictures of her. "What were we talking about?"

"Sex with Tessa," Fletcher restated. "Have you thought about it?"

Without a word, I shook my head.

"Not even once?" Maverick asked, narrowing his eyes at me. "I don't believe that."

Taking a deep breath, I stole the basketball out of Fletcher's hand and started dribbling it between my legs. "I've thought about her a few times."

"And?" Fletcher asked curiously.

"And I might have seen her naked," I said nonchalantly with a shrug.

"WHAT!?" Cash laughed while the other three stood wide-eyed in shock. "Details, man. We need details! What does she look like?"

I laughed, shaking my head. "I'm not going into detail about her. She didn't know I was home at the time."

"Go on," Fletcher said, waving his hand for me to continue.

"And apparently women do this thing where they enjoy dancing around the apartment nude?"

Fletcher and Maverick shared a laugh. "Oh yeah, Bayler walks around naked all time."

"So does Harper."

"Guys!" Carter snapped harshly. "Those are my sisters! I'd rather not hear about them being naked."

I laughed at the disgusted look on his face and then continued explaining how the incident went down. Once I was finished, I dribbled toward the basket and shot a layup.

"That's it?" Maverick asked, crossing his arms over his chest.

"Yep." I tossed the ball to Carter, and he looked around at the rest of the guys stupefied. "Why? What else did you guys expect?"

"You didn't do anything with her after seeing her naked?" Fletcher asked, brows furrowed.

Cash shook his head. "Please tell me you did not pass up an opportunity like that?!"

"What opportunity?" I asked, confused. "We ran into each other naked. It was more of an accident than anything."

"See," Maverick said, smiling. "That's your problem. The rest of us see it as an opportunity for you to make a move, and you just saw it as an accident that wasn't supposed to happen but did."

"What was I supposed to do?"

"MAKE A MOVE!" Fletcher shouted, throwing his hands up in the air. "Jesus, Jameson! Do we need to draw you a fucking picture? A woman is at her most vulnerable state when she's naked, and all you did was give Tessa some line about hoping to catch her next nude show. She's not a stripper."

"Let's just be glad he didn't pull out some ones and throw them at her," Cash muttered.

Anger filled my chest at their antics. "I didn't insult her if that's what you're saying."

"Well, I bet you didn't make her feel wanted either," Mav stated frankly.

Shaking my head, I wiped a hand down my face, completely overwhelmed by the turn of our conversation. I knew I didn't have the experience the rest of the guys had, but I wasn't a complete idiot when it came to women. Their comments and accusations caused a wave of anxiety to roll through me as I grew more frustrated. I recalled the last few weeks of living with her, and remembered the online dating, which just pissed me off more. "It doesn't really matter now, does it? She's my friend and roommate, and I don't really want to screw either of those relationships up by making a move on her. That's the last thing she needs right now as she goes on dates with complete strangers who are too self-involved to give two fucks about her!"

Silence greeted me as the four of them looked at one another, completely surprised by my outburst, and then burst into laughter.

"I think we hit a nerve," Carter said.

"I think we might have broke him," Maverick laughed.

I rolled my eyes. "Shut up."

Fletcher walked over to me and threw his arm around my shoulders. "Look, Jameson. Whether we like it or not, she's dating other guys, but that doesn't mean she doesn't want to date you."

"I just don't think now is a good—"

"Take it from someone who waited years to be with the woman he wanted," Carter stated in a serious tone. "If I could go back and redo things, I would've told Elly the minute I met her that I wanted to be with her. You're just wasting time contemplating things that don't even matter."

"Yeah, man," Maverick said, nodding. "You know Tessa's not the type of woman who would let a relationship ruin her friendships. She would never make us choose sides between you two if it ended up not working out."

"Guys," Cash stated, "we need to put this in terms he'll understand." His eyes fell on me as he crossed his arms over his chest. "Okay, if any of us were in this situation, what advice would you give?"

They waited as I thought about the question and how I would answer it. Once I had it, I knew they probably wouldn't like what I had to say since they rarely agreed with my advice. "I'd tell you to be there for her. She needs support right now. She wants to fall in love just like her friends have, so while she's looking for Mr. Right, you need to be Mr. There-for-Her."

"Okay," Cash deadpanned. "Not what I was expecting."

"I know," I said, glancing around at the four of them. "But it's the right thing to do. I think you all know that. I know we don't like the idea of her dating someone she meets online, but she doesn't need our negativity weighing her down. Just keep your thoughts to yourself. She's been supportive of all of us; she deserves the same from her friends."

"What about you?" Maverick asked. "Are you going to be okay watching her go out with other guys?"

I nodded, feeling somewhat conflicted as I tried to reassure them. "I have to be okay with it. This is her decision, and I don't want to be just another guy she dates. I've been friends with her for a long time, but it wasn't until after she moved in with me that I realized how much I need her to be more. If she's dating random guys off the Internet, she's not ready for more with me yet."

***

Tessa

The following night, I walked out of my room and started looking for my purse in the living room. Justin was seated on the couch watching TV, and I was getting ready to head over to Maverick and Harper's to babysit Seghen.

"Hey," Justin said, "What are you looking for?"

"My purse," I answered, checking the couch.

"Island barstool," he said, pointing toward the kitchen.

"Thanks." I slung the black cross-body over my shoulder and pulled on my heavy coat.

He smiled at me and ran his eyes over my hoodie and jeans. "Where are you headed?"

"Harper and Maverick are going to dinner tonight, so they've asked me to babysit."

"Really?" he asked, leaning forward. "I can't believe Mav agreed to leave Seghen for an evening."

I laughed. "It's just an hour or two. So, they won't be gone long."

He twirled the remote in his hand with excitement dancing in his eyes. "Do you mind if I come with you? I haven't seen her since she was born."

"No, I don't mind." The thought of seeing him hold Seghen made my lady box tremble with giddiness, and I couldn't think of a better way to spend my Sunday night.

"Great!" He clicked off the television, grabbed his coat and then locked the apartment behind us. "Maverick showed us a few pictures of her on his phone the other day at the gym. I can't wait to give him shit for leaving her."

Smacking him in the stomach, I turned around to face him, latching on to the material of his sweatshirt. "Don't give him any crap. It's hard on first-time parents to leave their little ones behind. Even if it is only for a short period of time."

"He would give me shit if the situations were reversed," he said.

"I know, but Harper didn't even think she'd get him to agree to dinner."

"Fine," he stated, running a hand through his hair. "I guess I can keep the jokes to myself until after they get back."

"Thank you." I turned around, feeling satisfied, and continued out into the freezing winter air. Justin hailed us a cab, insisting it was too cold to walk, and before I knew it we were headed across town to Harper and Maverick's penthouse.

When we arrived, Justin paid the driver, and we rushed into the building to escape the chill. Once in the private elevator, I tapped in Harper and Maverick's code, and it quickly ascended. The ding announced our arrival as the doors to the elevator opened up and Axel, Harper and Maverick's Great Dane, came running down the foyer toward us.

"Hey, bud!" I exclaimed, petting the massive pup's ears as he eagerly begged for attention, wagging his long gray tail.

"I swear, you get bigger every time I see you, Ax," Justin said. At the sound of his name, Axel jumped up, placing his paws on Justin's shoulders, and licked his face.

"I wonder how he is with Seghen."

"I'm sure he's great with her," Justin said, rubbing Axel's shoulders. "Great Danes are great people dogs."

"He's a little protective," Harper said, grabbing Axel's attention. The friendly pup ran to his master and greeted her with much more enthusiasm. Harper laughed, waving us toward her. "Come on in, guys. I'm sorry our big horse attacked you."

"It's okay," I said, shrugging off my coat. "Where's Mav?"

"He's feeding Seghen," Harper replied, leading us into the living room.

Mav sat on the couch holding an adorable baby girl decked out in a pink onesie in one hand and a bottle in the other, his tattoos and muscles on display with the sleeves of his button-down rolled up his forearms.

Justin joined him as Harper led me into the kitchen.

"She should be good since we're feeding her before we leave, but if she does get fussy and wants a bottle, you can give her one. I pumped earlier, so there's one ready to go in the fridge if you need it. She usually naps after eating, so I'm hoping she just sleeps while we're gone."

"I'm sure she'll be fine," I reassured, smiling as I admired Harper in her purple sweater dress. "You look great, by the way!"

"Thanks," she said excitedly. "It feels so good to be dressed up. Just ignore the baby weight."

"Oh, shut up," I deadpanned, rolling my eyes. "You seriously look amazing for just having a baby, and your boobs are huge."

She laughed, smiling down at her chest, unimpressed. "Yeah, they're also raw and sore, and they leak on occasion."

"The things we put ourselves through for kids," I stated.

"I know," Harper sighed, gazing back into the living room at Maverick and Seghen. "She's worth it."

"She's adorable," I said, rubbing my hands together. "I can't wait to hold her all night!"

Harper laughed. "I think you'll have to wait your turn."

We watched as Maverick cautiously transferred Seghen off to Justin, and then they picked up their conversation again.

"Damn him," I said dramatically, shaking my head. I felt Harper's warm gaze on me, and when I looked over at her, she was smiling wittingly. "What?"

"I think he's into you," she whispered in an eager voice. "Why else would he tag along to help you babysit?"

"Because your daughter has us all wrapped around her finger," I quipped, waving my pinkie finger in the air.

"True," she laughed with a proud shrug. "But I also think it's because he wants to be here, spending time with you outside the apartment."

I sighed, sneaking another wistful glance at him. I'd been excited at the thought of seeing him hold Seghen earlier. Now, the sight of them together was like a swift kick in the vagina, reminding me that he'd probably never hold our babies. Taking a deep breath, I turned my attention back to Harper and put on a smile for her. "I have another date later this week. He's an accountant, and he let me choose where to have dinner."

"That's great," she said, her smile weakening at the mention of my date. "But I'm still rooting for Justin and you."

So am I, I mused, looking back into the living room.

Justin caught my gaze and smiled.

"I think it's safe to say he's rooting for you, too."

"Why must they look so good with her?" I asked seriously, ignoring her remark. "What is it about guys with babies? Do you think it's them or her that makes the other cuter?"

"It's her," Harper answered undoubtedly. "She softens them up, makes them more vulnerable."

I nodded in agreement, loving the way Justin gave Seghen his full attention. "You're right."

"And now, I'm going to take my hot, vulnerable man out to dinner," she said, as she reapplied her lipstick. She checked herself in the mirror one last time before throwing everything in her purse and smiling back at me. "Thank you so much for babysitting tonight. We really need this. I can't even explain to you how excited I was to get dressed up. I love being a mom and wearing my comfy lounge clothes, but sometimes a woman just needs to put on a thong and a dress to feel sexy again."

"You're welcome," I said, stifling my laugh. "I'm happy to help out whenever you need me."

"You're a lifesaver, Tessa!" Harper said, leading the way back in the living room. "Mav, you ready to go?"

He stood from the couch and eyed me closely. "If you need anything, call us, okay? I mean it. If something happens, I want to know. If you can't reach us, call 9-1-1."

Harper laughed, wrapping her arms around Maverick's waist. "They will not need 9-1-1."

"You don't know that," Mav replied, pulling her closer.

"I pretty much raised my nineteen-year-old brother on my own; I think I can handle a four-week-old," I stated, in an attempt to relieve his anxiety.

"Let's just go," he said heavily, staring down at Seghen in Justin's arms. He leaned down and pressed a kiss to her forehead. "Take care of my girl, guys."

"She'll be fine," Harper said, threading her fingers through Mav's. She looked between Justin and me, smiling. "Call if you do happen to need anything, but I'm sure you won't."

"Will do. Have a great time."

"Get some alcohol in him, Harper!" Justin called as they walked away. "Maybe it'll loosen him up!"

"Fuck off, Jameson!" Maverick shouted from the foyer.

When I heard the elevator start to descend, I turned to Justin and shook my head. "You just had to say something, didn't you?"

"It was a joke!" he exclaimed, stroking his thumb over Seghen's back. "He deserved it for lecturing me on how to take care of a baby. I watched his hair gray while he babbled on about bottles and diapers and the meaning behind each one of Seghen's cries."

Laughing, I took a seat on the couch and brushed a finger over Seghen's beautiful dark hair that looked just like her mom's. "I think it's cute that he's so concerned about her; it means he cares. Most dads would just pawn all that stuff off on the mom."

"That's not my point. I think he's a great dad, but the way he kept repeating things to me . . ." Justin rolled his eyes. "I have an eidetic memory. He knows that."

Hearing our voices, Seghen turned her head toward Justin's neck and mewled quietly as she tried to find the perfect position to fall back asleep. Justin tried to soothe her by rubbing her back softly, while I tried comforting her with words.

"It's okay, sweetie," I said, scooting closer to Justin. "Just go back to sleep. You're okay."

But the sound of my voice wasn't a comfort to her as her face turned red and her cries grew louder.

"Oh, wow," Justin whispered. "She is not happy."

"She woke up just in time to realize Mom and Dad aren't here anymore," I said quietly. "Here, I'll take her and try walking with her."

Justin handed her off to me, and I stood from the couch and started walking around the living room, speaking to her in a soft voice in an attempt to calm her down. We made five laps around the living room, and she'd only grown angrier. I tried bouncing her, rocking her, singing to her, but nothing was working as her cries turned into wails, causing anxiety to wade in my belly.

"I have an idea," Justin stated, pulling his hoodie over his head.

"What are you doing?" I asked sharply, eyes wide as he continued taking off his undershirt. "Why are you taking off your clothes? What good is that going to do us?"

"I know how to calm Seghen down," Justin explained in a cool tone. "Now, get her down to just her diaper."

Exhaling a deep nervous breath, I slowly laid Seghen down on the area rug despite her loud, furious sobs. I felt like the worst aunt ever, but I proceeded to unbutton her onesie.

She felt hot and sweaty from her outburst, and I wanted nothing more than to make her feel better.

Picking her up, I found a shirtless Justin lying on the couch with a throw pillow situated behind his head. "Okay, let's see if a little skin-to-skin contact will calm her down."

Confused and tired of hearing her cries, I carefully carried her over to him and he took her from me. He whispered to her as he placed her against his bare chest, and her shudders simmered slightly at the feel of his skin against hers.

Justin smiled down at her and began stroking her back with his thumb again. He placed a soft kiss on her forehead and explained, "The contact triggers the release of a hormone called oxytocin inside her body, which will help calm her. It also helps control stress hormones, heart rate and temperature, also allowing her to relax."

"I'm going to go grab a blanket from her room," I said.

"Okay," he said, never taking his eyes off her. As I entered the hall, I stopped and listened as he spoke to her in a soothing voice. "Dad said you usually sleep after eating, but maybe you ate too much and your belly hurts. Don't worry, beautiful girl, that happens to all of us sometimes."

I smiled to myself and found a soft, pink blanket from her nursery and carried it back to the living room with me. I stopped short as I entered the room and leaned against the wall to listen. Her cries had minimized to a few whimpers as her breathing went back to normal, but it was the sound of Justin singing to her that mesmerized me. His tone was deep and soothing, hauntingly beautiful in a cappella, as he sang a song I barely recognized. I'd heard the song before, but I couldn't place it. I knew the words, they came so easily as I lip-synced along with him. Tears pooled in my eyes and a knot formed in my throat in disbelief of the talent before me. I had no idea he could sing so effortlessly. His raspy bass sent a delicious chill down my spine that made goose bumps pebble across my skin. Listening to him comfort her was such a harmonic pleasure, I swear I felt my ovaries swaying along to the tune.

He hummed the melody to her between verses before starting again, and finally, after five or six repeats, I remembered where I'd heard it before. It was the ballad from *Sleeping Beauty*, "Once Upon a Dream." It wasn't as cheerful or upbeat the way Justin sang it. His version was more swoony and mellow, and I had to capture it. I pulled my phone out of my back pocket and recorded a video of him soothing her back to sleep with his beautiful voice.

As I stepped closer, I noticed his eyes were shut and her cries had completely stopped as she slept soundly now. I switched to my camera app and snapped a picture of them lying together. They seemed so relaxed, handling each other with such ease. When I couldn't calm her down, he swooped in and saved the day, shirtless and singing. I felt a tear hit my cheek, and I quickly wiped it away, removing my evident weakness for him.

Tiptoeing around the couch, I knelt down beside them, leaning my head against the cushion to continue watching the show, totally captivated by his voice. His fingers stroked over her skin in rhythm to his words—the same words that reminded me of the actual dream I'd had about him. It was as if he secretly knew about it and decided to taunt me with this song.

When he finished another round of lyrics, he opened his eyes and smiled at me with pride. Whispering, he said, "It worked."

"You sang her the song from *Sleeping Beauty*," I stated quietly, still enamored by him. "I didn't even know you could sing. You're really good."

The grin on his face widened at my acknowledgement. "Did you know that song was inspired by a ballet?"

Of course not. I shook my head.

In a soft voice, he explained. "It was inspired by the music Pyotr Tchaikovsky composed for his ballet called *The Sleeping Beauty*. My parents wouldn't let me watch Disney movies; they considered them too mundane." He rolled his eyes and suppressed a laugh. "Instead, I attended operas and symphonies and ballets. I can't remember how old I was when I first saw the ballet, but I enjoyed the music. The Garland Waltz is the first dance in Tchaikovsky's ballet, and "Once Upon a Dream" from the movie was inspired from the composition during that dance. I didn't even know it was part of a Disney movie until I was in college. My grandma heard me humming the tune one day, and she started singing the words to it. She had no idea it originated from a ballet. Tchaikovsky also wrote the music for *Swan Lake* and *The Nutcracker*, but *The Sleeping Beauty* is my favorite of his ballets."

Most of our friends stopped listening when Justin went off on tangents like this, talking about topics none of us knew or really cared about, but I cared because it was obvious he did. "I've never been to a ballet, but I'd like to someday."

"Really?" he asked incredulously. "You have to see a ballet. I'll take you."

I felt my skin flush. "I don't think I own anything fancy enough to wear to a ballet."

"Sure you do," he replied earnestly. "You have that gray dress that matches your eyes."

He knows the contents of my closet and which pieces go with my eyes?

"You know the color of my eyes?" I teased in a soft voice.

He stifled more laughter to keep from waking Seghen, and looked down at me with that gleam in his eyes that he had when he talked about the ballet. "So, will you go with me to the ballet? *The Sleeping Beauty* won't be in production right now, but we could see *The Nutcracker*."

A smile spread wide across my face as I nodded. "I'd love to."

"And you'll wear the gray dress?" he asked, crooking a brow playfully.

"A fan of that one, are you?" I teased, nudging his arm.

"Yeah, I am," he answered honestly. His deep, seductive tone totally caught me off guard and electrified my body at the same time.

I nodded silently, too confused and aroused to reply. The more alone time I spent with him, the more I realized I would never get over him. No matter how many other guys I dated, none of them would compare to him. My mind and body were like magnets to Justin, fascinated by every piece he gave so freely each time he opened up. I'd been in love with his body for years, but falling in love with his mind seduced me now more than ever.

The heat from our close proximity fueled my desire to kiss him. Instead, I gave Seghen a chaste kiss on the top of her hand, and stood up and smiled at Justin. "Would you like something to drink?"

"Sure," he whispered. "I'll take a water."

"Okay." I headed into the kitchen, desperately in need of water myself, as I focused my attention on my surroundings. I was still amazed by Harper and Maverick's penthouse, despite having been here numerous times. Originally, it'd been Harper's, but Maverick moved in and now called this place home. It looked like the inside of a modern day castle with its limestone walls and marble flooring. Limestone pillars separated the kitchen from the open living and dining rooms, and the cream and brown colors made the space warm and inviting. I found the cabinet of glasses and filled two with water, and carried them back into the living room with me.

When I set Justin's down on the coffee table in front of him, he nudged the back of my thigh. Turning to face him, I was met with a cringe masking his features, and he nodded toward Seghen. "Do you smell that? Please tell me it's not her. Something so cute should not be able to smell that bad."

I took in the rotten smell and leaned down to sniff Seghen's diaper. "It's not her."

"Where is that smell coming from then?" Justin asked.

Pulling my sweatshirt up to cover my nose, I shook my head. "I don't know."

When a tail started pounding against the leather arm chair, Justin and I turned our heads to find Axel curled up in the chair, tongue out and panting.

"Seriously, Axel . . ." I whined, waving my hand in the air. "What did you eat? A carton of eggs?"

"I knew it had to come from one of Maverick's children," Justin muttered, shaking his head. "That's about how bad Mav's farts are."

"Gross," I said, wrinkling my nose. "I'm going to go find some spray to cover the smell."

"You might want to get yourself another glass of water, too," Justin laughed.

Twisting around, I found Axel drinking out of my glass, his big tongue sloshing water all over the coffee table. "You've got to be kidding me."

Walking into the kitchen, Axel followed close behind me like a miniature horse, just waiting to see how else he could get my attention. I grabbed a rag and cleaned up the water in the living room, and then filled a new glass with water and curled up at the end of the couch.

Leaning my head back against the couch, I sighed and closed my eyes. A paw tapped my leg and before I knew it, Axel jumped onto the couch, turned in a circle twice and sprawled out over Justin and me. He rested his back legs on top of Justin's, draping the rest of his body over my side.

"You probably thought we'd only be watching Seghen tonight," Justin said, smiling.

Axel rested his head on my shoulder and stared at me. I laughed and began rubbing his ears. "Clearly, someone wasn't getting enough attention."

"They treat him like a child."

"Most people do." At the sound of my voice, Axel scooted closer and licked my face. "Did you ever have a pet growing up?"

"No," Justin smirked. "Pets were considered a distraction. What about you?"

"We couldn't afford them." Petting his soft, gray fur, I showered Axel with my attention, remembering all the times I'd wished I had a dog as a kid. His big brown eyes shuttered closed as I continued rubbing his ear with one hand and his belly with the other. He made himself comfortable by stretching his front legs over my hips.

"He's in heaven right now."

"So is she," I said, eyeing Seghen still sound asleep on his chest with her pacifier hanging out of her mouth.

"Yeah, she is," Justin said, moving the blanket further up on her shoulders.

"You're really good with her." My gaze moved from Seghen up to Justin, and I found a weak smile pulling at his lips as he looked down at Seghen with admiration dancing in his eyes. "Do you want your own kids someday?"

He sighed. "Yeah, I do. I used to think I'd end up alone, and thought I'd be okay with that because I didn't have that many friends back then and I certainly wasn't having any luck with the ladies."

"But now?"

"Now, I find myself wanting the same things our friends have: love, kids, maybe even a dog who acts like a kid."

I laughed, nodding. "I know what you mean."

"I don't even have to ask if you want kids," he said, teasingly. "I'm sure you have the genders and names all picked out already, right?"

Maybe, I thought, as I replied, "I just want happy, healthy babies. Their names can be figured out later."

***

By the time Harper and Maverick got home a half hour later, Justin and I had fallen asleep with their children. Their whispering comments woke me up, and I found them both staring down at us.

"Look how cute they are, the four of them lying together on the couch," Harper whispered.

"What is our daughter doing naked on Justin's bare chest?" Maverick murmured.

I let out a laugh and nudged Justin awake. "Seghen's fine, Maverick. She got a little fussy after you guys left, but Justin calmed her down by laying with her."

"You could've let us know," Maverick said. "I told you to text if anything happened."

"Oh, Mav, enough," Harper laughed, rolling her eyes. She carefully took Seghen from Justin's chest and smiled at us. "I'm going to go put this little lady in her crib."

"I'll come with you," I said, maneuvering my way out from underneath Axel's weight.

When we entered Seghen's room, Harper sat down in the glider in the corner and began rocking her. I folded the blanket I'd grabbed earlier and put it back in its place near her crib.

"I missed her tonight," Harper admitted softly. "I took Maverick's phone away from him so we could enjoy dinner, but then I felt guilty for leaving her."

"She was fine, really," I said, admiring all the pretty pink decor of her nursery. "Did I tell you, I'm planning a gender reveal party for Elly and Carter?"

"No!" She exclaimed in a quiet gasp. "When did this get planned?"

"The night Seghen was born and Carter told all of us they were expecting," I said, smiling. "We went to Judge's afterward, and I asked if I could throw them a gender reveal party. She agreed since she wanted something different than a baby shower. So, I'm going with them to their next appointment, where I'll find out the gender, and go from there."

"So they won't know until the party?"

"Nope. They'll find out that night just like everyone else."

She hugged Seghen to her chest and sighed. "I love that idea, Tessa. Let me know if you need help with anything."

"Thanks," I said, excitedly. "I was going to ask if I should invite anyone else besides your immediate family from the Jennings' side?"

"No, parents and grandparents will be fine. Have you decided where you're going to have it?"

"Judge's. Fletcher is going to make sure we have the whole place to ourselves."

"Perfect!"

"Oh, I almost forgot! I have something to show you." I pulled my phone out of my pocket and hit play on the video of Justin singing. "The minute he started singing to her, she started to calm down."

She took the device from my hands and stared at the screen in awe of what she was watching.

"Wow," she murmured. "Will you send this to me? His voice is amazing." She pressed replay and watched it again. When it was over again, she looked up at me with tears streaked across her cheeks. "I think *I'm* in love with him. Who knew he could sing! How did you not jump him after witnessing this?"

"I know," I stated, blinking back tears of my own. Taking a seat on the ottoman, I took a deep breath and exhaled it. "I keep making all these stupid excuses, but I think I just don't want to screw up what we have now. Ever since I moved in, I've learned more about him. What if I tell him how I feel and he closes back up again? I don't want that to happen. I know he's quiet when we're all together, but when it's just us, he talks about everything."

She placed a kiss on Seghen's head and smiled. "That's understandable, but eventually, you'll have to tell him."

"I know." But eventually could be a while, until I was absolutely sure he wouldn't build his walls back up.

Chapter Eight

Justin

"How do I look?" she asked.

Tessa stopped in front of the couch where I sat and spun around slowly. She wore a maroon, long-sleeved dress that hit an inch above her knees with black tights and black high-heeled boots. I'd never seen the dress before, but it fit her perfectly, not too tight, not too loose, highlighting the slim curve of her waist.

"Beautiful," I replied, unable to take my eyes off her. "Fancy for Judge's?"

She grabbed her bag and smiled. "I'm not going to Judge's tonight. I have a date. I'm meeting him at the restaurant."

"Oh." Another date with a different guy. It took everything in me to smile and wish her good luck. "I hope you have a great time."

"Thanks. Me too." She applied lipstick to her already perfect mouth, and then looked herself over in her compact mirror one more time. "You think this is okay for dinner? It's not too dressy?"

How the hell am I supposed to know?

"I think it's great," I answered, trying my best to take away her insecurities. She looked exquisite. Her brown hair fell in big, soft curls over her shoulders, and her makeup emphasized the stormy gray color of her eyes. Her prominent peach scent couldn't be missed as she pulled on her coat and tightened the belt around her waist.

"Okay, good. I bought this dress back in the summer when it was on sale, and I've been dying to wear it ever since!"

Catching another whiff of her scent, which I'd grown to love, I readjusted myself and tried to focus on the TV instead. "So, will we see you at Judge's later then or . . ."

"I don't know," she stated hesitantly. "If Milo wants to, we will."

Milo? I wasn't an expert on names, but that one left a bad taste in my mouth.

"I'm going to go." She walked to the door, her heels clicking against the hardwood. "Have fun tonight!"

"Be safe," I muttered as she shut the door behind her.

Relaxing back against the couch, I exhaled a frustrated sigh, hating the fact that she was going out to meet a guy named Milo. I didn't even feel like hanging out with the rest of the gang at the bar now. My stomach hurt. My head ached. I wanted to sit on this couch and wait until Tessa came home, but I knew my friends wouldn't allow me to do that. They'd call me; I'd send them to voicemail. They'd text me, and I'd ignore them. Then they'd bust in here like a SWAT team ready to defuse a bomb.

There was no avoiding them.

So, I grabbed my jacket and locked up the apartment. When I arrived at Judge's, everyone else was already there, even Harper and Maverick sans Seghen. I took a seat at the end of the bar next to Elly, and Cash immediately brought me a beer.

I proceeded to sit and listen to the conversations around me without contributing. That was one nice thing about the gang: they didn't push me to converse. I often preferred to observe rather than chat. For instance, I could tell Elly was particularly tired tonight by the way she kept rubbing her bump and leaning against Carter. Maverick checked his phone every five minutes since Seghen was at his mom's. Paige seemed to be in a better mood tonight as she conversed with Harper about clothes. I had a gut feeling something was wrong by the way she'd distanced herself from the rest of us lately, so it was nice to see her here tonight. I turned my attention to the game playing on the flat screen, but when it ended an hour and three beers later, I tuned back in to my friends.

"Where's Tessa tonight?" Fletcher asked.

I took a long swig from my bottle and set it down on top of the bar, spinning it in my hands. "She met Milo for dinner."

"Milo?" Carter laughed. "What kind of name is Milo?"

I nodded with annoyance. "Right."

He turned to Elly and shook his head. "If we have a boy, we are *not* naming him Milo."

"Isn't that some character from *The Little Rascals*?" Fletcher asked.

"No, that's Alfalfa!" Bayler laughed, choking on her drink. "Not even close, babe."

"Whatever," Fletcher said, smiling at her. "Nobody should name their child after a crop."

"I guess it's better than Sorghum," I quipped, gazing around at the others. Confused stares greeted me instead of laughter, since none of them understood my joke. "Milo is actually another name for sorghum. It's grown in areas prone to drought."

"Well," Cash said, raising his bottle in the air. "Here's to hoping Milo's sex life is prone to a lot of drought, too!"

Everyone laughed and raised their drinks in a toast as I went back to watching TV. A few minutes later, Elly's phone chimed on the bar next to my elbow. Peering down at it, Tessa's name appeared with a new text notification.

"Elly," I said, nudging her arm. "You have a text from Tessa."

"Thanks," she said, grabbing her phone. "I texted her to see how her date was going."

As she unlocked her phone, I mentally told myself not to look at her screen. It wasn't any of my business. If Tessa wanted me to know, she'd tell me herself. But when Elly opened the message and I watched her shoulders slump, I read Tessa's response.

Tessa: He didn't show up.

"What an asshole," I muttered, shaking my head.

"Agreed," Elly said softly. She sent a reply and then locked her phone again. Running her fingertips around the top of her water glass, her mood turned pensive. "As much as I didn't really like the idea of her trying online dating, I hate how badly her dates have gone."

"Me too," I admitted under my breath.

She shoved my shoulder and laughed. "Then what are you still doing here?"

I downed the rest of my beer and narrowed my eyes at her. She knew about our conversation from the gym. "Carter told you, didn't he?"

"We took vows," she explained with a shrug.

"Which means?" I smirked, shaking my head.

"It means he tells me everything!" she exclaimed through laughter. "So, yes, I know what you guys talked about after basketball the other day, and I still don't understand why the hell you're sitting here talking to a pregnant, married woman when there is a woman at your place drowning her feelings in ice cream."

I threw a handful of bills on the bar top and glared. "I hate you all."

"You love us!" she exclaimed, patting me on the cheek. "Now, go cheer her up, and let us know how it goes!"

"I definitely won't."

***

When I arrived home, I found Tessa sitting on the couch, her feet perched on the coffee table, still in the outfit she wore for the date. Her coat was thrown over the ottoman. Her purse was tossed on the floor next to the couch. She held a pint of Ben & Jerry's in one hand, a spoon in the other. The glass blender jar, nestled between her thighs, was filled with an unidentifiable orange slush.

"She told everyone?!" she shrieked, sounding completely mortified.

I shrugged out of my coat and shook my head. "No, I happened to be sitting by her and saw your text."

"Oh." She shoved a spoonful of Half Baked into her mouth as I walked over and sat next to her. "You didn't have to come home. I'm fine."

"The bar wasn't that interesting." Before I walked through the door, I expected her to be in sweats, crying to some chick flick, but she wasn't. She still looked absolutely beautiful in her dress and tights, with her black boots kicked off and crumpled beneath the coffee table. She was watching *The Expendables*.

Not what I expected at all.

"A guy stands you up and you watch *The Expendables*? A movie full of men," I stated, amused.

She shot me a half smile and shrugged. "I wanted to watch good guys kill the bad guys."

"Understandable." I untied my boots and stretched my legs up onto the coffee table next to hers. "What's in the blender?"

"Orange juice margaritas," she replied, never taking her eyes off the TV. "We were out of margarita mix."

My stomached clenched at the idea of mixing orange juice and tequila. "Sounds awful."

"Might as well drink how I feel," she mumbled, spooning another bite of ice cream into her mouth. "What's wrong with me? Did he show up, see me and leave, or did he forget? When did dating become so difficult?"

"I don't know, but there's nothing wrong with you." Grabbing the pint from her hand, I scooped up a bite for myself and smiled. "Everyone gets stood up."

"Oh, whatever!" she quipped, taking a long sip from the straw in the blender. "Have you looked in a mirror? I bet you've never been stood up!"

"You'd bet wrong," I said, smiling.

She curled her legs up underneath her as she turned to face me. "Go on . . ."

The last topic I wanted to delve into tonight was my dating life in college as a teenager, but I would if it meant cheering her up. "Well, for starters, I didn't look like this when I was younger."

"Wow, I'm surprised you could get your big head into the apartment," she teased.

"You know what I mean," I laughed, rolling my eyes. "I didn't have the shaggy hair or any muscles. I had a buzz cut, and I looked like a twig weighing in at ninety-eight pounds."

"Okay," she laughed, squinting her eyes at me. "I can't really picture you like that, but I'll try."

Sighing, I leaned my head against the couch and studied the ceiling as mental flashbacks from those early college days entered my mind. "The first girl to stand me up was this blonde who cheated off me during every statistics test. I offered to tutor her, and she took me up on it. We set up a time to meet at the library, but she never showed. She continued cheating off me. The second girl was one I thought actually liked me. She'd always ask me to explain what the professor was talking about, which I took as her flirting with me. I asked her out to see a movie; she agreed but never showed up at the theater. The third girl was in a sorority. She invited me to a frat party after I helped her ace a test, but when

I got to the party, she wasn't there and her boyfriend ended up pouring a beer on my head. The fourth—"

"Justin," Tessa interjected softly. She placed her hand on my right cheek and turned my head toward her. Her skin felt so soft and warm, I had to mentally tell myself not to cover her hand with mine. Her beautiful eyes glistened with sincerity instead of pity, which made me want to grab her neck and pull her in for a kiss. "How many times have you been stood up?"

"Seven."

She smiled weakly and ran her hand through my hair. "Some girls are assholes."

"As are some men," I replied, unable to resist touching her. I pressed a quick kiss to the inside of her wrist and then let her go. "You know it's not your fault he stood you up tonight, right?"

She nodded silently, smiling back at me.

"Then don't give him the power to make you feel awful."

Taking a deep breath, she brushed a hand through her curls and exhaled. "Thanks."

"Do you want to do something besides sit here and drink and eat ice cream? We could go out. You were so excited to wear that dress tonight, I'd hate for you to waste it on a night in with Sylvester Stallone and his mercenary buddies."

"No, I want to stay here," she laughed, leaning her head against my shoulder. "Because they're *hot* mercenaries!"

"My bad," I chuckled.

She lifted her head, leaned in and kissed my cheek. I gazed into her bloodshot eyes, warning me of her apparent drunkenness as my eyes drifted down to her soft pink lips and settled.

Do not kiss her, Jameson.

Her own gaze studied my face and ended up on my mouth.

Don't kiss me either, Tessa. I won't be able to stop if I get a taste of you.

"You're the best, Justin." Skimming her fingertips over the scruff of my beard, she giggled. "I like the facial hair you have going on right now, too. The way it feels against my skin . . ."

Holy shit.

"So rough yet soft at the same time," she continued, like she had no idea of how effective she was. "It's a good look on you."

"Thank you. I'm glad you approve." I grabbed her wrist abruptly and pulled her hand away from my face. I stood up fast, before she could make another move, and glanced down at her. Confusion marred her face, causing a dull ache to pound in my chest as I tried to get us back on even ground. "Should I make us some more orange juice margaritas? Maybe we can find another action movie to watch."

"No," she yawned, raising her hands above her head. "I think I'm going to go to bed."

"Okay." I picked up the ice cream container and the blender and carried them into the kitchen. I tossed the empty pint in the trash and rinsed the spoon and blender jar in the sink, storing them in the dishwasher.

"Could you unzip me?"

Turning around, I found Tessa standing near the hallway with her back to me, her long hair pulled over her right shoulder. Her sweet words sent a shiver down my spine, and I had to remind myself that she was drunk. No matter how much I wanted this with her, I wouldn't take advantage of her.

Not now. Not ever.

"Sure." I wandered over to her and reached for her zipper, hands slightly shaking. The peachy, cherry scent of her made me smother a groan, and I felt my control weakening.

What is she doing to me?

As I unzipped her dress, I tried to think about less arousing topics like my grandma, work, and orange juice margaritas. In an attempt to respect her privacy, I stopped before her bra strap, though the zipper traveled all the way down to the small of her back.

"All the way, please," she requested, smiling back at me over her shoulder. "The zipper gets stuck."

I unzipped it the rest of the way, feeling tortured in my jeans the farther south I went. The smooth, pale flesh of her back peeked through along with the gray lace of her bra, and I grew eager to see her without the dress. The heat coming off of her made me want to bend her over the kitchen island and trail kisses down her spine before ripping the dress off completely.

"Thanks!" she said, holding the dress in the front.

"Goodnight," I offered, admiring her backside one last time before she entered the hall.

"Sleep tight!" she cheered drunkenly.

I'm tight all right.

Chapter Nine

Tessa

The next morning, I woke with a hangover from hell. My cheeks felt like they'd been lined with cotton balls. Every time I blinked, an obnoxiously painful set of fireworks went off behind my eyeballs and they weren't pretty. The headache pounding through my temples made getting out of bed for yoga nearly impossible, but I did it.

I threw on a tank and yoga pants, gathered my hair up into a ponytail and slipped on my tennis shoes. I grabbed my coat and purse and walked out into the hall, where I heard voices.

Who would be here this early in the morning?

Sliding my arms into my coat, I rounded the corner to the kitchen and saw Justin sitting at the island having coffee with a woman wearing only a towel. Her dark hair was still wet from a shower, and her face appeared absolutely flawless even without makeup. I had no idea who she was, but I instantly grew self-conscious of my yoga look, knowing without a doubt that I looked terrible this morning.

"Hey," I muttered, walking over to the fridge without making eye contact with either of them. "Don't mind me. Just grabbing a water." As I crossed by them quickly, the distant scent of my shower gel filled my nostrils, and anger poured into my veins. *Did she use my stuff? Who the fuck does that?*

"Tess—"

"Gotta go. I'm going to be late for yoga." I grabbed a water bottle and slammed the fridge door. I rushed out of the apartment even though I really wasn't running late. Seeing him with another woman, especially one that oozed sex appeal like her, made me forget all about my hangover as a new pain settled in my chest and my stomach twisted into a million knots. Did he invite her over after I went to bed last night? After I practically threw myself at him, he denied me and made a booty call instead? Why else would she be hanging out in the apartment wearing just a towel?

I ran all the way to Jones Jym in the freezing cold to stop my mind from wondering about the two of them. How could Justin be so stupid? He was turned on last night. I knew it. He knew it. The bulge in his pants knew it! What was his deal? Why couldn't he see how much I wanted him? Instead, he called another woman. Maybe I really wasn't good enough for him.

A few blocks away, my phone beeped with an email notification. A new message from a different guy interested in setting up a date sat at the top of my inbox. Without another thought, I clicked on it, read his profile and then replied agreeing to dinner.

Third time's a charm, right?

Wrong. I only set up that date to rid my thoughts from Justin and the woman in the kitchen, which only pissed me off more.

"Hey, Tessa," Maverick called, as I stormed through the doors of the gym. "What's up?"

"What's up?" I sneered, narrowing my eyes at him. "What's up is that I live with the stupidest smart guy! Seriously, what the fuck is wrong with him?"

"Whoa," he said, pulling me off to the side. He wrapped his arms around my shoulders, and I hugged him back as I burrowed my head into his shoulder. "What happened?"

"It's stupid," I said, shaking my head. Tears filled my eyes and before I knew it they were falling onto my cheeks.

"Tessa," he whispered, brushing my tears away. "Tell me what happened so I can go kick his ass."

"Mav, I really don't want to talk about it," I mumbled, drying my face with my hands. "I just want to go to yoga and forget about men altogether."

"Will you at least talk to the girls about it?" he asked, eyeing me closely.

I nodded and gave him a weak smile. "Yeah."

"Good."

***

We were seated in meditation, but I was far from relaxed. With my eyes shut, I kept replaying this morning over in my head and comparing the woman to myself. Where I had fair skin, she had naturally sun-kissed skin like Justin's. She had an organic, sexy rasp to her voice that I lacked, which made me even more envious of her since she didn't sound like she smoked a carton of cigarettes a day.

"Okay, now let's move into downward dog," the instructor stated in a soft, annoying voice.

"I can't do this today," I complained, stretching out flat against my mat. Lying on my back, I stared up at the ceiling, fully intent on staying like this for the rest of class.

"If I have to do this," Elly muttered, struggling into the position. "You have to do it."

Shaking my head, I disagreed. "I'm hungover."

"I'm pregnant!" she exclaimed, laughing. "I win."

"Not happening today, Jennings," I said, in a sour tone.

"So, Justin left the bar early last night and you guys got drunk?" Bayler teased. "Did anything else happen? Please tell me something happened!"

"Unfortunately, no." I swallowed around the ball in my throat and crossed my ankles. "He came home. I'd already been drinking from being stood up—"

"Wait, you were stood up last night?" Harper asked, completely confused.

"By who?" Paige continued. "The Milo guy?"

"Yes, Milo," I stated, rolling my eyes. "Anyway, when Justin got home, I was already pretty tipsy, and feeling sorry for myself. He told me about all the times he's been stood up, and I ended up giving him a kiss on the cheek and running my hand through his hair. He practically jumped off the couch like I was some infectious disease he couldn't wait to get away from, even though I could tell he was turned on."

"He probably—"

"Oh no, it gets worse," I stated, twirling my ponytail around my finger. "This morning, I woke up and heard voices in the kitchen. When I walked in, I found some bitch in a towel sitting at the island with him having coffee. Her hair was still wet from a shower, and she smelled like me!"

"Ladies!" the instructor barked. "Quiet, please!"

Elly furrowed her brows and shook her head. "Are you saying Justin had a girl over last night?"

"Yes!" I whispered loudly. "After he unzipped my dress for me—"

"Nice," Bayler smirked. "I can't believe he didn't jump you after that. Fletcher knows when I ask him to undo my dress, it's on."

"Right?" I reiterated. "Most guys do."

"We're not talking about most guys here though," Elly explained.

"Elly's right. This is Justin," Paige stated, as they all changed into the next pose. "He's not going to take advantage of you, drunk or not."

"And I can't see him making a booty call either," Harper continued. "He's too nice to make a booty call."

"Well, how else do you explain the woman this morning?" I asked, rolling my eyes. "She didn't magically appear out of thin air. He had to invite her over after I went to bed."

"What did she look like?" Elly asked and then huffed out an exasperated breath. She turned her attention to her belly. "I love you, kid, but I don't like you kicking me in the bladder."

"You okay?" I asked, rubbing her back.

"The kid's just really active this morning," she said, turning onto her back next to me. "Go on. What did she look like?"

I sighed. "She looked like Mila Kunis' doppelgänger!"

Paige and Elly started laughing, and then Paige asked. "Are you sure it wasn't Whitley?"

"She does look like Mila," Elly smirked.

"Who the hell is Whitley?" I asked, brows furrowed, matching Bayler and Harper's.

"Whitley lives across the hall from Justin," Elly explained.

"How have you lived there for a month and not met her?" Paige asked, shaking her head.

I sat up and stared at the four of them. "I don't know. I haven't even heard of her until now. How do you two know her?"

"We don't really know her," Elly said, rubbing her belly. "I've only seen her once, but I've heard Mrs. J. mention her a few times when she's brought food over."

Mrs. J., also known as Janice Jameson, was Elly's neighbor before she and Carter moved into the penthouse in their building. Mrs. J. liked to spoil us all like we were her other grandchildren.

"Doesn't she have a kid?" Paige asked.

"Yeah, I think his name is Zane."

"Okay . . ." Bayler moved into the next pose and then continued, "That still doesn't explain why she was at Justin's place this morning . . . in a towel."

"I think you need to ask Justin about it," Harper said with a smile. "He'll tell you why she was there, and he's not going to lie to you. It's your place now, too. You have a right to know why someone was using your stuff in the shower."

"Did she use your razor, too?" Bayler asked with a cringe. "Because that's gross."

"I don't know," I answered, feeling annoyed. "I didn't check before I left."

"Well, throw it out if she did."

I laughed, shaking my head at her. "Thanks, Bayler. That's the best advice I've heard all day."

"You're welcome," she said, smiling proudly.

Elly reached for my hand and placed it on her belly. "Are you going to be okay?"

I felt Baby Jennings kick against my hand and smiled. "Yeah, I already have another date set up for Sunday."

All four of my friends' eyes glared back at me, clearly trying to kill me with their stares.

"I know!" I cried, covering my face with my hands. "But I was pissed off at Justin this morning, and I had a message from a guy wanting to grab dinner."

"Please tell me this is the last one," Elly warned. "I don't know if I can take listening to anymore of your awful dates."

"Yeah, I'm going to close my account on the dating site after the dinner date."

"Thank God!" Paige, Harper and Bayler muttered in unison.

Elly pulled my hand away from my face and shot me a comforting smile. "We love you, Tessa, but we already know which guy will make you happy. You just need to give him the opportunity to do so."

"Talk to him," Harper reiterated. "Maybe Whitley just needed sugar for her coffee."

"The minute she got out of the shower?" Bayler asked incredulously, shooting her sister an annoyed glare.

"Hey, I'm trying not to jump to conclusions here," Harper stated.

Bayler rolled her eyes. "And the rest of us are trying to be realistic. Please, do join us."

Harper shoved Bayler off her mat and smiled at us. "All I'm saying is that Mav would be pissed at me if I accused him of sleeping with a woman before talking to him about it. It's all about trust. If you can't trust him, it's never going to work."

"She's right," Elly said, nodding. "Carter would be mad, too."

"Ugh," Bayler groaned. "I learned my lesson with Fletcher."

"You'll feel better after you talk to him," Paige insisted.

They smiled at me, which did nothing to ease my anxiety as I thought about how Justin might react. He'd probably be hurt, and the last thing I wanted was to become the eighth woman to let him down. "I'll talk to him later."

***

Justin

Saturday afternoon, I walked onto the basketball courts and was met with a strong, hard shove from Maverick. He pushed me up against the wall and pinned me there, his angry eyes glaring at me.

"What the hell, man?" I asked, pushing him off of me.

"What happened with Tessa this morning?" he asked, crossing his arms over his chest. "She came into the gym crying."

"I don't know what you're talking about," I said, completely taken aback by his words. "She ran out of the apartment this morning like her ass was on fire, so I didn't even get a chance to talk to her."

"Did something happen last night after you got home?" Carter asked, seeming just as confused as me.

I leaned my head back against the wall and sighed. I'd just about hit my limit with these guys and their meddling. "When I got home, she was already pretty drunk, but we talked and she seemed like she was in a better mood. She thanked me with a kiss on the cheek, asked me to help her with her dress, and then she went to bed. Nothing happened."

"Nothing happened?" Cash asked incredulously.

"You really are the stupidest guy ever!" Fletcher exclaimed, throwing his hands in the air.

Maverick sighed, shaking his head in disappointment, while Carter just looked at me in disbelief.

"Do you like her?" Cash asked, harshly.

"What kind of question is that?" I asked, glaring at him. "Of course, I like her, but I'm not about to take advantage of her."

"She was giving you the advantage!" Fletcher insisted bitterly. "I'm sorry, but this wasn't just some accident where you ran into her naked. If she didn't need your help getting the dress on, why would she need your help getting it off? She wanted you to take it off her. Jesus, Jameson, do we need to make you a playbook for how to get women?"

I rolled my eyes at him. "She said the zipper stuck."

The four of them smiled at one another and then laughed. "Zipper's stuck, my ass."

I pushed off the wall with my foot and glared at them. "Is it so awful that I actually want her to have a good time with me? I don't want to be the guy she uses to get over some asshole who stood her up. Look, I appreciate all the help you guys think you're giving me, but I don't need it. What I need is for you all to back off." I made eye contact with Carter and added, "And maybe stop telling your wife everything we talk about!"

"Hey," Carter said, pointing at Maverick. "He tells Harper shit, too."

"What about this morning?" Maverick asked quizzically. "Why would Tessa have walked in here so upset?"

"I don't know. Like I said, she barely talked to me this morning. She didn't even give me the chance to introduce her to Whit before she stormed out of the place."

"Wait," Cash said, holding his hand up. "Whitley was there?"

"Yeah, she came over this morning because the drain in her shower stopped working, so she asked if she could use ours."

Maverick thought about the situation for a second and then asked, "So, had she already taken a shower or—"

"Yeah, she stayed for a cup of coffee."

"Jameson," Fletcher muttered in a chastising tone, running a hand through his hair.

"What?" I asked, growing more irritated with them by the second. "What did I do wrong now?"

"Can you describe what Whitley was wearing while you two had coffee together?" Cash asked, laughing hysterically. "Please say just a towel!"

Oh fuck, I thought as I pictured the scene in my head, trying to imagine how Tessa might have seen it when she walked into the kitchen. It wasn't pretty. I saw myself talking with a gorgeous woman clothed in just a towel. Even though I hadn't given the towel much thought when I was actually talking to Whit, Tessa wouldn't have missed it. "She must've thought Whit and I—"

"Exactly," Maverick interjected.

"Why would she think that though?" I asked sharply, scowling. "I would never hang out with a woman and call another one for sex. She should know that!"

"Well, she has been screwed over by guys lately," Carter explained.

"I don't care!" I zipped my coat up harshly and looked at my friends. "She knows me. You guys know I would never fucking do something that shitty."

They nodded, glancing at one another silently.

"I have to go," I stated, shaking my head. "I have to talk to her. I can't believe she'd think I'd do that to her."

***

After running all the way back home, I'd calmed down from my initial outburst in the gym and found Tessa in her room. She was still in her yoga clothes, standing next to her bed, folding laundry. When she noticed me standing in the doorway, she dropped the shirt in her hand and shot me a weak smile. Her sad eyes gave her away, and I knew, despite it being the afternoon, this morning was still fresh in her mind.

"Hey," she said in a soft voice.

I walked toward her, determined to ease her troubled thoughts as I explained. "The woman I had coffee with this morning was Whitley Gonzales. She lives across the hall from us, and called this morning asking if she could use our shower because her drain is broken. So, I let her use ours, and she also used your shower gel because she thought it smelled nice. She has an eight-year-old son named Zane. She works part-time as a nurse and spends the rest of her time doing volunteer work."

Tears took over her eyes as she looked away from me, realizing that I knew.

I stalked closer and sat on the edge of her bed. "I wanted to introduce you to her this morning, but you ran out of here so fast, you didn't give me the chance."

"I'm sorry," she said, turning her gaze down to the floor.

"For what? For thinking I'd hang out with you all night and then invite a different woman over for sex, or for not sticking around this morning to meet our neighbor?"

She worried her lip with her teeth. "Both."

My hand curled around her neck and turned her face to look at me. "I would never treat someone like that, especially you."

"I know," she whispered, blinking away tears.

My other hand settled on her hip and pulled her in between my thighs. God, she looked so beautiful and raw standing in front of me right now. I wanted to crush my mouth to hers and show her all the ways she should be treated, but I knew I couldn't.

Not right now.

Caressing my thumb over her cheek, I continued. "I'm not going to be the guy you use to get over another one. I'm not going to take advantage of you after you've been drinking."

"Justin—"

"Please let me finish," I insisted.

She nodded silently.

"I'm not going to be the bad guy, Tessa. You can do whatever you want to me. Put on every single dress you own and ask me to unzip you out of it. Run around the apartment stark-ass naked. I still won't make a move on you. Not because I don't want to, but because I respect you."

"I wasn't running around the apartment naked!" she insisted with an eye roll and a flush of her cheeks.

Laughing, I dropped both hands to her waist and then stood up. "I know, but don't think I'm letting you live that down."

I turned to walk out of her room, but she grabbed my hand and stopped me. Glancing over my shoulder, I noticed contentment in her eyes. I felt all the satisfaction I needed from her right then with that one look.

"Thank you, Justin."

"For what?" I asked, curiously.

"For being the good guy."

Chapter Ten

Tessa

I spent the following evening with a guy named Mitch. We'd met at a nice restaurant in Midtown and had dinner. It wasn't anything too special, mostly because I was still reeling from my moment with Justin yesterday. The way my thoughts kept wandering back to him during my dinner conversation with Mitch only confirmed how awful I was at online dating. I couldn't wait to get home and tell Justin I was officially done with it.

Mitch hailed a cab outside of the restaurant and held the door open for me. I crawled in and told the driver my address as Mitch slid in next to me. He was around my height with dark hair and pale skin. He worked as a mechanic and mostly talked about cars throughout our entire meal. Still, he had passion for his job that a lot of people lacked, and I appreciated that.

When we arrived at my building, Mitch got out and offered to walk me to my door, even though I insisted he didn't need to.

"I want to," he said, smiling.

So, I let him, even though he'd been somewhat touchy during the cab ride back to my place, making me feel uneasy as he brushed a piece of hair out of my face, his hand lingering too long for my liking.

"Good evening, Miss Wilder," George said as we walked in.

"Thanks, George."

Once Mitch and I arrived at my door, I started digging through my purse for my keys. I smiled at him and said, "Thank you again for dinner. I had a great time."

"Me too," he said in low voice. "Maybe we can do it again sometime."

"Oh, uh—"

"Or maybe we can continue inside your place." He placed both hands next to my face and caged me in, pressing his body up against mine as he leaned in to kiss me.

"I-I'm sorry, Mitch," I said, turning my face away from him. "I didn't mean to give you the wrong impression. I just—"

"You just what?" he spit out angrily, his breath hot against my skin. "Do you enjoy teasing men for a free meal?"

"What?" I asked, completely confused. "That's not what I—"

"Oh, save it, bitch!" Before I could move, he swung his hand in the air and let it fly across my cheek in one quick slap that immediately sent me back to the past.

He grabbed my chin roughly and turned my face to look at him. "It's women like you who don't know when to shut the fuck up and just take it."

As his grip on my chin tightened and he shoved me back against the door, I reached into my purse and grabbed the mace. I watched him raise his hand again in the air, but I was quicker. I lifted the bottle and sprayed him in the eyes before he had a chance to hit me again.

His hands clawed at his eyes as he cried out in pain, so I grabbed ahold of his shoulders and kneed him in the groin.

He moaned louder. "You fucking bitch!"

Hunched over with one hand over his eyes, the other holding his crotch, he eventually fell to the ground in the fetal position, too weak to stand.

"You maced me!"

"You deserved it." I squatted down beside him, pulled the knife out of my purse and flipped the blade out. With my glove-clad hand, I opened one of his eyes with my fingers and twirled the blade in front of his face with my other hand.

"Fuck, fuck, fuck!" he shouted, twitching in pain. "I'm sorry! Please, let go of my eye! Please!"

"If I ever see you again, I swear to God I will use this knife here to carve your pathetic excuse of a penis into unidentifiable flesh. Do you understand?"

"Yes, God, yes!"

"Remember that the next time you think about raising a hand to a woman." I released him, shoving his head to the floor before standing up to catch my breath. I was still tightly clutching the knife in my hand. My body trembled as adrenaline rushed through my system, making it almost impossible to breathe. Numb, I stared down at the groaning asshole, rolling around on the floor in pain. I blinked once, but when I opened my eyes, I saw Trey's dad lying in a pool of his own blood.

"Tessa," Trey said, his voice shaking with fear. "You're bleeding. What do you want me to do? Tell me what to do."

"Call 9-1-1," I answered, unable to take my eyes off the motionless body only a few feet away from me.

"But what about your cut?"

Removing my hand from the injury on my stomach, I found my palm lined in blood and immediately put it back on my cut, applying as much pressure as I could. "Get me a towel and then make the call, okay?"

"I'll be right back." He ran to the bathroom and came back with a trail of towels falling behind him. "What now?"

I grabbed one of the longer towels and sat up straighter, swallowing back the agony as it cut further into my system. With the bloody knife still clenched in my right hand, I finally let it fall to the floor beside me. Wrapping the ragged cotton around my waist, I tightly secured it over the cut and fastened it into a temporary bandage.

"There's so much blood," Trey stated, clearly shocked.

"Don't look at it," I advised, pulling his attention away from the maroon puddles that now hid our kitchen tiles.

His eyes rimmed with tears as he looked at me. "He could've killed you."

"Tessa?" Justin asked, bringing me back to the present.

His hands covered the knife, and he took it from me. I studied my hands to make sure there wasn't any blood on them, and found them still enveloped in the warmth of my gloves. I quickly untied my coat and pressed a hand to my side. It also came back clean.

Thank God.

"Come on," Justin said, wrapping his arm around my shoulder. "Let's get you inside."

I nodded, and without a word, he walked me back into our apartment. Visions of the past mixing with the present flashed in my mind, causing me more paranoia with each step. Mitch's words were on replay, but I saw my stepdad saying them.

Once inside, he closed the door and secured the lock. I quickly rid myself of my coat and gloves, and Justin pulled me into his arms for a tight hug. "Jesus, you're shaking right now."

He pressed a kiss to the top of my head as his hands caressed up and down my arms. I focused my attention on Justin. On the sound of his voice. The scent of him surrounding me. His beautiful features distracted me from my greatest fear. "Are you okay? I heard a noise out in the hall, but by the time I opened the door, he was already on the ground complaining. What happened?"

"He hit me," I uttered, my voice raw in shock.

"What?" He pulled away to look me over, and I saw it in his eyes when they landed on the mark on my face. The sting from the slap still sizzled over my marred flesh, and it obviously didn't look any prettier by the alarmed look on Justin's face.

"Does it look bad?"

"There's going to be a bruise," he confirmed, causing tears to pool in my eyes as he led me over to the couch and sat me down next to him. He brushed my hair back out of my face and caressed my neck. "Are you okay?"

One glance at his worried face and I broke. The tears rushed out of my eyes as I shook my head, and then he gathered me up in his arms and began trailing his hands up and down my back. He held me as I sobbed for the eighteen-year-old girl who killed out of self-defense and for the twenty-four-year-old woman who still carried weapons with her because she was terrified she'd have to do it again. I cried until I was completely out of breath and the streams of tears ran dry.

"You're safe now," he whispered, pressing another kiss to my forehead. "You defended yourself, and I am so proud of you."

A powerful sniffle rocked through my chest as I took a deep breath. "I shouldn't have let him walk me to the door."

"No, this was not your fault," he said, running a hand over the back of my head.

"He was mad because I didn't want to let him inside." I pulled away from him and settled back against the couch. "He said I was a tease: that I teased men for a free meal."

"He should've respected your decision and left." He shook his head, gliding his thumb back and forth over my knuckles. "Do you want some ibuprofen? Maybe an ice pack?"

I wanted neither. I wanted to pretend none of this ever happened. After spending the last six years keeping them caged away, the demons ran wild again tonight. "I want to take a shower and go to bed."

"Okay." He grabbed my hands and helped me up. Holding my hand, he walked me back to the bathroom and started the shower for me. "If you need—"

"I know," I said numbly, staring at my reflection in the mirror. I dropped his hand and walked closer to the vanity.

The image transposed back to that night, a girl wearing a ripped shirt stained with blood, face smudged with tears, eyes wide in fear.

"Tessa?"

Shaking my head, the reflection blurred away to the present, and I surveyed the large red mark on my cheek. It'd already started to bruise. Speckles of black and blue filtered in under the red; spots of broken blood vessels had risen to the surface of my skin. Turning my face to the side, it felt hot as I ran my fingers along the tender flesh and assessed the damage. This was nothing compared to what I'd endured in the past.

I noticed Justin standing behind me and focused my attention back to him. I shot him a weak smile through the mirror and ran a hand through my hair. "Nothing a little makeup can't cover up."

He moved closer, placing his hands on either side of me. He rested his chin on my shoulder, his voice warm and comforting in my ear as he spoke. "All I see is how strong you are. Don't think for one second you need to cover that up."

If he only knew what I saw.

"I'll let you shower," he said, backing away from me.

"Thanks." I waited until he closed the door behind him to undress and step into the shower. When the hot water hit my skin I felt like I could finally breathe again. Too raw to move, I stood beneath the rushing water and closed my eyes. I imagined the water washing away all of my anxiety, taking every bad memory and scar with it as it spiraled down the drain, but I knew that was wishful thinking.

I opened my eyes, ran my fingers through my drenched hair, and trailed my eyes down my body. That's when I saw it. Red streams, mixing with the water, fell down my legs and settled around the drain before disappearing completely. I stumbled back against the wall, away from the water, but the steam billowing around me felt suffocating. It was impossible to escape the panic trembling through my body.

Breathing hard, I rested my head against the tiles and grabbed my shower gel. I scrubbed my arms and legs hard, determined to wash the memories away, but when I brushed the loofa over my side, I saw the scar. His inch-long tombstone permanently etched into my skin. Something I carried around with me every day. As if the mental scars weren't enough.

I washed my hair, rinsed off, and quickly got out of the shower and began drying off. I couldn't decide if I really wanted to go to bed now. I knew what awaited me when I fell asleep, especially with all the flashbacks I'd experienced already. The horrific night from years ago would play out in full detail, like a home movie my mind kept on hand whenever tragedy struck.

I wasn't ready for it.

Leaving the bathroom, I went to my room and threw on my pajamas. I sat on the bed and brushed my hair out, avoiding the mirror on my dresser.

A knock sounded at the door. "You decent?"

"Yeah," I called, laying my brush on the nightstand. I pulled back the covers on my bed and crawled underneath.

Justin came in carrying a glass of water in one hand and an icepack in the other. "I thought you might want these later." He pulled a couple of ibuprofen out of his pocket and set them next to the other items on the nightstand. He sat on the edge of the bed and smiled. "What are you reading tonight?"

He knew I read every night before bed, and that my Kindle could usually be found charging on my nightstand. "I'm in the middle of a second-chance romance, but I don't really feel up to reading tonight."

"What if I read to you?" He unhooked the device from its charger and turned around so he was sitting next to me with his back against the headboard. "Would that be okay?"

"You want to read a smutty romance novel aloud?" I asked incredulously, smiling.

"If it would make you feel better, maybe take your mind off things, then yes, I want to," he replied, unlocking the Kindle.

"Okay." I inched farther down the bed so I could get more comfortable. He did the same, propping a pillow up behind his head.

He opened the book I was currently reading and started on chapter ten. I focused on the deep, soothing tone of his voice more than the words he read. The warmth of his presence made me more comfortable than the pillows or sheets around me. I felt safe here with him, protected by his arm wrapped around my shoulders. He ran his fingers along the length of my arm and the soothing motion, combined with the sound of his voice reading to me, lulled me into a light, peaceful slumber I knew wouldn't last.

Chapter Eleven

Justin

Her scream woke me up.

The abrupt, alarming nature of it sent an immediate chill down my spine that made me jump out of bed and pull on my sweats. I ran into her room and found her sobbing hard in her sleep. She was lying on her side, and the moonlight coming in through her window highlighted the sweat lining her skin. The covers shifted closer to her feet the more she kicked.

Sliding into bed beside her, I was careful not to disturb her. Waking her up could possibly cause her more panic and confusion. She likely wouldn't remember any of this. Trey had been wrong about her nightmares. Nightmares usually occurred toward the end of the sleep cycle, and it was still relatively early. She'd fallen asleep not long after I started reading. When I left her room thirty minutes later, she was still sleeping peacefully.

She was experiencing a night terror: the sweating, the rapid breathing, the increased heart rate, the screaming and the crying. All happening while she slept.

I slowly placed my hand on her back, and her kicking stopped almost immediately. The sobs continued as I trailed my hand up and down her back tentatively. The more she calmed down, the closer I scooted toward her. I brushed her damp hair off of her forehead and studied the distraught features of her face. Her lips trembled as she whimpered and her eyes moved rapidly underneath their lids. Even with my hand on her back, I could feel her heart racing.

Laying my head on the pillow next to hers, I considered the cause of her terror. My thoughts immediately went to her date. She'd been abused earlier, and I noticed right away when I opened the door and found her in the hall that something wasn't right. She appeared more paranoid than scared. The way she studied her hands after I took her knife away, and the way she peered at herself in the bathroom mirror was so unlike her. She'd been so shaken yet detached at the same time.

But paranoid of what? The guy? The knife? Defending herself?

Whatever the cause, it was disturbing her sleep even if she didn't know it, and there was a good chance she'd wake up tomorrow and not remember any of this. But I needed her to remember it so I could talk to her about it tomorrow. Not only was talk therapy one of the best ways to treat night terrors, but I also needed her to talk about everything for my own sake. I'd been worried about her ever since I witnessed her wielding a knife. Seeing her so tormented while she slept completely gutted me. The scream from before still rang out in my head and gave me chills. All I could do was lay here with her. The unknown made me feel helpless.

No matter what frightened her, I wanted to know so that I could help her feel safe again. She was the one in our group of friends who'd had it the hardest. The one who grew up in a scary part of the city with parents who cared more about their vices than their children. Whatever demons she carried had come alive again tonight, and I hated watching her fight them alone, even though I knew she could.

Tracing her spine with my fingertips, I thought, *You're the strongest woman I know, Tessa Wilder.*

Ten minutes after lying down beside her, her cries simmered and her breathing stabilized. My hand continued soothing her back, but eventually the episode ended with her drifting off into a peaceful slumber again.

***

When morning came, I felt her roll over, but it was her sharp intake of air that woke me up.

She scooted away from me quickly, covering herself up with the sheets despite being fully clothed in her pajamas. "What are you doing in my bed?"

Not knowing exactly how to answer her, I sat up, rubbed the sleep from my eyes, and gazed over at her. She still looked tired with dark circles under her eyes and her hair a mess around her face. The curiosity furrowing her brows gave her an adorable smirk as she waited for me to speak, but it quickly faded into a perceptive glare the longer I took to answer.

"He told you, didn't he?" she asked, immediately crawling out of bed.

"Yes," I replied, running a hand through my hair.

She paced over to her closet and began rummaging through the clothes. "I can't believe he would tell you something so private."

"He's your brother," I said, placing my feet on the floor. "He worries about you."

"Well, he doesn't need to." She found an outfit, threw it on the bed and then studied her shoe rack.

"Tessa." I stepped toward her, but she moved past me and grabbed her door.

"I really need to get ready for work," she insisted coldly, avoiding eye contact with me. "So, if you could—"

"No," I said abruptly, shaking my head. "I really need to talk to you about last night."

"Well, I don't want to talk about it right now!" she exclaimed, waving to the hall. "I want you to get out so I can get dressed for work."

"Okay," I said, which seemed to appease her since she finally looked at me. I planted my ass on the edge of her bed and crossed my arms over my chest. "I'll talk while you get dressed for work. It's not like I haven't seen you naked already."

"Why are you being like this?" she asked with a scowl, pulling her tank over her head. Her small, perky breasts bounced as she wiggled out of her shorts and sauntered over to her dresser wearing nothing but a thong.

Jesus, look at her. She carried a strong presence about her that I found absolutely breathtaking, marching around the room, naked and pissed off.

Focus, Jameson.

"I'm worried about you," I replied, holding her gaze in the mirror as she slipped her arms through her bra straps. "Do you remember last night? Do you remember what the terror was about?"

"Of course I do," she said, rolling her eyes. "It's the same every time. Now, could we please drop it?"

"No, I want to know. What was it about?"

She scoffed, shaking her head as she pulled on a pair of navy dress pants. "Trust me, you don't, and I'm not telling you."

Feeling defeated, I stewed quietly and watched as she finished getting dressed. She pulled a green print sweater over her head and stepped into a pair of heels. She spritzed on her signature scent, and went to work on her hair, powerfully brushing the strands in an attempt to rid them of their knots. She seemed to avoid the mirror at all costs.

As I stood up and walked over to her she turned around to face me. My eyes immediately went to the black-and-blue mark on her cheek and wondered if that's why she couldn't look in the mirror. "Why won't you look in the mirror?"

"What?" she asked, feigning confusion. "What are you talking about? I've looked in the mirror."

"This entire time you've been brushing your hair, you've been looking down at the floor," I explained, caressing my thumb over her unmarred cheek. "You've been standing in front of the mirror, but you won't look in it. Why?"

"Because I don't want to see the mark he left on my face!" she replied angrily, turning her head away from my hand. "Will you drop it now?"

"That's not it! You could look at it last night, but not now? You're stronger than that, Tessa," I said, gritting my teeth. "It's something else, and I want to know what it is."

"It's none of your goddamn business!" She went into the bathroom, and I followed close behind. She flipped on the vanity light and started applying makeup. "See, I'm looking in the mirror just fine. Please, Justin, just let it go. I'm fine."

You're not fine, I thought, feeling beyond irritated. "This isn't over."

***

A few hours later, Carter and I walked into Elly's clinic for lunch. Part of me had been dreading coming here all morning because I'd texted Tessa and she never responded. I worried she might be pissed at me over our morning discussion, which only pissed me off because she'd evaded most of it. But Elly sat at our usual table alone with her lunch already out on the table.

"Where's Tessa?" I asked, sitting down across from her.

She glared at me. "What the hell happened to her face?"

"What's wrong with her face?" Carter asked, seeming confused.

Elly sighed and rolled her eyes. "She has a bruise on her left cheek, and she thinks makeup is doing a great job of covering it up but it's not. I was waiting to talk to her about it over lunch, but she left to have lunch with her brother."

"Oh." I opened my bag of chips and ate a couple.

"Justin!" Elly exclaimed, kicking me under the table. "You have to tell us what happened. She's supposed to come with us to our doctor's appointment this afternoon. I need to know if I should talk to her about it before or after."

"I'd wait until after." I uncapped my water bottle and took a drink. "Even though you probably won't get much from her. I tried talking to her this morning, and she dodged almost every question I asked."

"So, you don't know how she got the bruise?" Elly asked.

Taking a deep breath, I leaned back in my chair and exhaled. "I'm not a hundred percent sure how it all happened. All I know is that she came home from a date, the guy called her a tease and hit her because she didn't want to invite him in, and when I opened the door to the commotion in the hall, I found her threatening to shred his manhood with a knife."

"Holy shit," Carter muttered, dropping his sandwich. "A knife?"

"Yeah, a fucking knife," I said, shaking my head. "He kept complaining about his eyes, so I'm assuming she sprayed him with mace first."

"Fuck," he said with a shudder.

"She was defending herself," Elly contended, glaring at us. "What was she supposed to do? Just stand there and take it?"

"God, no," I retorted with a scowl. "But why does she need mace *and* a knife?"

"I don't know." Elly shrugged and turned her attention back to her food. "Maybe she feels safer with two forms of protection."

Carter excused himself to use the restroom, and the minute he was out of earshot, I pointed at Elly. "You know something."

"I do not," she insisted.

"You met Tessa during a counseling program, right?" I asked, knowing for a fact that was true. "Why was she in the program?"

"Justin, I can't tell you that. Even if I knew why, it would be unethical."

"I know." I stared down at the wood tabletop and traced the design with my finger. "I think last night triggered something. She did things that don't add up for me."

"What do you mean?" she asked curiously.

"She studied her hands," I said, holding my hands out in front of me like Tessa had done the night before. "Like they had something on them. She patted her shirt and then stared at her hand again, like she was looking for something even though she was the one who had the knife, not him."

"What are we talking about now?" Carter asked as he sat back down at the table.

Elly hushed him with a glare and then waved her hand at me to continue. "Go on."

"Before she took a shower, she studied herself in the mirror and she wasn't just looking at the mark on her face."

"Sounds like she was in shock," Elly speculated.

I nodded, leaning my elbows up on the table as I ate a few more chips. "Then she had a night terror last night. I mean, full on crying during her sleep. Her scream woke me up. If Trey hadn't told me she had nightmares, I wouldn't have known what to do to calm her down. He said she has them every once in a while, and that he didn't know what triggered them. But I think that guy hitting her triggered it."

"Did she remember any of it this morning?" Elly asked.

"Yes, she knew exactly what it was about," I said, growing more frustrated. "But she wouldn't tell me. She avoided talking about it, and now she's not here for lunch. I bet you she didn't even have lunch with Trey. She was pissed this morning about him telling me about the night terrors. I think she's displaying symptoms of post-traumatic stress disorder."

"Justin," Elly stated warily.

"What!" I shoved away from the table, screeching my chair across the floor. Treading around the small space of the lobby with my hands resting on the back of my head, I thought out loud. "She told me it was none of my business, but it is my business! She made it my business when she moved in and made me fall for her! I can't help her if she won't tell me what's wrong!"

"Have you told her how you feel?" Elly asked.

"What? No," I answered with a grimace. "I mean, I've eluded to it, but I haven't come right out and said it to her."

Carter smirked. "You have to tell her, man."

I stopped pacing and looked at the two of them huddled close together, smiling at each other. Carter's hand rested on Elly's pregnant belly as she leaned in and kissed him.

"Can we please focus on the real issue here?" I bit out in an irritated tone.

They broke away laughing, and Elly rested her head on Carter's shoulder. "Justin, did you ever stop to think that she might open up to you if she knew how you felt?"

"Are you kidding me?" I asked, astounded. I pulled my chair back up to the table and sat down. "I'm surprised she doesn't know already since you two gossip like a couple of schoolgirls."

"She's my best friend," Carter said, kissing his wife. "Of course, we're going to talk about the rest of you."

Elly smirked. "And we weren't really sure."

"Thanks." I continued eating my lunch, overwhelmed with curiosity. "How am I supposed to tell her?"

Carter grinned at Elly. "I think you tell her the same way you told us."

"But I was angry," I replied, significantly confused. "I don't want to scare her."

Elly giggled and rolled her eyes. "There's this thing called passion, Justin. You may have heard of it before."

"And?" I deadpanned.

"Falling in love will bring out the passion in you," she explained, smiling at Carter. "Cherish it."

Chapter Twelve

Tessa

I was feeling ecstatic as I arrived back at the apartment after Carter and Elly's doctor appointment. I was the only one who knew the sex of their baby, and I couldn't wait for them and the rest of our friends to find out what they were having at the gender reveal party I was planning. I spent the whole way home brainstorming reveal ideas and how I could decorate Judge's. I even sent Paige a text to get her opinion on one of my ideas, but I'd yet to hear back from her.

Listening to the heartbeat and watching how amazed both Elly and Carter were over the sound of it made me feel both inspired and sad at the same time. I wanted what they had, that endless love that continuously radiated between the two of them. They gazed at each other, and anyone who witnessed it knew they were still falling in love. I wanted that kind of love: the kind that kept a person falling for another over and over again, knowing their feelings were reciprocated.

I also wanted a baby. It was hard not to with Harper and Maverick's little angel already around, and Carter and Elly's arriving in a few months. Before their appointment, Elly and I had been shopping online for baby clothes. The adorable outfits made me want a baby of my own, but I'd happily play aunt, spoil those babies the best I could, and dream about motherhood in the meantime.

"How'd Elly and Carter's appointment go?" Justin asked as I walked through the door. My joy turned to uneasiness.

"Great," I said, slightly on edge. I'd avoided him today, mostly because I didn't want to talk about the topic from this morning, which only caused me more anxiety. He was hard to ignore. The texts he'd sent went unanswered, even though I took solace in them because his words meant he cared. I'd left for lunch, too worried we might pick up where we left off this morning.

Those same worries ate at me again now that we were alone together.

"I ordered a pizza for dinner," he said, sitting down on the couch. "I hope that's okay."

"That's fine." I tossed my coat and purse over the back of a bar stool at the island and took a seat at the other end of the couch. The tension between us was growing more evident by the second with his clipped phrases and my short answers.

We sat in silence, watching *American Pickers* on The History Channel. It was one of his favorite shows, and I blamed Mrs. J. for that. It was like the man version of *Antiques Roadshow*, and she'd gotten him hooked on it. But I couldn't totally blame her. Justin was addicted to The History Channel, so he would've found it one way or another. The fact that these guys enjoyed digging through other people's junk grossed me out, and the fact that they almost always found a pot of gold amidst all the garbage pissed me off, too. But the way they rattled off historical information reminded me of Justin, and that was the only thing I liked about the show; I learned something new each time I watched.

When it cut to a commercial, Justin turned the volume down and shifted towards me, placing his arm over the back of the couch. "I'm sorry about this morning. I wasn't trying to interrogate you. I just think you deserve so much more than everything you've had to deal with lately."

"You think I don't know that?" I asked fervently, shifting my body to face his. "I know I deserve more, but I don't know how to deserve a guy like you! I know more about drugs and alcohol than I do about things like the ballet or any of this antique crap! I can roll a joint or get away with stealing a bottle of liquor because those are the things I watched growing up." Resting my elbow on the couch next to his hand, I ran a hand through my hair as tears threatened my eyes. "After you offered me a place to stay, I decided to try online dating because I was trying to get over you. Now, you want to know my darkest secret, and I'm scared to tell you because I'm not over you, not even close. How can I be when you send me lunch, or when you leave the bar early to come hang out with me after I've been stood up, or when you read to me in bed because I'm too shook up to read myself? You're the perfect guy, Justin. You're sweet and caring, and I know you would never do anything to hurt me." I brushed away a fallen tear and gazed back at him. "But I don't know how to be good enough for you. All I know is—"

"You can't get over me," he interjected, before grabbing the back of my neck and covering my lips with his. He stole my breath away in an instant, kissing me back with the same fervor as if he couldn't breathe without me. Scooting closer, he eliminated the space between us and tilted my head so he could devour me at a different angle, tangling his tongue around mine and sucking in sweet, smooth motions that made my insides tremble with need. He was all I could focus on. The delicious cinnamon taste of his gum still lingered in his mouth, and his clean, masculine scent enveloped me. His touch electrified my senses, awakening a passion that couldn't go unnoticed. I never wanted this kiss to stop, yet at the same time I did, so it could start all over again with him desperately grabbing me and taking what had always been his. My lips have always had his name on them, and now he knew it. He massaged the back of my neck with his fingers before breaking away with that boyish grin spreading across his face. "You can't get over me because I'm falling in love with you."

Relief flooded my system, and my heart ached hearing his words. "You are? Since when?"

"Do you remember that day I freaked out about the food and laundry?"

I nodded with a laugh, cupping his face in my hands. "Like it was yesterday."

"I've wanted to kiss you ever since," he admitted, pressing a chaste kiss to my lips. "You've never tried to change me, and I love that about you. So, you have to know that I don't want to change a thing about you. No matter what you've been through, it's not going to affect the way I feel about you. You're a strong, beautiful woman because of everything you've had to endure, and that's enough for me." He lightly brushed his thumb over the bruise on my cheek and looked me in the eyes. "You just don't have to brave it all alone anymore."

Wrapping my arms around his shoulders, I pulled him into a hug. "I don't want to be alone anymore, but I don't know if I can tell you what happened, why I have the nightmares. I've never talked about it out loud."

He brushed a hand over the back of my head soothingly. "I think talking about it might help them go away. Release those demons so they can't haunt you anymore."

I pulled away with tears threatening my eyes and studied his features. He stared back at me with those bright blue eyes shimmering with understanding and care, his mouth lined with a delicate smile. Reaching out, he brushed a fallen tear off my cheek and held my gaze.

"You don't have to tell me right now," he murmured against my lips. "But I do want to know because I love you."

"Promise me, when I tell you, it won't change the way you see me," I whispered, sealing my lips over his.

His lips brushed over mine once and then twice before he muttered, "I promise."

Then he lifted me into his lap, and our mouths collided, hard and demanding, securing our promises to each other. Eventually, I'd tell him about the nightmare, but right now, I just wanted to drown myself in his touch for the night, and live out every pleasurable dream and fantasy I've ever had about the one guy I've always wanted.

Straddling his hips, I ran my fingers through his soft, sandy hair and tugged, eliciting an amorous moan that vibrated from him all the way down to my lady box. He anchored his hands to my waist as I rocked myself against his erection and continued devouring his perfect mouth. He was an excellent kisser. His tongue worshipped mine like it was the holy grail, drinking every ounce of pleasure I offered and giving it back to me fruitfully. We were licking and sucking until neither one of us could breathe. Never in all the years of our friendship had I experienced Justin so wanton and needy like he was now, and I felt victorious for making him lose control.

Creeping my hands underneath his shirt, I grazed my fingers over his sculpted abs as a knock sounded at the door. He broke away from my lips and rested his head back on the couch.

"That's the pizza," he sighed, his eyes dark with desire as a wicked smile played at his lips.

Jesus, he's hot when he's turned on.

I smiled down at his arousal and climbed off of him. "I'll get it."

"Good idea." He pulled out his wallet and handed me a fifty. "Tell him to keep the change."

I scoffed, rolling my eyes. "I'm all for tipping generously but that's way too much."

He reached for my hand and pulled me in between his legs. "If it means getting you back in my lap quicker, I'll give him a hundred."

"Who are you, and what have you done with Justin Jameson?" I asked incredulously. Seeing him this turned on by simply making out made me more eager to experience how amazing he must be in bed.

He laughed, pulling me down for another quick kiss. "What have I done? I let myself fall for you. I think it was the best decision I've made in a long time." He gave my ass a light tap and smiled. "Grab our pizza and get back here."

"Okay, okay," I twirled around and opened the door. I paid for our pizza and just as the delivery guy started to walk away, Whitley exited her apartment across the hall wearing a pair of dark green scrubs.

"Hey, Tessa," she said, offering me a smile, even though I didn't deserve one from her.

"Hi," I replied, leaning against the doorframe.

She eyed the box of pizza and laughed. "Looks like Justin cooked tonight, huh?"

"Yeah," I said with a shrug. "I couldn't completely break him of his takeout habit."

"How he doesn't gain weight eating out all the time, I'll never know."

"Right?" I laughed along with her. An awkward silence hung in the hallway between us for a few seconds and I finally broke. "Whitley, I'm really sorry about the other morning. It was a misunderstanding on my part, and I hope you can forgive me for acting like a bitch. I had no idea you were our neighbor. I thought you were some girl he hooked up with, and I'm woman enough to admit that I was jealous."

"It's okay. I completely understand." The smile on her face widened as she stepped closer to me. She motioned me forward like she had a secret to tell me, so I gave her my ear and she whispered. "Just don't hurt him. He's a great guy, and I know he really likes you."

"I won't because the feeling's mutual."

"Good," she said, backing away. "Have a good night, Tessa."

"You too, Whit."

Walking back into the apartment, I found Justin still sitting on the couch. The bulge in his pants was still quite evident.

"Come here," he said.

I dropped the box of pizza on the coffee table and hopped back into his lap and pressed my lips to his, unable to get enough of him. The scratch of his stubble branded my skin, creating a beautiful contradiction to the way his mouth gently glided over mine as our kisses deepened. I couldn't wait to discover the rest of him. The way he felt in my hands. How he sounded when he came. The way he looked during sex. The idea of us in bed together made me want to drag him back to my room and find out the wonders I still had yet to discover about him.

Toying with the waistband of his sweats, I ran my hand down the front of them and traced the outline of his cock with my fingertip.

"Tessa," Justin groaned, leaning his forehead against mine.

"What?" I teased, gripping his length through the material. "You're commando underneath here. Do you know how hard it's been living with you knowing you walk around in sweats commando?"

"Yes, I do," he laughed, grabbing my wrist. He pulled my hand away from his shaft and lifted it to his mouth. Pressing a soft kiss to my palm, he smiled. "Almost as hard as it is living with you in the scanty clothes you call pajamas."

"What's wrong with my pajamas?!" I exclaimed, laughing.

"You don't wear a bra, and the shorts are damn near underwear."

"They're called boy shorts," I explained, linking my hands around the back of his neck. "You don't like them?"

"I love them," he said, raking his hands through my hair. "What I don't like is the idea of other men seeing you in them."

With his admission, I softened in his hands like putty. "You don't have to worry about other guys. You're the only one I want seeing me like that."

"No more dating?" he asked, curiosity lining his voice.

"I'm done with online dating."

"Good." He dragged me back in for a quick peck on the lips and then pulled away wearing a big grin. "Because I bought tickets to the ballet, and I plan on making it our first date."

"Really?" I asked eagerly. "You're taking me to the ballet."

"I told you I would," he said, caressing my cheek. He studied my bruise and then gently pressed a sweet kiss below it. "I want to do this right with you."

"So no bedroom shenanigans tonight?" I asked jokingly.

Instead of laughing like I thought he would, he trailed his lips along my neck up to my ear. "No bedroom shenanigans. Trust me. It'll be worth the wait."

"Pretty sure of yourself there, Dr. Jameson?" I asked, biting back a moan.

He chuckled against my ear and then sucked on my lobe. "I'm sure if I reached into your pants and pulled your thong to the side, I'd find you soaking wet for me."

My heart rate escalated with his hot, wanton words as heat flushed over my skin and need pounded between my legs. *Holy shit, he talks dirty, too.* He hardly said anything around all of us, but secretly had a filthy mouth when it came to sex. Jackpot.

"Am I right?" He teased me, sucking on the skin beneath my ear as he caressed a finger down the center seam of my pants. "Tell me I'm right."

"You're so right," I said, in a breathy voice I didn't even recognize as I rocked against his hard-on.

"See," he quipped, halting my hips with his hands and pulling back to face me. "Anticipation is half the fun."

"Tell that to my lady box," I murmured to myself.

Or so I thought.

Justin lifted me off his lap and threw me back down on the couch with ease. I laughed loudly, completely surprised by his actions. Sliding in between my legs, he pressed a kiss to the inside of my covered thigh and then smiled at me before speaking directly to my lady box. "Look, I know we both want to have some fun right now, but I'm trying to show your owner the respect she deserves. My dick is just as devastated as you are, trust me, but work with me here."

The sight of him between my legs, so close to the place that I needed him most, coupled with his warm, sexy voice vibrating against my sensitive flesh, turned me on even more. My yoga pants did nothing to block his charms.

"She drives a hard bargain," he said, pressing a kiss to my stomach. He crawled up my body and hovered over me. "I could smell how aroused you are."

"And you're not going to do anything about it?" I asked, pouting slightly.

"Not tonight." That devilish smile played on his lips again as his eyes danced with excitement. "Are you hungry?"

"Pizza will have to do," I said, shoving him off of me.

***

Justin

I came back into the living room with plates and beers, and set them on the coffee table next to our pizza. Loading each of our plates with a couple of slices, I sat back down next to Tessa and pulled her close to my side.

Tonight had gone a lot better than I thought it would. I expected more yelling and another fight about her night terror. I had no idea she would confess her feelings for me, and I couldn't stop the elation pounding in my chest from her confession. But some of the things she'd said still bothered me. Even with the raging hard-on I was trying to overcome, her words echoed in my mind.

"Can I ask you something?" I asked, relaxing back against the couch and gazing over at her.

"Yeah," she said, swallowing a bite of her food.

"You said earlier that you didn't know how to be good enough for me," I stated, running a hand down her arm. I linked our fingers together and asked, "Why'd you think that? Did I do something to make you feel like you weren't?"

"No, you didn't." She took a deep breath and rested her head on my shoulder. "For years, I thought you wouldn't want me because of my past. I dropped out of high school, so I don't have several degrees like you do; all I have is my GED. I'm not as smart as you, and I don't come from money like the rest of our friends. I'm just a receptionist. I thought you'd want someone more like yourself."

"You're perfect just the way you are, and that's enough for me. No degree or amount of income is going to change that. You're more than just a receptionist, too. You know if it weren't for you, Elly's clinic wouldn't run as smoothly as it does. But I also know it's not your dream job. You should do what you love. What do you love?"

She thought about my question for a minute while chewing, and then her face lit up with a smile as she stated, "I love planning events."

I shot her a smile and nodded. "So, you start your own business. We have plenty of friends who run their own businesses, so you won't have to do it alone. Maybe you can start out gradually, gain a few clients, and then you'll be able to quit the receptionist job."

"I've only planned a few things," she said with a shrug. "I don't know if I can make a career out of it."

"You never know until you try," I said, placing my hand on her chin. I lifted her lips to mine and gave her a kiss.

"Just like this thing between us. I'll be honest. It wasn't until you moved in with me that I started thinking about you as more than a friend. Before, my history with women made me give up on the idea of dating. Now, I've tried sitting back and pretending to be okay with you dating other guys, but I haven't been okay with it at all. It's killed me to watch other guys hurt you, and after the other night when that guy hit you, I couldn't pretend anymore. So, I'm going to try my best to be the man you deserve because you are enough for me. I need you to believe that. Believe in yourself, because I do."

"Okay," she whispered with a smile as tears pooled in her eyes.

"Do you want another slice?" I asked, nodding toward the food.

She shook her head. "No, thanks."

I grabbed another slice for myself, took a bite and then watched as she placed her empty plate on the coffee table and wiped her eyes. She took a deep breath, gathered herself, and then shot me a weak smile over her shoulder. I knew by the way her smile didn't reach her eyes that something was still bothering her.

"What is it?" I asked, running a hand down her back.

"I don't want to ruin tonight by talking about my nightmare, but I don't want to wait to tell you about it either," she confessed, bouncing her leg nervously. "After everything you've done for me, you deserve to know what happened."

"You're not going to ruin our night." Setting my plate on the table, I carefully placed my hand on her knee to ease her nerves, then I pulled her into my side and relaxed back against the couch with her. My stomach flipped knowing I was about to find out what terrified her so much during sleep, but I pushed the anxiety away and focused on her. If she had the courage to tell me, I needed to endure whatever I heard, regardless of the horrible scenarios formulating in my mind. "I want to know. I want to know everything about you, even the dark stuff you've never told anyone."

She nodded and swallowed hard before starting, avoiding eye contact with me as she stared down at her lap. "It happened a couple days after my eighteenth birthday. My mom had already died a few years earlier, so Trey and I were still living with his dad. I'd dropped out of school two years prior because Mom was no longer around to take care of things. That's when the abuse started. His dad hadn't started abusing us until after Mom died. She'd been his punching bag when she was alive, so I wasn't surprised when he started in on us after she died. I just tried my best to protect Trey from him.

"Anyway, I was washing dishes that night when Trey's dad came into the kitchen asking me for money. I waitressed full-time at a diner, and he was always asking for money for either alcohol or drugs. Since I started working, I'd been hiding money, in hopes of saving enough to get Trey and I out of the shithole we called home. So, I told him I didn't have any extra to give him, which was the truth. I was planning on taking what I had and leaving with Trey the following day while his dad was out.

"But that night, his dad kept harassing me for the money. He even brought up how he knew I was hiding some, but that he didn't know where. He ransacked the apartment looking for it. I tried to ignore him as I finished the dishes, but then he grabbed a knife and threatened to kill me if I didn't tell him where the money was."

"Did you tell him?" I asked.

"No," she replied, wiping away a tear. "I worked my ass off for that money, money that I dropped out of high school for so we would have food to eat and a roof over our heads. I wasn't giving him shit just so he could piss it away on booze or drugs."

I held her tighter and encouraged her to continue. "What happened next?"

"He threw me up against the fridge and hit me. He called me names, slapped me around, but when I didn't fess up, he took the knife and stabbed me in the stomach. Then he threatened to hurt Trey if I didn't tell him where the money was. The second he brought up Trey, I lost it because I knew he'd hurt him if I didn't do something. So, I kneed him in the groin and pushed him off me. The knife dropped out of his hand as he fell to the ground in pain, and then I grabbed it and put it right through his heart without even thinking about it. I felt nothing when I stabbed him. I just did it. I killed him."

Holy shit. "Tessa . . ."

A tear streamed down her cheek as she continued. "It wasn't until Trey came into the kitchen that I realized what I'd done, that I was bleeding, too. He helped me bandage the cut on my stomach and called 9-1-1. They didn't charge me with anything because it was in self-defense, and we had neighbors who heard the whole ordeal. But I had to go through a counseling program to make sure I was fit to be a guardian for Trey. That's where I met Elly. She was an intern for one of the counselors at the time."

She exhaled a shaky breath and dried her face with her hands. "After that, I started carrying mace and a knife with me because they made me feel safe. I think that's what scares me the most, the thought of being attacked again and knowing that I have the ability to do what I did. That I would do it all over again if it meant protecting the people I love and myself. I think that's why I still hold on to it, because I'm afraid it's going to happen again, and the other night, it started to. After my date hit me, it just took me right back to that night. I knew I wasn't going to actually use the knife on him, but once I had it in my hand, I felt safer.

"Situations that remind me of that night usually trigger nightmares. I can still hear his threatening words and see the blood covering the kitchen floor. I can see myself in bloody clothes with the bruises he gave me. I remember Trey being so incredibly scared for me that he could barely dial the phone to call for help."

All I could do was stare back at her in admiration and understanding. Now, I understood why she reacted the way she did the other night. This beautiful woman sitting next to me had lived in hell and fought her way out, and she thought it would make me think differently of her; how incredibly wrong she was. She was the strongest woman I knew, and if anything, hearing what she's been through, what she did to survive, just made me fall deeper in love with her.

"Say something," she urged anxiously, nudging my arm.

I moved her into my lap so she faced me and I asked, "Can I see the scar?"

Anger quickly masked the anxiety gracing her gorgeous features. "After everything I just told you, you want to see the scar he left me with?" she asked incredulously.

"Yes," I said, pressing a chaste kiss to her lips. "I promise to say something clever then."

She rolled her eyes and lifted her shirt up, pointing to the left side above her hipbone. I ran my finger over the inch-long linear scar that marred her pale flesh. I'd seen her in a bikini numerous times and never noticed this scar, so I leaned over and kissed it, showering it with the attention it deserved. "You probably hate this scar, don't you?"

"Of course I hate it," she muttered hastily. She tried to pull her shirt back down to cover it up, but I caught her hand and stopped her. "He gave it to me. It's like I'm constantly carrying him around with me."

"Have you ever admired it? Touched it and really looked at it?" I asked, gazing up at her.

"Why would I do that?" she questioned, furrowing her brows. "I just told you I hated it."

The last thing I wanted to do was upset her, but if she didn't know how to be proud of herself, I would show her. Taking one of her hands in mine, I slowly guided her finger over the raised skin on her stomach. "This scar is proof that you're stronger than him. When you look at it, when you feel it, you should remember the strength you carry with you every day. Not everyone would've been able to do what you did to protect the people they love."

"I know," she stated, staring down at her stomach with me. "I've just hated him for so long, for everything he put us all through, that I'd look at it and feel like he was still harassing me. Sometimes I wish it never would've happened, but I know if it hadn't, I wouldn't be where I am today."

"Exactly," I said, caressing her cheek. "You fought your way out of a bad situation, and you should be proud of that. I know I am."

"Thank you." Her eyes connected with mine as she leaned into my palm and smiled, the cloud of worry dissipating from her gray irises. "Thank you for listening, for always being here for me, and for not running away from all of my baggage."

"You made me fall in love with you by simply being yourself." Cupping the back of her neck, I drew her in for another kiss. "Which means I'm going to love you along with all of your scars, even the ones I can't see or touch."

She leaned her forehead against mine and sighed. "The more you talk, the deeper I fall for you."

"Good. My plan's working," I teased, smiling against her mouth. "Now, tell me about the party you're planning for Carter and Elly's baby. I know you've already thought of ideas. I want to hear them."

"I can't tell you!" she exclaimed, her body melting against mine as she wrapped her arms around my neck. "Telling you about my ideas won't do them justice. You'll have to come to the party to really experience them."

"You're not even going to tell me the gender of the baby?" I asked in disbelief.

"Nope," she said, crushing her mouth against mine. "But I will spend the rest of the night making out with you. Will that do?"

"I suppose," I said, feigning disappointment before slipping my tongue into her mouth.

Chapter Thirteen

Tessa

Our dynamic quickly changed in regard to our living situation. We couldn't keep our hands to ourselves anymore. We spent our nights sleeping together in one of our rooms. Any free time we had usually turned into a make-out session that grew more intense each time. We hadn't had sex yet, which was perfectly fine since tonight was our first date. Justin had gotten us tickets to the ballet, so I skipped the gym after work and immediately came home to start getting ready. I'd never been to the ballet before, but I knew I wanted to stun him in the gray dress he wanted me to wear tonight.

Tonight, I wanted all of him.

So, I primped myself. I took a long shower, shaving everywhere and exfoliating my face. I spent extra time on my hair, blow-drying it and styling it in big, soft waves that hung over my shoulders. I rubbed my favorite lotion on my smooth skin, knowing the smell would drive him crazy. I even threw on my nicest set of lingerie: a matching black bra and thong. The gray cashmere dress he wanted me to wear was short, falling a few inches above my knee, so black stockings were a must this evening, but I decided to forgo the garter belt. Sure, it looked sexy, but it was just another item he'd have to take off me later, canceling out its sex appeal.

I slipped into the dress and admired myself in the mirror. I understood why he loved this dress so much. The dark gray material hugged my slim figure, but was looser than some knit dresses with its material twisted down the center for a flattering, edgy look that ended in a small slit. The deep V in the front was so dramatic it showed off the minimal cleavage I had, and it scooped low in the back showing off more skin. Its long sleeves were perfect for winter though, and knowing he wanted me in this dress made me feel even more excited for our date.

The bruise from my assault had vanished over the week, so I thankfully didn't need to spend any extra time covering it up with makeup; the last thing I wanted him to see when he looked at me tonight was a bruise another man gave me.

No, tonight, when he looked at me, I wanted him to know that I was his, that I took the time to look good for him and only him. That I was so grateful he was taking me some place I'd never been before for our first date. But most importantly, that I knew deep down in the very marrow of my bones that he would never lay an abusive finger on me or string together a verbal attack toward me.

With minutes to spare, I stepped into my black high-heeled booties and put in a pair of silver earrings. I grabbed my black pea coat and clutch and quietly made my way into the living room, where I found him ready to go. He hadn't heard me come out of my room, so I took a moment to take in his gorgeous appearance. While I enjoyed the commando-in-sweats look he sported on a regular basis, he cleaned up nicely, which I appreciated just as much. He wore gray dress pants with a navy blazer over a light blue button-down that made his hazel-blue eyes pop against his naturally tan skin. His dirty blond hair was pulled back in its signature man bun, and his clean, aquatic cologne with a hint of musk lingered in the room as he paced back and forth nervously.

My heart swelled watching him move, knowing he was just as eager for tonight as I was. He checked his watch a couple of times and stopped to study my brother's photographs as he walked by them. It was obvious he had no idea I was watching him because he rarely ever showed this much emotion. It was cute knowing he was nervous for our date, even though he had nothing to worry about.

"Looking good there, Jameson," I called out as I stepped into the living room.

He turned toward my voice and smiled away his nerves, bringing out those drop-dead sexy dimples he masterfully owned. His eyes studied my body, leaving behind a warm trail of lust that made my body ache for his touch. "You look absolutely breathtaking."

I twirled around for him and laughed. "You like?"

"I love," he replied, pulling me closer. He wrapped his arms around my waist, settling them on the small of my back. "Are you ready for the ballet?"

"As ready as I'll ever be," I answered.

"Let's get you into your coat."

He grabbed the garment from my hands and helped me into it. With my back to him, I placed my arms in the sleeves and tied the belt around my waist. Reaching for his hand, I threaded my fingers through his and smiled up at him. "Don't be nervous."

"You saw me pacing?"

"I did." I pressed a kiss to his cheek and then wiped away my lipstick stain. Cupping his face in my palm, I reassured him, brushing my fingers over his stubble. "You already have me. I'm not going anywhere."

"It's been a long time since I took a woman out on a date," he admitted, shaking his head.

In all the years I'd known him, I had never heard of him going out on a date, so I already knew it'd been a long time for him.

"I just want you to have a good time."

"I'm with you," I stated, resting my head on his shoulder, "so I already know I'll have a good time."

He pulled me close and walked us to the door. "Okay, but don't say I didn't warn you."

"Oh whatever," I laughed, sauntering out of the apartment in front of him. I dragged him out by his lapels and whispered, "I wore the dress for you. If all else fails, you can score points for getting me out of it later."

"I'm holding you to that," he quipped, catching me around the waist.

He led us down to the street where a black town car idled at the curb instead of a cab, and I already knew this was going to be the best first date of my life.

***

After taking us through the Upper West Side, our driver finally stopped in front of the David H. Koch Theater at Lincoln Center, home to the New York City Ballet. Justin helped me out of the car and up the steps to the building with his hand resting at the small of my back. The building looked breathtaking at night with its steps and fountain illuminated. All the lights from inside were visible through the massive windows, making it that much more inviting, and I couldn't wait to get inside.

"It's beautiful," I whispered.

"Just wait until you see the inside," he said, opening the door for me.

I stepped in and continued to gawk at my surroundings while Justin dealt with the usher. The promenade was decorated in winter-themed decorations along with *The Nutcracker* propaganda. People wandered around the area dressed for the occasion. Some were still in their coats like us, some were already carrying around a glass of champagne and conversing with people they knew.

Justin grabbed my hand as well as my attention. "Time to show you off in your amazing dress. The coatroom's this way."

He led me over to the room and took my coat for me, handing it over to the attendant and slipping him a tip. I admired all the other women in their outfits and couldn't help comparing myself to them. Apparently, the ballet wasn't as big of an occasion to dress up for as I thought it was. There were women in pantsuits, while other women went all out in long, designer dresses. Then there were some dressed like me, in a simple dress perfect for any occasion.

I felt Justin's hand on my lower back again and smiled up at him. "Now what?"

"Would you like a drink?" he asked, excitedly. "We still have some time before the performance starts."

"Sure," I said, clutching my purse in my hand.

As he led us over to the bar, I watched him acknowledge people he knew with a head nod and listened as he explained to me who they were. Most of them were people he knew from working at the college, but so far, none of them were too important for us to stop and chat with. Even as we walked through a sea of people, his attention never broke away from me. I could feel him touching me at all times, making me feel like the most important person in his eyes tonight.

He grabbed two glasses of champagne and handed one to me. I took a sip of the bubbly concoction and nodded. "It's good."

"It is," he replied, tipping his glass back for a drink.

"Justin!"

Both of us turned at the sound of his name and found an older couple headed our way. The woman waved at Justin, dragging her husband along with her as she walked.

"Oh, God," Justin laughed, shaking his head. "You're in for a treat with these two."

"Can't wait," I teased, snaking my arm inside his jacket and around his waist.

Finally, the couple caught up to us, and the guy immediately headed toward the bar and ordered two drinks.

"Justin Jameson," the lady said excitedly. "I'm sorry to interrupt, but I just had to come over and meet your beautiful date! In all the years you've worked with Burg, I don't think I've ever seen you bring a woman to anything!"

The more she talked, the more noticeable her Brooklyn accent became, making me like her even more for being loud and obnoxious at such a sophisticated event. She grabbed her husband, pulling him into the conversation, and turned to me wearing a big smile as she gave me a once-over. "Burg, isn't she just gorgeous?"

Justin laughed and tightened his hold on my waist. "Tessa, this here is Dr. Burgess Gustafson and his wife, Mitzi. Burg is one of the heads of the Psychology Department at NYU."

"It's nice to meet you both," I offered politely, smiling back at them.

"Burg, Mitzi," Justin stated, motioning to me. "I'd like you to meet my girlfriend, Tessa Wilder."

"Girlfriend!?" Mitzi exclaimed, smacking Burg in the arm. "Did you hear that, Burg? One of your co-workers has a girlfriend, and you didn't even tell me!"

"I didn't know!" he declared, rolling his eyes at her. He flashed Justin and me a smile and shook his head. "She won't shut up about this until something new and exciting happens to someone else we know."

"What? I can't be excited for him?" Mitzi quipped, glaring at her husband. "He's a beautiful man! He shouldn't be single for the rest of his life!"

"She's right. He shouldn't be," I added, biting back my laughter. These two were hilarious with their back and forth jabs at one another. I loved how curious Mitzi came off, eager to know more about her husband's co-workers and their love lives. A true romantic at heart. She seemed like one of those elderly women who grand-mothered everyone, always knowing what's best for them. Even with her rounded waist and small stature, she appeared fashionable in her red pantsuit and pearls. Her white hair was styled to perfection with enough hairspray in it to ensure it didn't stray.

"Don't encourage her," Burg said, before taking a sip of his amber-colored cocktail. He seemed more laid back than Mitzi. Sarcasm dripped from his words, showcasing a playful side to him that I instantly appreciated. Next to his wife, he looked good in a brown suit and tie, with his silver hair combed over in an attempt to hide any bald spots.

"Oh, don't listen to him." Mitzi waved him off and clinked her champagne glass against mine. "So, what do you do, Tessa?"

"I'm a receptionist at a clinic," I answered, feeling inadequate just stating the words.

"And . . ." Justin added, rubbing my back for encouragement.

I smiled up at him and glanced over at Mitzi. "I also plan events on the side. It's something I've always enjoyed doing, and I like to think I'm pretty organized."

"Mitzi is the exact opposite of organized," Burg teased.

The three of us laughed as Mitzi shrugged and tossed back the rest of her champagne. "Unfortunately, he's right. Our fiftieth wedding anniversary is coming up, and I've been thinking of ways to celebrate. Do we throw a party? Do we go on a vacation? Or do we just go on pretending like we haven't been with the same person for the last fifty years? I don't know!"

More laughter ensued, and then Justin spoke up and gave his opinion. "Fifty years is a milestone to celebrate. You should throw a party. Hire Tessa here to help you plan everything. She's planned a wedding for one of our friends as well as a baby shower, and she's now in the process of planning a gender reveal party. An anniversary party would be right up her alley."

"Yeah?" Mitzi asked, smiling at me. "Would you want to plan an old people's party?"

I laughed again and nodded. "I would be honored."

"Okay then!" she exclaimed, cheerfully. "You're just too pretty to disagree with, Justin, so if your girl is as good as you say she is, I'm in."

"Great!" he proclaimed, patting Burg on the shoulder. "I'll give Burg her information on Monday."

"Perfect!" Mitzi said, setting her glass on the bar top. She pulled lipstick out of her purse and proceeded to reapply it effortlessly. "Now, Burg, finish your whiskey. It's about time for us to go in."

Burg leaned into Justin so his wife couldn't hear him. "I'll be dead by the time you celebrate your fiftieth wedding anniversary, but don't think I won't come back and haunt you for this very moment, son."

Justin and I tried our best to smother our laughter as Burg knocked back the rest of his drink.

"It was very nice to meet you, Tessa," Mitzi offered. "I look forward to working with you."

"Likewise," I said with a nod.

"Justin," she stated maternally, patting him on the cheek. "As always, it was nice to see you too, and I'm so thrilled you finally found yourself a woman! It's about time you settled down."

"Thank you, Mitzi," he said, smiling down at me. "I'm pretty thrilled about her myself."

She grabbed Burg's glass from his hand and set it on the bar, linking her arm through his. They started to walk off together, but before they got too far, Mitzi waved back at us. "Have a good evening, kids!"

"You, too!" I cheered, leaning into Justin. "I like them."

"They're fun." He took our empty drink glasses and set them aside. Holding his arm out to me, I weaved my arm around his. He threaded our fingers together and led us toward our seats. "Can you imagine being together for fifty years? Isn't that amazing?"

"It really is." Then it hit me. That I just landed another party to plan. "Did I just get my first event client?"

He laughed. "I believe you did, Miss Wilder."

I stopped in my tracks and covered his lips with mine. "Thanks for pimping me out."

"Anytime, panion."

"Panion?" I asked, amused by the pet name I'd never heard before. "Where did that come from?"

"You're mine," he explained. "My companion—panion for short. Is that okay?"

The smile on my face widened as I leaned in and kissed him again. "It's perfect."

We continued into the auditorium, and again, the beauty of the room swept me away as the usher led us to our row. The bright lights made the plush red seats pop against the gold trim of the ceiling and leveled rings. A gold curtain hid the stage and as we sat down, the lights fell, darkening the room; I tightened my grip on Justin's hand in anticipation of the opening act as the orchestra started playing.

***

I sauntered into the apartment with so much energy, it felt like I was riding on a magic carpet and never wanted to get off of it. After watching the performance, I was energized, abuzz with excitement over what I'd just seen. The smile hadn't left my face since we gave the performers the standing ovation they deserved, and I spent most of the elevator ride up to our place twirling in Justin's arms, completely in awe of how the dancers moved. They had such discipline to dance on the tips of their toes. The ballet was amazing, and I hadn't shut up about it since we left the theater.

"So, I take it you enjoyed it?" Justin laughed.

"Hell yes, I enjoyed it!" I replied, latching onto his lapels. "Don't you just love the way they move so flawlessly to the music? The story they told was just so entertaining, and I loved the music more than I thought I would."

"It's not as good as *The Sleeping Beauty*'s music," he said with a shrug. "But I knew there would be parts of it that you'd recognize."

"Like the one toward the end? What'd you call it?" I spun around in his arms and laughed as I tried to hike my leg back up into what Justin called an arabesque. He knew so much about the ballet, specifically the music and the orchestra and even some of the dancers' moves, that he spent most of the intermission and the whole way home teaching me all the technical terms.

"The 'Dance of the Sugar Plum Fairy'?" he laughed. "The one you thought was the theme from the movie, *Home Alone*."

"Yes, that one!" I quipped, wrapping my arms around his neck. "I could never be a dancer; I like ice cream too much."

"I like that you like ice cream," he replied, his tone turning more serious as his mouth hovered over mine. He reached for the belt on my coat and started to untie it as he walked us back into the hall. The material easily fell from my shoulders, so I pushed his blazer off and let it accompany my coat on the floor. We stopped in front of my bedroom, and I leaned back against the door, pulling him close with my hands on his waist.

"Thank you for tonight," I said earnestly, smiling up at him. "Did you have a good time?"

"I did," he answered, his eyes studying my lips.

Reaching back, I turned the knob and pushed the door open. I stepped back into my room, the smile on my face instantly growing mischievous as I pulled him in by the waistband of his pants. "You know what would make this night even more perfect?"

"What's that?" he asked, his deep voice a stabbing, sensual exhilaration to the nerves situated between my legs.

"If you lost all these clothes, helped me out of my dress, and gave me the best goodnight kiss ever." I untucked his dress shirt and began unbuttoning it, thinking back on all the times I imagined doing this with him. I wasn't as insecure now as I had been in my daydreams. He empowered me to take what I wanted without hesitation, to be open with him and trust him. I felt comfortable with him, like I could be myself and not have to worry about being perceived a certain way. We'd only been dating a few days, but years of friendship had brought us to this moment, and I knew he would be well worth the wait.

A wild amusement danced in his eyes as he grazed his hands down over my ass and grabbed the hem of my dress. With his mouth right next to my ear, his breath warm and sensual against my flesh, he asked, "And where exactly would you like me to kiss you? On the lips?"

Before I could answer, he tugged my dress up over my hips, and I reflexively lifted my arms for him to pull it all the way off. He tossed the garment to the floor, and his gaze immediately zeroed in on my chest. His hands slowly skimmed up my sides and around to the back clasp of my bra, where the lacy material fell from my body, leaving me completely bare to him.

He cupped my small breasts in his warm hands and began kneading them as a wicked smile spread across his lips. "Maybe you'd like me to kiss you here?"

I nodded silently, totally speechless right now. I'd never heard Justin speak so erotically. His words mixed with his touch sent me into a mindless stupor where all I could do was watch and listen.

His hands left my chest and trailed down my stomach where they toyed with the waistband of my thong. Then he wrapped his fingers around the material and the muscles in his arms bulged as he pulled hard, tearing the small piece of cloth away from my body, tossing it on the floor with the rest of my clothes.

Sweet mother of sex, he just tore my panties off!

"Or maybe you'd like my mouth here?" He reached in between my thighs and cupped my lady box, immediately sending a piercing shudder through me as I imagined him kissing me everywhere. With his other hand, he tilted my chin up so I was looking at him. His eyes were dark now. The erection in his pants was remarkably noticeable. He was just as worked up over his actions as I was. "Your lips, boobs, or pussy?"

"All of the above," I answered, hastily undoing his belt. I led him over to my bed, but before I could further help him out of his clothes, he tossed me on the bed with such swift force that I squealed as I landed on top of the duvet.

I started to move toward the edge of the bed so I could continue undressing him, but he grabbed one of my heels and shook his head. "Lie back and relax."

Doing as I was told, I rested back on my elbows and watched as he shrugged out of his dress shirt. With his abs on full display, I couldn't help but lick my lips at the thought of getting my mouth on his hard stomach. Justin was leaner than the other guys in our group of friends, but good God, he had the most beautiful muscles I'd ever seen. No tattoos. Just smooth, tan skin and a body he maintained very well. His pectorals stood out against his lean chest. His forearms flexed and exposed veins, begging for my tongue to trace them. But his dimples, etched into his adorable face whenever he smiled, were my complete undoing.

He kicked off his loafers and socks, and then shucked his pants, showing off thick thighs of a runner and hips that directed my eyes right down to his groin. He crawled onto the bed still wearing his navy boxer briefs, and I felt like I'd died and gone to heaven just admiring his taut, sun-kissed body. He removed my heels and kissed his way up the inside of my stocking-clad legs until he got to the top of the hosiery. Dragging his fingers under the black material, he began pulling them down my legs. "I saw a peek of these when you crossed your legs in the car, and it took everything in me not to put my hand up your dress."

"You could've," I offered, relaxing back into the mattress. "I would've let you."

"I know," he said, wearing a deliberate smile. "But then I probably would've had to have you naked."

"I'm naked now," I quipped, running my hands down his exquisite stomach and into the band of his boxers. "And you're not. Take these off or let me take them off for you."

He removed his shorts and crawled back over me and smiled. "Now, what would you like me to do?"

"I believe we were talking about kissing," I said, linking my hands behind his neck. I drew him down and covered his lips with mine. The kiss started out sweet and innocent, just two consenting adults showering one another with affection, but it quickly turned hot. Tongues twisted and sucked. Legs tangled and hands grabbed. Need flourished between us as our breathing escalated and our bodies melted together.

His lips broke away first, and began trailing a line of kisses down my chest as he spoke. "I need you; I need all of you. Tell me you need me, too."

Running my fingers over his ponytail, I tugged on it and arched my body into his mouth as his lips wrapped around my nipple. "I need—oh God," I cried out. "I need you." His teeth grazed my tender flesh and bit at it lovingly, causing a moan to escape from my throat while my hands held his head to my chest.

He switched over to the other side, and I threw my head back and stifled an even louder moan when he started tweaking one nipple with his fingers and sucking on the other. His mouth was lethal, but I'd let it kill me if it meant dying such a pleasurable death.

His mouth tore away from my breast and he flashed me that grin of his I loved so much. "Two down, one to go."

"Yes," I begged breathlessly, smiling down at him weakly as he settled in between my thighs. I was on the brink of an orgasm from his mouth alone, and he looked like a kid in a candy store, eager to devour it all.

"I'm not going to stop until you come," he warned, pressing a kiss to the inside of my thigh. "I want to feel these legs wrapped tight around my shoulders, squeezing me so hard as you come. What do you think?"

"I want that, too," I cried, writhing beneath him.

His chuckle vibrated against my skin, sending a tingle down my spine as he placed another kiss above my pubis. "You are so sexy, Tessa. So wet and ready for me. I knew you would be, but reality just doesn't do my imagination justice."

"Y-yeah?" I asked, barely able to form words. "You've . . . thought about me . . . like this?"

"Of course, I have," he muttered, dragging a knuckle through my wetness. "Since the day I saw you naked, I've thought about all the ways I could cherish this body of yours."

Then he kissed me there, and I groaned at the brush of his tongue gliding through my wetness and devouring it as he pushed deeper. Soon, I was rocking my hips against his face, winding up tighter and tighter with each stroke of his tongue and fingers.

When his thumb found my clit and started massaging, I came undone. My legs tightened around his neck as the orgasm rolled through me like a fallen ball of yarn unraveling into a mess on the floor. My body trembled. My vision blurred for a few seconds. My lungs tensed from the inability to catch my breath.

By the time it was over, I felt free and satisfied, with a smile covering my lips and sweat dotting my forehead.

"That was . . ." I shook my head, unable to find the right word.

"Unbelievable?" Justin finished, laying a kiss on my lips.

"Best. Kiss. Ever," I said, reaching for his dick. He'd already sheathed himself with a condom, so I took him in my hand, dragged the tip through my wetness and began stroking his rigid length. I already knew he had a gorgeous dick, but the way he felt was new to me. The weight of him against my palm as he thrust his hips spurred the need for him all over again.

He gazed down at my hands stroking him and smiled back up at me. "You feel so good, but . . ." Grabbing my hand, he stopped my motions and threaded his fingers through my hands, pressing them in the mattress as he hovered over me. "I'd rather be inside you when I come."

I curled my legs around his waist and urged him in with the heels of my feet. "Me too."

He positioned himself at my opening, and then he pushed inside, nuzzling my neck and showering me with kisses as he went. "God, Tessa."

"I know," I sighed, completely infatuated with every sensational inch of him. Once he was fully seated inside of me, he gave me a moment to adjust to his size.

"Tell me how you want me," he said, pulling out slightly. "Hard and fast?"

He thrust back in harder to emphasize his words, eliciting a playful yelp of approval from me as I flushed with need.

"Or slow and sweet?" he asked, retreating in such a slow motion that I whined in frustration.

"Just take me!" I begged, digging my nails into his hands. "However you want, just take me."

His lips crushed against mine, and his hips went off like a gun, firing his length into me with such hard precision, he hit the bullseye immediately.

"Oh . . . my God, Justin." He felt so good. I tightened my legs around him and matched each one of his drives with the same amount of vigor he possessed.

"You feel incredible," he grunted, hiking my legs up higher around his body. "But I want more. I want to go deeper."

"Yes!" I cheered, tossing my head back. "Deeper!"

"Don't hold back."

When he plunged back in, he struck deeper, causing his body to stimulate my clit as he rocked in and out of me, bringing forth the first beautiful hit of my impending release. He massaged my flesh, unable to keep his hands off me, and ran his lips over my collarbone, muttering succulent words as he worshipped me.

"You're so beautiful," he groaned, sucking on the tender skin of my neck. "So flushed and turned on for me. I want to feel you come around me."

Once again, his words and his actions were my undoing. I'd never had a lover speak so carnally during sex, but oh my God, was it hot. For someone who hardly spoke outside of the bedroom, Justin was surprisingly chatty during sex, and I cherished it. I relished in his sinful words, got off on them and handed myself over to him like I was the last supper and he was starved.

"Keep talking to me like that," I roused.

"You like that, huh?" he teased, nipping my earlobe with his teeth. "There are so many things I want to do with you, Tessa. I want to watch you lose control. I want to give you all the control. I want to bury myself so deep inside of you that you'll never want me to leave. I want you every way I can get you, in every position you'll try. I want your lips on mine. Your hands clawing at my body. Your mouth sucking me off. I want you on your knees, ass up in the air, so I can watch myself move in and out of you as I fuck the orgasm out of you."

"Justin!" I cried, clenching hard around him. The more he talked, the harder he thrust, punctuating each phrase with his hips, quickly causing me to erupt. I praised his name again as the orgasm blew through me, and just as I entered the universe again and my vision cleared, he tensed above me, grunted my name along with some expletives, and came with a final jolt of his hips.

We broke through our releases like a couple of sprinters crossing the finish line after a race: winded, proud and eager for more, despite our tired limbs and the soreness I'd surely feel tomorrow morning.

"That . . . that was amazing," he said, tumbling against my body.

"Yes, it was," I cooed, running my fingers along the hard planes of his back. "Best. Kiss. Ever."

He laughed and pulled himself up on his elbows, satisfaction splashed across his handsome face. Brushing a few pieces of damp hair off my face, he leaned in and gave me a soft kiss on the lips. "Are you okay? I didn't hurt you, did I?"

"No," I said, pulling his lips back to mine. "I'm perfect."

"Good," he said, smiling. "Let me just go get cleaned up."

"Okay." I watched as he crossed the hall to the bathroom, and then I crawled under the covers, all the while thinking about everything he'd said.

"What's with the mischievous smile?" he asked, slipping into bed with me. "My refractory period isn't god-like or anything, so it's still going to be a while."

"Ha! Good to know," I laughed, tangling my body with his. "But I was actually just thinking about what you said earlier, about cherishing me." I glanced up at him to gauge his reaction. "Were you serious about that, that you've thought about all the ways you could cherish my body?"

"Absolutely," he replied unabashed, furrowing his brows. "You don't believe me?"

"It's not that I don't believe you," I said, running my fingers through the golden dust of hair on his chest. "I've just never had a guy say things like that to me before."

"Well, I can prove it to you." He leaned over the bed to my nightstand and started opening the drawers.

I froze, knowing the bottom drawer held my vibrator.

"That's okay," I stated nervously, shaking my head. "You don't need to prove anything. I believe you."

"Oh, no," he insisted, gazing back at me over his shoulder. "I'm going to prove it to you."

He closed the middle drawer, and I slumped back into the mattress and felt my face turn red when I heard him open the last drawer.

Justin twirled the pink sex toy in his hand, smiling proudly. "Jackpot."

Tucking the sheet under my arms to hide my nakedness, I tried not to smile at him. "How do you know where I keep that?"

"Good question," he said, eyeing the device closely. "I probably should've told you when you moved in that the walls are pretty thin in this place."

"Are you kidding me?!" I shrieked, smacking him in the arm. "So for the past month, you've heard me using it, and you didn't think to say anything to me?"

"What was I supposed to say?" he quipped, humor lingering in his voice. "'Oh hey, by the way, I can hear you masturbating.'"

"You could've at least said something!" I said, burying my head under a pillow. "This is so embarrassing!"

"Tessa." He put the toy back in its drawer and pulled the pillow and sheet away so he could hold me. "You have nothing to be embarrassed about. It's a turn on knowing a woman isn't afraid to masturbate, that she knows exactly what she likes and how she likes it. Would it make you feel better if I told you I thoroughly enjoyed it and that I joined you? Because I did. Every damn time. I'd hear your vibrator and the occasional moan from your side of the wall, and I'd get off to it. I'd spend those nights imagining what you looked like while you got off and thinking about what it'd really be like to be with you and how I'd make love to you." He moved the hair on my neck out of the way and kissed me there. "So, I'm not bullshitting when I say I've thought about loving you."

I smiled at him, feeling less ashamed than before, and then I kissed him. "I thought about you, too."

An agonized groan fell from his lips as he playfully rocked his groin against me. "Give me a few more minutes, and then I want to hear every detail while I make love to you again."

Chapter Fourteen

Justin

The following Saturday, I invited Tessa and Trey over to my grandma's house for Thanksgiving. Grandma and I had made a pact a long time ago that we wouldn't spend Thanksgiving Day together because I enjoyed spending the day watching football while she enjoyed spending it with her friends and watching the Macy's parade. It was how we'd been celebrating the holiday for years now but this year, I wanted to include Tessa and Trey, especially since Tessa had implied that they'd never celebrated the holiday before. Sure, she'd celebrated it by going Black Friday shopping with the girls, but that was the extent of her Thanksgiving celebration. While the rest of us had families to go home to for the holidays, Tessa and Trey only had each other. I wanted them to know that now they had us.

We walked up the flight of stairs to my grandma's place carrying the containers of food Tessa insisted on bringing, even though cooking was Grandma's specialty. The whole time I listened to Tessa's entertaining conversation with Trey. I was thoroughly captivated by their fun yet frustrating sibling dynamic.

"Please try to be respectful," she murmured, glaring up at her brother. "We are guests in her home."

"I thought you said you knew her," Trey replied, confusion furrowing his brows. "I thought you said this Mrs. J. was cool."

"I do know her, and she is cool," Tessa said, rolling her eyes. "But what I don't know are the ridiculous words that might come out of your mouth at any given moment. So, please, try to use a filter today."

"Hey!" he exclaimed, proudly. "Women love me. I'm sure I can charm the granny panties right off her."

I laughed as a sigh of frustration fell from Tessa's lips and she glanced up at me with a look of defeat. "Tell me again why we invited him?"

Wrapping my arm around her waist, I pulled her into my side and comforted her. "Because he's your brother, and he deserves a home-cooked meal?"

"He can cook his own meals," she said, shaking her head.

Trey lifted the lid to the container he'd brought with him. The smell of freshly baked bread drifted into my nostrils, causing my stomach to rumble. "I made my infamous braid bread you like. Just like you asked me to."

Dammit, I thought. *Even the kid knows how to cook well.*

"I know," Tessa said, smiling weakly.

"It smells really good," I added, rapping my knuckles on Grandma's door. "She's probably going to say something when she sees how much food we brought. Just warning you now."

"See," Trey whispered, nudging Tessa. "I told you we didn't need to bring food with us. Old ladies always cook a lot of food."

"It's impolite to show up empty-handed," Tessa snapped at him.

"You brought three different things!" Trey insisted, shaking his head. "She'll probably tell Justin to dump you for insulting her."

The horror that crossed Tessa's face when she turned to me almost made me laugh, but I knew better.

"Is she going to be insulted by all of this?" Tessa asked in a worried tone. "I never even thought about that. I just didn't want her thinking she had to do a turkey and everything else all by herself. I should've called her and asked, or—"

"Tessa," I stated, grinning proudly. It made me happy that she was fretting over my grandma's reaction. "She's going to say it wasn't necessary, but she's still going to appreciate the gesture. You have nothing to worry about."

"Except when my braid bread wins her over faster than your pumpkin pie," Trey quipped.

"Hey," I retorted, smacking him on the back of the head. "*I* made the pumpkin pie."

He recoiled with an incredulous smirk on his face. "You made a pumpkin pie? I thought Tessa said you didn't know how to cook."

"She helped me," I said, giving her a chaste kiss on the lips.

"Now, I'm really not going to eat it," he said, wrinkling his nose. "God knows what happened in the kitchen while she *helped* you."

"Trey," Tessa chastised, elbowing him in the stomach. "This is what I mean about your mouth. Please don't say shit like that in front of Mrs. J."

When the door finally opened, my grandma appeared wearing her blue-and white-checkered apron over a nice shirt and pants. Her orthopedic tennis shoes donned her feet, and her white curly hair was styled the same way it's been all thirty years of my life.

"Well, what do we have here?" she questioned, taking the pie container from my hands. "You guys didn't need to bring anything with you."

"It's just a pie," I stated proudly, walking into her place. "That I made."

"With Tessa's help," Trey added as he followed in behind Tessa and me. He held out his hand to my grandma and smiled. "I'm Trey Wilder, Tessa's younger brother. I heard I'm supposed to call you Mrs. J., is that right?"

"Yes, it's nice to meet you, Trey," she said, the smile on her face widening. "And what did you bring? Is that bread I smell?"

"I'm glad you asked," he replied, leaning toward her like he had a secret to tell. "This here, Mrs. J., is the best bread you've ever tasted."

"Is that right?" she asked, amused by his antics.

"Yep," he said with a resolute nod. He lifted the lid and showed off his masterpiece. "It's braided Nutella bread. Chocolate and hazelnut goodness in the form of bread. I hope it's okay that I brought a dessert, too."

"We can never have too many desserts!" She laughed, patting him on the shoulder. "Now, come in and make yourselves at home. The turkey just finished, so I hope you're all starved."

"Always!" Trey cheered, rubbing his belly.

"Mrs. J., do you need any help in the kitchen?" Tessa asked, following close behind her.

"I could always use the help of a great cook," Grandma said, waving Tessa in for a hug. "I hear you helped my boy make a pie?"

"Yes," Tessa answered, glancing at me over Grandma's shoulder. "I mostly advised. He did all the hard work."

Grandma pulled back and smiled proudly. "In all of my years, I never once got him to actually cook anything."

Trey murmured under his breath, "Getting laid on a regular basis will do that to a guy."

I grabbed the back of his neck and turned us both toward the living room to watch television and give the women time to chat. "What did Tessa say about your comments?"

"Filter them," Trey sighed, plopping down on the couch.

"Show her some respect, would you?" I asked, taking a seat in the recliner. "She's nervous enough today. Why, I don't really know, but she doesn't need you adding to her stress."

I clicked the TV on, which immediately greeted us with the TV Land channel. As I flipped through the channels, I felt Trey's eyes on me. "What?"

"You really like her?" Trey asked.

When I looked over at him, his eyes were glued to his sister in the kitchen. My eyes followed his, and I couldn't help the grin that spread across my face. Tessa had thrown on one of Grandma's aprons over her sweater dress, so they were in their element as they removed items from the oven. The two of them shared their love for cooking, taste-testing all the different foods before we actually sat down to eat them. Tessa awed over Grandma's stuffing while Grandma taste-tested the side salads Tessa had brought, eventually requesting the recipe for both. Just watching the two of them interact so effortlessly together, laughing and smiling one minute, serious and curious the next as they discussed ingredients, mesmerized me. They fed off of each other's sentences and listened so closely to what the other said. It was as if Tessa had finally found the grandma she'd never had, and Grandma could finally share her cooking secrets with someone who actually understood what the hell she was talking about.

"I more than like her," I confessed, looking back at Trey. "Is that a problem?"

"No," he said soberly, shaking his head. "She deserves a guy like you, someone who's going to treat her well."

"Thanks."

"I think she's good for you, too," he continued. "You haven't seemed like such a robot during your lectures lately. It's like you're a real person up there now, babbling about psychology stuff."

"A robot?" I asked, entertained by his description. "What the hell is that supposed to mean?"

He laughed. "I don't know. You show more emotion when you lecture now. Like if some asshole comes in late or leaves early, you react to it, or when that girl's cell phone went off during class and you answered it, that was awesome. Before, you wouldn't even give those types of distractions the time of day."

He was right. Before Tessa, I observed but kept most of my reactions to myself, specifically my nerves or frustrations. Remembering my first date with her, I laughed. She saw right through me, noticed how anxious I was, and she immediately calmed me down. Her love opened me up, wrapped its arms around my soul, and welcomed all of my eccentricities without judgment.

"You seem happier with her," Trey concluded with a shrug. "I think that's great because she's happy with you, too. I mean, look at her; I don't think I've seen her smile like that in years. She loves this stuff though, planning get-togethers and cooking a bunch of food. When we were really little, she used to make me attend her fake tea parties, even though she didn't have a tea set. She used the disfigured, microwaved Tupperware, the best china we owned back then. We didn't have dinners like this, where our family gathered around a table to eat together. The one time Tessa tried to make that happen, my dad passed out at the table and Mom was too high to function.

"So, I know today means a lot to her, because this is something she's always wanted. To celebrate the holidays together, do it up big with food and people and fun. We never celebrated anything growing up, not even birthdays, until it was just the two of us."

That explained her love for planning events, I thought.

He glanced back at me and laughed. "I'm probably going to try and extort an A out of you for sleeping with my sister. But all in all, I'm happy for you guys."

I cocked an eyebrow at him. "Hence the word *try*."

"I'm a photography major," he stated, relaxing into the floral furniture. "Cut me some slack, man."

"Psychology plays a huge part when it comes to photography." I shot him a smile, and the smirk on his face instantly dropped.

"Go on . . ."

Resting my ankle over my opposite knee, I continued channel surfing as I explained. "As a photographer, you have the ability to impact people with your work. You create a relationship between yourself and the viewer, whether you want it or not, which means you need to understand your viewer. Photography isn't just about taking a great picture in the technical sense. It's about telling a story to the viewer, evoking some sort of emotion out of them with just a photograph, and essentially revealing some part of yourself, too. Photography is a visual means of communication, and what's great about it is, no photographer can take the same photo. The minute you pick up your camera, you're putting your own unique stamp on whatever you capture. Being able to relate to others and understand them as well as yourself will give you the ability to not only take great pictures, but also capture timeless moments that affect people. You want to be great, you need to understand your own mind if you want to affect the minds of others."

"Shit," he muttered, running a hand over his face. "I've never thought of it like that, like getting into other people's minds."

With nothing on TV, I set down the remote and smiled at him. "You're good, Trey. You know your way around a camera, and how to work with lighting and angles and all that."

"But..."

"If you want to make photography a career, you need to be great," I reiterated. "And I know you have an eighty-eight point nine percent in my class right now, so—"

"Do you memorize everyone's grades?" he interjected warily.

"Photographic memory," I said, tapping my head. "So, I know you're a good student. You come to class. You turn in assignments on time, and you do fairly well on the tests. If you study your ass off for the final, you could easily bump that B up to an A."

"Okay, okay," he said, smiling weakly.

"I also teach a perception course in the spring that I think you'd benefit from. You should enroll in it."

"I'll check it out."

I smiled, humored by his aloof personality. "You should start thinking about your career now. It's never too early to start putting your work out there, make a name for yourself. Maybe even put together a gallery."

That piqued his interest as he raised his brows. "Really? You think I could showcase my work?"

He didn't even realize how good he was already. I nodded. "Some of our friends have asked about the photographs we have hanging in the apartment. So, I know plenty of people who would pay hundreds for your pictures. You put together a show, advertise it and yourself, and I know people will come to it. If you want to make money doing what you love, you have to start somewhere. Tessa could help you put it together, find a gallery that'll treat you with respect. Like you said, she loves planning things."

"Thanks, man." He stared off into space, with a goofy grin plastered on his face, probably thinking about his work and how he could show it off.

"Anytime," I offered as I stood. "Now, let's go see if they need help setting the table. I'm starving."

He jumped up from the couch. "Me too."

***

Once the table was set, the four of us took our seats. Grandma and I took up the ends with Tessa and Trey sitting across from one another on the sides. I uncorked the wine and filled our glasses, even Trey's, despite him being underage. Grandma and Grandpa Jameson had started offering me wine with holiday dinners at a very young age, so filling every glass at the table with pinot noir was tradition.

However, the look Tessa threw my way didn't go unnoticed as joy spread across Trey's face.

"So," Grandma started, setting her wine glass down in front of her. "We usually go around the table and say what we're most thankful for this year, and then we dig in."

"Okay," Tessa said with a nod.

"I'm not going first," Trey stated, peering around at the four of us.

Grandma laughed and covered his hand with hers. "I'll go first."

Taking my seat, I took a sip of my wine and ran through the list of things I was grateful for this year, as Grandma started in on hers.

"First off, I want to thank Tessa and Trey for being here with us today," she said, smiling at the two of them. "It's a joy to fill this table with not only food, but people who appreciate all the hard work that went in to making this meal. I'm so thankful that my grandson has you both in his life. It gives me a reason to spoil his friends like they're my own family, and that's what I'm most thankful for this year. I'm thankful for my friends who have turned into family."

After Grandma finished, she looked across the table at me and smiled. "Justin?"

Taking a deep breath, I exhaled with a nod, acknowledging my turn. "I'm grateful for the people in my life who accept me for who I am." My eyes found Tessa's, and I reached out and threaded my fingers through hers. "Who love me in spite of my quirks."

She smiled, blinking back tears as she lifted our joined hands to her mouth and gave mine a kiss. Glancing back at my grandma and her brother, she laughed. "My turn?"

"Yes," Grandma answered, shooting me a wink.

"I'm thankful to have a friend who opened his home and welcomed me without hesitation." Tessa's grip on my hand tightened as she spoke, her beautiful gray eyes full of appreciation as they gazed back at me. "But what I'm most thankful for this year is the man who opened his heart to me."

"Way to make a brother feel bad for wanting to live alone," Trey quipped, before taking a drink of his wine.

"I didn't mean to make you feel bad!" Laughter ensued around the table as Tessa added, "Okay, I'm also thankful for a brother who pushed me to live a little this year by wanting to live on his own."

Trey nearly spit out his wine. "You can't just add me in like that."

"Yes, I can," she threw back, the smile on her face widening as she turned to Grandma. "Right, Mrs. J.?"

The wrinkles on Grandma's face stood out the harder she laughed. "There's already one Jameson in the middle of this. Keep me out of it!"

Tessa and Trey turned to me. "Well?"

I glanced between the two of them, and pretended to think about the question while studying the burgundy liquid in my glass. "I think it's Trey's turn to tell us what he's thankful for."

"Great answer," Tessa said victoriously, smirking at Trey.

"Okay, let's see," Trey contemplated aloud, relaxing back in his chair. His playful gaze jumped from Grandma to me, but eventually settled on Tessa. "I'm most thankful for my sister, who has always put me and my wants and needs before herself or anyone else. Until just a few seconds ago."

"Treylor," Tessa begged, demanding his serious answer.

"I know, I know," he continued, rolling his eyes. "What I'm trying to say is, I'm thankful for everything you've done for me and everything you continue to do. You've worked so hard to give me the opportunities you weren't given, and I just want you to know that I'm thankful for that."

With his response, tears took over Tessa's eyes, and I took her hand in mine again to comfort her as she attempted to blink them away.

Trey grabbed his napkin and placed it in his lap. "Look, I didn't say that to make you cry, okay?"

"I know." Tessa ran her index finger under her eyes to catch any fallen tears. "It was just really sweet."

"It was very nice," Grandma added, commending Trey by raising her drink to him.

"Whatever," Trey muttered around the lip of his wine glass. "Can we eat now? I'm starving."

Grandma laughed again. "Yes, let's eat!"

For the next ten minutes, the four of us filled our plates with turkey and the many sides spread across the table. Serving dishes were passed around. Condiments were asked for and received. I topped off everyone's wine. And for a while, we ate and drank in comfortable silence, the only sound an occasional clanking of utensils hitting the porcelain plates.

"So, Mrs. J., what do you guys usually do for the Christmas holiday?" Tessa asked, smothering her turkey in dark gravy.

"Justin and I usually attend the Christmas Eve service at my church, and then we come back here for dinner. One of my favorite things during the Christmas holiday is seeing all the people who hardly ever come to mass during the rest of the year. Justin's guilty of being one of them."

"Hey," I scoffed, pointing my glass at her. "I attend more often than some of them."

"But you could attend more often," she quipped, raising her brows teasingly.

Trey laughed. "I don't think we've ever been to church, have we Tessa?"

Looking over at Tessa, I saw her pushing food around with her fork, her cheeks flushed a soft shade of red as she shook her head. "Nope."

"That's okay," I said, in hopes of steering away any shame she might feel. "It's not for everyone. Plus, Grandma here really only goes for the social aspect of it. You know, to get all the gossip."

"Justin Jameson!" she chastised harshly, tossing her napkin onto the table. "You know that's not true."

"You walk by the funeral home on your way to church just to see who's on the menu," I retorted.

"On the menu?" Tessa asked, horrified, furrowing her brows.

Grandma narrowed her eyes at me and then turned to them and explained. "The funeral home has this board outside where they list the names of the recently deceased and the date and time of their wakes."

"Seriously?" Trey asked, wide-eyed in disbelief.

"Yep," I answered, leaning back in my chair. "Grandma and her buddies call it the menu."

"That's awesome!" he exclaimed with a chuckle.

Tessa crinkled her nose as she stared at my grandma. "That's kind of awful."

I nodded, further teasing Grandma. "So is making fun of all the irregular churchgoers."

"Oh, hush!" she snapped, grabbing her wine glass. "When you get to be my age, you'll understand that walking by the menu is like flipping off death every Sunday morning."

Trey smacked the tabletop with his hand, his face beet red from laughing so hard. "I'm sorry. I just keep picturing a bunch of old ladies ordering from the dead people's menu. 'I'd like a Reuben with a Caesar salad, and a Tom Collins to wash it all down. No, you better make that a Shirley Temple. I never liked that bitch.'"

The three of us instantly cracked up, breathlessly entertained by Trey's imitation of Grandma and her friends. My cheeks tightened the more I laughed, and Tessa's face turned the same color as Trey's. Even Grandma was wiping her eyes as our amusement finally simmered.

Once we settled down, we went back to eating our dinner, quietly stuffing ourselves with the delicious food, heaping more portions onto our plates, and allowing our faces to relax back to normal.

Then Grandma broke through the silence. "But like I was saying, you two are more than welcome to join us for Christmas."

And the laughter started up all over again.

***

By the time Tessa and I got home, we were stuffed and tired. We changed into sweats and fell into my bed together, too tired to do anything else but cuddle, which was fine with me. I found out very soon after we started dating that being around Tessa stimulated me, dominating me in a whole other way than when we were just living together as friends. My mind continuously thought of her like a song it had on repeat; her voice was a harmonious tune I could listen to forever. Her tousled brown hair twisted up into a bun made my fingers itch to run through it and make it messier. With her face free of makeup, her naturally pale skin held the same soft glow as the moon peeking through the window. She had the ability to make sweats and an old tee look just as sexy as a tight dress and heels, and I found myself falling for her effortless beauty and low maintenance ways more and more every day.

"What are you smiling about?" she asked curiously, running her hand up my chest.

"You," I answered, pressing my lips to her temple. "And how beautiful you are just like this."

She laughed and shook her head slightly. "Don't be cute right now. I feel like I've gained ten pounds, so I don't feel beautiful."

Turning on my side, I faced her and tightened my arms around her waist. "I don't feel so hot either. I probably didn't need that third piece of pie."

"But it was so good," she giggled, nuzzling my neck. "All of the food was good. I'm going to have to spend the next few weeks working off the food from Thanksgiving to prepare for the Christmas meal."

The thought of us spending Christmas together made my chest tighten, but in a good way. It also prompted me to make a mental note to go Christmas shopping for her gift. I wanted us to spend every holiday together. I never knew what it was like to spend a holiday with a girlfriend, but today, after saying what we were thankful for, I knew Tessa Wilder was the one I wanted to spend the rest of my holidays with. "I want us to spend Christmas together."

She pulled back from me slightly so she could get a good look at my face. "I want that, too. Your Grandma's cooking is amazing, and she's so funny. I'd love to spend Christmas with you guys."

"Then why were you so nervous earlier today?" I asked, finally voicing the question that had been bugging me most of the day. "You've known my grandma for years. Why would you be nervous about spending the holiday with her?"

She exhaled a sigh and rested her head back on the pillow. "Well, I was mostly nervous because of Trey and his mouth. I didn't raise him to be disrespectful, but somehow he grew up into this charming young man without a filter. Most of the time, he uses his sarcasm and humor to entertain, but sometimes people can find it insulting."

"Janice Jameson doesn't insult that easily," I said, making her smile. "Neither do I."

"I know," she laughed, tangling her legs with mine. "But I was also worried your parents might show up, and that's who I was most nervous for him to be around because I don't know them."

I propped myself up on my elbow and ran my hand along her side as I recalled the last time I saw my parents. "You don't have to worry about them ever showing up to anything."

"What do you mean?"

"John and Leslie Jameson are very self-centered people. Always have been, always will be," I stated, as the last memory of them played in my mind. "The last time I saw them was when they dropped me off at my grandma's because they'd been invited on an expedition to the North Pole to study string theory. While they were gone, which was a total of six months, they never once called to check on me or to say hi. During that time, I graduated from middle school and tested out of high school, so Grandma was stuck with helping me choose a college to attend. My parents were Harvard alums, but I knew I didn't want to go there. I didn't want to become like them. So, I chose NYU because it was a college close to Grandma. I also chose to major in psychology because I enjoyed studying people.

"When my parents got back and heard about my choices, I overheard them fighting about it with Grandma, even though she never swayed me in making my decisions like they would've, had they been home. Grandma was upset with the way they neglected me, claiming she didn't raise her son to choose work over his family. But in the end, they gave Grandma full custody of me, and I haven't seen them since."

"I'm so sorry, Justin," she said, rubbing my arm. "I had no idea you guys had such a falling out with them."

"Don't be," I stated, shaking my head. "We're better off without each other, and I've made my peace with that. They can focus on their work, and I can be who I want to be.

Grandma, on the other hand, is still upset about it all, so we don't discuss them."

"Understandable." Her hand moved into my hair and brushed it off of my face. "Can I ask why you have their textbooks on your bookshelf?"

I laughed lightly and nodded. "I'm still proud of them, even if they can't be proud of me and the work I do. They don't consider psychology a science, so they'll always be disappointed by the fact that I didn't follow in their footsteps and study physics. I also know that they still care about me, even if the only way they know how to show it is by putting money into a trust. They're not bad people, just bad parents. Some people weren't meant to be parents, and they're the perfect example. There are a thousand awful things they could be doing, so I'm glad they choose work instead of engaging in other activities that could potentially harm themselves or others. I still love them because they're my parents; I wouldn't be here if it weren't for them. So, I buy their work and put it on my shelf."

She laughed. "You've never read any of it?"

"God, no. Why would I? Maybe when they write an autobiography and explain why they are the way they are, I'll read it."

"So, you haven't reached out to them since?" she asked, inquisitively.

"Nope." I slipped a hand underneath her shirt and trailed my fingers up and down her spine. "I have no desire to have them in my life now. I already have everyone I need."

"Is that so?" she asked, linking her arms around my neck as she arched into my touch.

I nodded and covered her lips with mine for a slow, easy kiss. "You, Grandma, and all of our friends, including Trey, are all I need right now."

She perked a brow, even with her eyes still shut from our kiss. "Right now? You say that like you've thought about the future."

Of course I'd been thinking about my future. Ever since she moved in. The first time I'd seen her naked. That brief second right before I grabbed her face and kissed her for the first time. The moment I told her I was falling for her. Every minute spent with her shined a light on my future, and she stood right in its spotlight.

"I have." I flushed her body up against mine and held her close, the two of us sharing the same pillow with sleep just minutes away from abducting us.

Her soft hands settled on my chest and she quietly asked, "Am I in your future?"

Closing my eyes, I smiled and kissed her forehead. "You're my leading lady."

Chapter Fifteen

Tessa

Tonight was the night!

In a few minutes, Elly and Carter would walk through the door of Judge's, eager to find out the gender of their baby. Everyone else—their families, friends, and colleagues—was already here, standing around the bar with drinks in their hands and placing their bets on the gender of Baby Jennings. So far, a majority of people were betting on a girl, while Fletcher was still hounding me for any sort of hint at which way he should bet.

"Blink once if it's a boy. Twice if it's a girl," he said, as I double-checked the flagged banner hanging above the archway. The banner had red and blue flags to match the color scheme Elly and Carter had chosen for their gender-neutral nursery. The flags displayed alternating baby pictures of the proud parents from their infant days.

"Fletcher," I warned, rolling my eyes. "For the last time, I'm not telling you. Just go with your gut."

"My gut says girl," he stated, glancing over at Harper and Maverick, who were showing off Seghen. "Didn't Justin say something about the odds being greater for a girl?"

Justin laughed behind me as his arms wrapped around my waist. "The odds are still fifty-fifty, man. What I said was, there is a correlation with a Jennings' first child being a girl. Harper was the first child in her family, and then she also had a girl. Elly was the first and only child in her family. Those aren't odds. It's just a correlation."

"Well, that's not helpful at all!" Fletcher exclaimed. "I bet she's already told you since you're sleeping together now."

He shook his head and laughed. "I swear, she didn't tell me."

"But he did try his best," I added, laying a kiss on his cheek. "I'm going to go do a sweep to make sure everything's ready to go. They should be here soon."

"Everything already looks perfect, Tessa," he said, smiling proudly as I walked away. "Don't worry about it."

"Just one more check." I skipped back to him, jumped into his arms, and kissed him hard, wrapping my arms around his neck and kicking one leg up in the air. "You know how these obsessive-compulsive things go."

"Yes, I do." He gave my ass a light spank as I walked toward the obstacles I had set up.

For Elly and Carter's gender reveal party, I went with a sports theme and called it The Jennings Olympics, since they're both athletic. I even had shirts made for Carter and Elly that had the *American Gladiators'* stars and stripes triangular logo on the front with JENNINGS OLYMPICS taking the place of the show title. The backs were customized with the nicknames "Daddy Diaper Changer" and "Mommy Milk Maker." Elly damn near peed her pants when I gave them to her at work and told her to wear them to the party.

CHERISHED BY YOU

As I went through each station I had set up throughout the bar, I watched the reveal play out in my head to make sure everything would work properly. If it didn't, the reveal wouldn't go as planned, and I couldn't have that happen. Thankfully, Fletcher let me move some of the bar's furniture around and decorate however I wanted. I converted the stage into the first two obstacles Carter and Elly would have to complete to make it to the final challenge, which was located on a smaller platform toward the back of the bar. With Justin and Cash's help, we moved the pool tables and set up for the final reveal. I'd flagged off most of the stage area and created a flagged aisle for Carter and Elly to easily use to get to the back obstacle as well as an aisle that led from the entrance up to the stage. The object was simple: complete an obstacle to reveal a word. The last obstacle would give them the sex of their baby.

After I finished triple-checking it all, I headed back toward the bar where Justin sat with Fletcher and Bayler. Cash was helping out behind the bar, and Paige sat on the other side of Justin nursing a drink.

"Hey!" Bayler exclaimed, wiggling in her seat and waving her phone. "I just got a text from Elly saying they are close."

"Ooh, good to know," I said, as I waved Cash down. "Hey, Bayler just said they're close."

Since he had all the right music and knew how to cut it, Cash was my emcee for tonight. "Great! I'll wait for them outside."

"I'll be out there in a minute."

"This is going to be awesome," Maverick stated, taking a seat at the bar with Seghen in his arms.

Harper laughed. "Elly is going to be so excited."

I smiled at all of my hard work, eager to see all the guests enjoying themselves with finger foods and alcohol. While waiting for our guests of honor to arrive, Justin pulled me to him, anchoring me between his thighs.

"This is really great, Tessa," he whispered, kissing me beneath my ear.

His stubble tickled my skin, causing a shiver to dance down my spine. Before we started dating, I wondered what type of guy Justin was. Would he hate public displays of affection, or would he participate in them freely? Now that I knew he wasn't averse to some PDA, I took pleasure in letting everyone know he was mine. So, I turned around in his arms and drew him in for another kiss. "Thank you."

As our kiss deepened and Justin's hands skated down to my ass, Bayler stated, "Nice to see he woke up and smelled the pussy!" I glanced over at her, and she had her cocktail raised in the air to us. "It's about fucking time!"

"Amen!" Maverick and Fletcher said in unison.

Justin chuckled against my mouth. "What is she talking about?"

"I'll explain later," I laughed, resting my forehead against his. "I have a party to host."

"Okay, go host."

I smiled at the gang and headed out the front door, where I found Cash standing with Elly and Carter, who were wearing their customized tees with jeans.

"Why are you making us stand out here in the cold?" Elly asked, rubbing her hands together. "And why did the lights in the bar just go out?"

The red and blue spotlights came on, highlighting the entrance to Judge's.

I laughed. "You have to make a grand entrance, right?"

Cash hit the play button on his remote. The bells rang inside and sports announcer Michael Buffer's voice boomed over the speakers, welcoming everyone to the event as 2 Unlimited's "Get Ready For This" started playing. I took Elly and Carter's coats and nodded at Cash.

He opened the door for Elly. "Weighing in at one hundred and sixty-five pounds, standing at five feet, seven inches! Due on or around February 23rd, 2015! Ladies and gentlemen, put your hands together for Ellyson 'Mommy Milk Maker' Jennings!"

Elly waddled—yes, she waddled—into the bar, showing off her huge baby bump as she went, slapping the hands of guests who held them out to her.

"And now, weighing in at one hundred and ninety pounds, standing at six feet, two inches. The sperm donor who probably hasn't read a single baby book! Folks, I give you, Carter 'Daddy Diaper Changer' Jennings!"

Carter ran in after his wife, high-fiving guests and waving. He met Elly at the bottom of the stage and helped her walk up the steps. Cash and I walked in as the lights came back on. The crowd clapped for Elly and Carter as they took the stage together hand-in-hand.

Cash lowered the music's volume when we joined them on the stage. He let the cheers and clapping die down before he took to the mic again. "My name is Cash Donovan, and I'd like to welcome you all to the first-ever Jennings Olympics!"

More cheers and whistles sounded throughout the room as people raised their glasses in the air.

"Tonight, the gender of Baby Jennings WILL be revealed!" he continued, rousing the crowd even more. "But first, our expecting parents will have to complete three obstacles to find out the gender of their baby! Put your hands together for your host tonight, Tessa Wilder!"

Clapping ensued as I took the mic from Cash, laughing at his fun antics. "Cash Donovan, everyone!"

The cheers grew louder for him as he exited the stage.

"Okay," I started, grabbing everyone's attention, "the Jennings Olympics will include three obstacles Elly and Carter must complete to reveal the gender of their baby." I led Elly and Carter over to the hanging tire on the left side of the stage. "Your first obstacle is the football toss. You both must throw a football through this hanging tire a combined total of twenty-three times to reveal your first word and move on to the second obstacle." I walked across to the other side of the stage where I had an arcade-styled double hoop shoot set up. "Your second obstacle is the hoop shoot. You each must make twenty-three baskets to reveal the second word and move on to the third and final obstacle." I motioned for them to stay put on the stage as I jumped down and ran over to the other platform. Pointing to the dart machine situated on the wall, I smiled, knowing full well they both sucked at darts. "In the final obstacle, you must take turns standing behind the designated throw line and play a regular five-oh-one game of darts, where you'll both start with five hundred and one points and must work your way down to twenty-three points instead of zero. When you both hit twenty-three points, the gender of your baby will be revealed! However, if either of you pass twenty-three, you bust and have to start over.

"Who's ready to find out the gender of Baby Jennings?" I asked enthusiastically, heading back to the stage.

Hoots and hollers lit up the room again. I looked over to the bar to see our gang causing most of the ruckus. Even Maverick had Seghen's little baby hand cheering, gently waving it in the air.

I took my place next to Elly and Carter and smiled at them. "Before we start, is there anything either of you'd like to say to the audience?"

Elly grabbed the mic and laughed. "I'd like to apologize right now to our baby as well as everyone here for any expletives that may come out of my mouth once we get started."

Carter smiled and took the mic from Elly's hand. "Yeah, what she said, but I'd also like to remind my wife . . ." He turned to Elly and smiled. "That we're not competing against each other tonight. This is a team effort."

Elly rolled her eyes and took the mic back. "I know, so you better not slack or else you're on diaper duty for the first month after birth. Sound reasonable, ladies?"

The women in the room cheered her on, and Elly laughed as she leaned into Carter and gave him a kiss.

"Okay, so we're going to get you mic'd up—"

"We're really going to be wearing a mic?" Elly whispered. "I was serious about the cursing thing, Tessa."

I nodded mischievously and waved Cash back on stage, where he proceeded to wire them up with a small mic that clipped on to the neck of their shirts.

"I think I'm going to need a drink," Carter muttered, signaling one of our friends at the bar.

"Make that a water for me!" Elly added.

Their drinks were handed up to them, and I led them back over to the football toss. A football was handed to each of them. Carter spiraled his in the air, but Elly practiced, going through the motions of her throw.

"Okay, when you hear the whistle, you can start!" I cheered, subtly nodding at Cash as I gazed out at the crowd. "So, grab yourselves a drink and some food—"

"There's food?" Elly quipped excitedly.

"You can eat later," Carter said, shaking his head.

I laughed and continued. "Sit back and enjoy the Jennings Olympics!"

Cash played the music again and the Quad City DJ's hit boomed from the speakers. The whistle sounded and Carter tossed his football first, immediately scoring their first point.

Elly went next and her ball ricocheted off the tire and fell to the ground. Cash tossed the balls back to them, and for the next few minutes, we watched as Carter scored point after point while Elly continuously failed to get the ball through the tire.

"Seriously, Elly?" Carter laughed. "Could you at least try to get it in the hole?"

"That's what she said!" Fletcher quipped loudly from the bar.

"I've never thrown a football before!" she exclaimed, brows furrowed. "And that's a small hole!"

Carter fixed Elly's hands on the ball, just the way he held it with his fingers on the laces, and he showed her how to throw it. "Just like that, babe."

"We don't have time for a teaching lesson, professor!" Elly stated, shaking him off. She aimed, took a step with her left foot, and threw the football at the tire. Spiraling toward the hole, we all watched closely as Elly scored their final point.

A banner fell from the ceiling with their first word and the crowd read it aloud: "IT'S!"

Carter smiled at her, but instead of celebrating, Elly dragged him across the stage to the double hoop shoot.

"Come on, come on!" she said, waddling in front of him. "Don't you want to find out what we're having?"

"Yes," he laughed. "But it's not a race."

"Whatever."

The song changed to Tag Team's "Whoomp! There It Is" as they took their places and grabbed their basketballs. They immediately started shooting, but this time the tables turned. Elly sunk every shot she took, while Carter's ball hit the rim and bounced out.

I leaned down to Elly's NBA legend dad, who stood in the front row with some of his old teammates, smiling proudly. "Keith, any words of encouragement to your son-in-law right now?"

He laughed. "A little more arch, Carter!"

"More arch, my ass!" Carter shouted, shaking his head in frustration. "This is shorter than a normal free throw distance!"

"Exactly!" Elly snapped, impatiently waiting for him to finish. "Which means you should be making them easier."

"You're not helping!" he stated, shooting her a glare. "Some of us didn't spend our youth winning free throw competitions."

She smirked over her shoulder at the crowd. "He's right. I still have the trophies, too."

Finally, Carter made his twenty-third shot, and a second banner fell from the ceiling, revealing the second word. "A!"

"IT'S A! . . ." Elly cheered, grabbing Carter's hand as he helped her down the stage. She looked back at me and asked, "Do we have bets going for the gender?"

"Of course we do, Mommy Milk Maker!" I said, pointing toward the bar. There was a chalkboard easel set up on the bar with the bet totals for each gender. "A majority of the crowd is betting girl, but someone did place a bet for twins!"

"Oh, God!" she shrieked, throwing her head back in laughter as she rubbed her belly. "There's definitely only one in here! We checked!"

Carter helped her up on the platform and they took their places behind the throw line for darts. Cash handed them three darts each and smiled as Rob Base and DJ E-Z Rock's "It Takes Two" came over the sound system.

Elly looked at Carter with a cringe as she cracked her neck and stretched her arms. "You ready for this?"

"They know how bad we are at darts, right?" he whispered to her.

"Yes, we do!" I answered. "Remember your mic'd, so we can hear everything you say, even the stuff you whisper."

"Fuck," he muttered, smiling. "Okay, let's do this."

For the next five minutes, Elly and Carter took turns throwing darts. They were doing surprisingly well, with Elly in the lead and thirty points shy of hitting twenty-three, which was much better than how they usually performed when we hung out and played darts.

Carter got a triple, bringing his score down to thirty. Then Elly hit two fourteens and a two, completing her part of the darts challenge by reaching twenty-three. Her buzzer went off, firing up the crowd even more as she performed a happy dance and threw her arms around Carter.

"Come on, babe!" Elly cheered, kissing him hard on the lips. "Only seven points to go!"

He focused hard, studying the board closely as his face grew more serious. Looking down to make sure he was behind the throw line, he placed his left foot in front of his right and rolled his shoulders to relax.

The more he concentrated, the more eager the crowd became. I could practically hear my heart pounding in my ears as the suspense of his next three shots boiled through my system.

His first throw landed on a one. The second hit the board and fell to the ground, leaving him still in need of a six. Taking a deep breath, he cocked his arm back and launched his third throw. The room fell silent as we watched the dart fly toward the board and eventually hit the ten.

The machine wailed in disappointment as the crowd sighed, and Carter's score reverted back to 501.

"Are you fucking kidding me!?" Elly shouted, putting her hands on her hips and glaring at him. "You were this close!"

"Hey!" Carter retorted with a smile, pointing one of his darts at her. "You knew how terrible I was at darts when you married me. Don't act like you're surprised I fucked this up!"

"Well, don't do it again!" she said, gesturing toward the board.

"You got this, Carter!" Maverick yelled from the bar.

Fletcher raised his beer in the air. "Make that board your bitch, man!"

As Carter started throwing again, Cash changed the song to Europe's "The Final Countdown," and the crowd went absolutely nuts. Bayler started clapping to the beat and everyone joined her, turning the bar into a powerhouse riot as they sang along to the 80's classic.

By the time the guitar solo started, Carter's score was already down to fifty. Then he lowered it to thirty-six. When Cash dropped the vocals on the music and cranked up the instrumentals, we all watched intensely as Carter went for thirteen.

The first dart hit a four. The second landed on a two.

"Here we go, again," Elly smirked. "Seven points, Carter!"

"Come on, man!" Cash said, patting him on the shoulder.

"Do this for your baby!" Elly encouraged him by grabbing his free hand and putting it on her belly. "Do you feel that? It's kicking up a storm in here for you!"

Carter laughed and pulled his wife in for a kiss. "I'm going to rub it for good luck."

He rubbed the bump and then turned his attention back to the task at hand. With only one dart left in his hand, he positioned it between his thumb and fingertips and took aim. He launched it into the air and everyone held their breath.

It stuck on a seven, and the machine went wild! A shower of blue confetti fell from the ceiling as the last banner dropped, revealing the gender: BOY!

"IT'S A BOY!" The crowd cheered. Elly wrapped her arms around Carter's neck. He lifted her up, spinning her pregnant ass around in a circle and then carefully lowered her feet to the stage.

"We're having a boy!" he yelled, before tossing back the rest of his beer.

Smiling, I walked over to them. I was completely thrilled that everything had gone as planned, with no glitches or injuries. Gazing into the crowd, I found Justin looking right back at me, and a swarm of giddiness fluttered in my belly. He was still sitting at the bar, drink in hand, as he gestured to the excitement around him and pointed at me proudly.

"Names!" Bayler yelled through cupped hands. "We want to know his name!"

I laughed, turning my attention back to Elly and Carter. "Now, everyone wants to know if you guys have a name picked out?"

Elly shot Carter a knowing look, and he nodded. "We do."

The crowd zipped their lips.

"We were inspired by our moms, the women who brought us into the world," Carter said, smiling down at his mom in the crowd. "So, we went with their maiden names."

"If we were going to have a girl," Elly stated, grasping Carter's hand tightly, "We were going to use Lucy's maiden name and call her Copelan Karen Jennings."

"But since we're having a boy," Carter continued, placing a chaste kiss on Elly's lips. "We're going with Karen's maiden name: Cooper Keith Jennings."

"To Cooper!" Harper proclaimed, raising her glass in the air.

"To Cooper!"

Cash helped Carter and Elly remove their mics, and then Elly asked for mine. "Carter and I just want to thank everyone for coming out tonight and celebrating with us. It means the world to us to have you all here, continuously showering us with your love and support. We also want to thank our good friend, Tessa, for putting all of this together tonight. The Jennings Olympics was absolutely brilliant, even if I did want to kill Carter toward the end there!"

Carter laughed, taking the mic from her. "We had fun, and we hope you all did, too! Please stick around for more drinks and food!"

"Ooh yeah, food!" Elly exclaimed, as she sauntered away from him.

"And she's off to eat," Carter muttered, handing the mic back to me. He leaned in and gave me a hug. "Thank you for making tonight special for us."

"You're welcome," I said, patting him on the back. "It was my pleasure. Just a reminder, Olympics usually happen ever four years, so . . ."

He laughed as he pulled away from me. "Let's see how the first kid goes, and then we'll talk about baby number two."

"I love his name," I said, gazing over at Elly, who was hugging her dad.

"I can't believe I'm going to have a son," he stated heartily, the smile widening on his face.

"You're going to be a great dad, Carter." I started toward the bar to join Justin, but before I got too far, I glanced over my shoulder and added, "But you might want to let Elly teach him how to shoot hoops."

"Ha ha, very funny!" he smirked, shaking his head.

When I reached the bar, Justin took me in his arms. I instantly felt like I was home again, melting into his warmth as I grabbed his face and pulled his lips down to mine.

"I'm so proud of you," he murmured, holding me tight.

"Thank you." I ran my fingers through his soft hair and cupped the back of his neck.

His mouth found mine again, causing a fury of want and need to swirl deep in my belly as his tongue gracefully coiled around mine. I sighed into him and handed over the rest of my breaths as I deepened our kiss, delighting in the yummy tart taste of the whiskey sour lingering on his tongue. His hands crawled down my back and latched onto the globes of my ass.

"I can't wait to get you home and show you just how proud I am," he said, in a seductive tone that made my cheeks blush.

Leaning into him, I kissed my way to his ear, so only he could hear me when I asked, "How do you plan to show me?"

"Mmm," he hummed, pondering the idea. "I'd like to strip you out of these tight-as-hell jeans and the rest of your clothes, and then get you on all fours and take you from behind."

God, I loved his mouth and his words, and the way they riled me up. Knowing how he talked during sex only made me eager to keep him talking about it. "Would you pull my hair?"

With a brow cocked in amusement, he wrapped my hair in his fist and angled my head up to him. "Would you want me to?"

Hearing his words in that deep, confident voice of his stirred a fire inside me that had me clenching my thighs together to simmer it. He could recite his lectures in that voice, and I'd get just as turned on as I was now.

"Maybe," I replied, my lips curling up into a devious smile. "I guess you'll have to find out later."

"I'm ready to leave whenever you are," he gritted, adjusting himself in his jeans.

"One drink," I said, threading my fingers through his. "That's all I want, and then we can go."

"Okay." He gave me another quick peck on the cheek. "I'm going to go congratulate Carter and Elly."

I let him go, but watched his sexy, laid-back stride as he walked toward the food table where Elly and Carter were standing. In his jeans, boots and flannel shirt untucked over a white tee, he looked so brawny and bronze. When his hair was down and framing his beautiful face, he was a lean cut of handsome that did silly things to my insides. I felt like the luckiest girl in the room even without him by my side.

Turning back to the bar, I took the seat next to Paige, waved down the bartender and ordered a margarita.

"The Olympics idea was great, Tessa," Paige offered with a weak grin. "Everyone seemed to really enjoy it."

I glared at her with my brows furrowed. "No thanks to you."

The smile disappeared from her face as she looked down at her drink.

For weeks, I'd been feeling angry with her, but she wouldn't know that because she hardly spent time with us anymore, always claiming she was busy with work. "You know, when I came up with the idea, you were the first person I wanted to tell because I thought you might want to help, but you ignored my calls and texts. You've been avoiding all of us lately, and I really don't understand why. I get you have some weird phobia of pregnancy and babies, but two of our best friends are expecting their first child together, and all you can think about is yourself or work." I shook my head and reached for my margarita. "You could at least pretend to care like you did for Harper's baby shower. You think I haven't noticed how you haven't moved from that seat all night? I have, which means I'm sure others have, too." I took a deep breath and exhaled, trying to calm down and continue without making a scene. "I don't know what's going on with you, Paige, but you haven't been that great of a friend lately."

She glanced up at me with tears glistening in her eyes that she attempted to blink away before she whispered, "I know."

The hurt I saw in her eyes punched me right in the gut. She was the one out of all of us who always seemed so together—Paige could handle anything and everything—but tonight, she looked like an emotional mess and I had no idea why. That's what worried me the most, that I didn't know what was wrong with one of my best friends.

Taking her hand in mine, I leaned my head against her shoulder. "I'm sorry. I didn't mean to make you feel bad. I just . . . I've been angry with you for avoiding Carter and Elly and the rest of us. I've missed you at our lunch dates. The only time I ever see you anymore is for our Saturday morning yoga sessions. Whatever it is that's bothering you, I want you to know that I'm here for you. We all are. You don't have to push us away to deal with whatever you've been dealt."

"Thanks, Tessa," she said, patting me on the arm.

"We don't have to sit around and talk about baby stuff all the time now just because our friends are having them." I took a sip of my drink and smiled at her. "We can talk about other things, like how talkative Justin is during sex."

Paige laughed in disbelief. "Really?"

"Oh yeah," I said, wiggling my brows excitedly.

We both turned to gaze at him, and the smile on her face widened. "Wow, I never would've taken him for a talker."

"Right?" I mused, nodding. "It's the best thing ever. He talks, and I'm instantly on the train to orgasm town!"

Laughter bubbled out of her, and I caught a glimpse of the woman I recognized as we clinked our glasses together. Once our giggles ceased, she traced the rim of her glass with her finger and sighed. "I'm sorry for being such a terrible friend. I've missed so much lately. I mean, Seghen's practically grown out of her newborn clothes already, and you and Justin are doing it like bunnies."

"What have you been so busy with at work?"

"There's a promotion up for grabs, so I've been pulling extra hours and giving my clients extra attention." She knocked back the rest of her drink. "But I've also been using the extra time to avoid Elly."

"Why? What is it that bothers you so much?" I asked, looking over my shoulder at Elly holding Seghen.

"I can't explain it," she said irritably, as she ran a shaky hand through her blond bob. "I mean, I can; I know what it is. I'm just not ready to talk about it."

"Well," I stated calmly, consoling her with a hug. "When you are, know that I'm here for you."

"Thanks." Paige pulled out my grasp and grabbed her purse. "I'm going to make the rounds real quick, and then head home. It's been a long week, and I'm tired."

"Promise to answer my calls and texts?" I asked, as she hopped off her barstool.

"I promise." With that, she moved away from the bar and started to walk toward the stage where Cash and Justin were conversing.

Despite her promise, I still didn't feel any better after my conversation with her. Something was going on with her, and her demeanor tonight—her unshed tears and the sad tone in her voice—watered the seed of worry planted in my mind.

Then Justin caught my eye and started toward me, so I put my worry to the side, grabbed my margarita and hopped off my seat to meet him and socialize with our friends.

***

Later that night, after Justin and I found out just how much I enjoyed having my hair pulled, we laid in bed together, completely exhausted from the night's activities. As our heartbeats slowed from their racing pace and our lungs retreated back to normal, my mind immediately went back to Paige and replayed our conversation from the bar.

She could explain it, but she wasn't ready to talk about it. What was *it*? Did Elly know what it was, and that's why she was avoiding her more so than when Harper was pregnant? She barely avoided Harper when she was pregnant with Seghen. And what was that she said about Seghen? That she looked like she'd grown out her newborn clothes? Paige did love fashion, so maybe she was just making small talk about Seghen? In the only way she knew how to talk about babies?

Fuck, this is going to drive me crazy.

"What is going on in there?" Justin asked, caressing his thumb over my cheek. "I can practically feel the wheels turning in there with your head on my shoulder."

I sighed audibly and shook my head. "It's Paige. I'm worried about her. Did you talk to her tonight?"

"No," he said, furrowing his brows. "Now that I think about it, she was relatively quiet most of the night. She barely spoke to any of us while we were all sitting at the bar."

"See," I said, leaning up on my elbow. "That's just not like her, especially on a night like tonight. The Paige we know would've been walking around, socializing with everyone and networking. She's a publicist, a workaholic; she knows how to handle herself and the public well. She did say she's been working hard for a promotion at work, so maybe tonight she just didn't feel like working, but that's not like her at all. Tonight, she just seemed so . . ."

"Depressed," Justin said, finishing my sentence.

I snapped my fingers and pointed at him. "That's it. But what could she be depressed about? When I asked her what bothered her so much about pregnancies and babies, she said she wasn't ready to talk about it. There's something she hasn't told us, and it's bothering her. I just wish I knew what it was so I could help her, so she wouldn't feel like she has to avoid all of us. That's what she's been doing for weeks now, and when I called her out on it, she had tears in her eyes! Real, sad tears, Justin. I've seen her cry happy tears, like at Carter and Elly's wedding, but I've never seen her eyes fill with sad tears. Something's going on with her."

"There's lots of things that could trigger depression, but a loss of interest in normal activities is a sign of it." He held me closer in an effort to comfort me. "As are feelings of sadness, fatigue, irritability . . ."

"I did seem to upset her when I asked what was bothering her," I added. "I just wish she wouldn't push us away. I mean, she's got two friends with doctorate degrees in psychology. She doesn't have to tell me what's wrong, but she could at least try talking to you or Elly."

"Tessa, have you met Paige?" he quipped sarcastically. "She's not going to ask for our help because she thinks she's strong enough to handle whatever it is on her own."

"I know, but that's not going to stop me from worrying about her."

He kissed my temple. "Do you think she'd harm herself or others?"

I shook my head adamantly. "No, of course not."

"Then, right now, I'm okay with letting her think she's strong enough."

"Okay." I ran my hands up and down his back in an attempt to relax my mind. "I'm sorry I brought her into bed with us."

"Don't apologize." He pulled the covers away from us, crawled on top of me and moved in between my legs as he reached for a condom. "One of your best qualities is that you have a great heart. You're always thinking about others instead of yourself, and I love that about you. But I obviously didn't work you over enough if you still have the ability to think right now."

I hummed a pleasurable moan as my legs curled around his waist and I felt the weight of his sheathed cock pressing against my pussy. "You do have a way of shutting up my mind."

And he did just that the second time around.

Chapter Sixteen

Justin

It was the last day of finals before winter break. I spotted Trey talking to a blond chick near the exit of the Psychology building. I'd just finished administering the final to my General Psych class, the one Trey's in, and I figured he must have done well. There wasn't a question that stumped him while taking the test, unlike some of the students who stared off into space thinking the answer would come to them. Now, he seemed relaxed as he flirted with the girl. Typical Trey Wilder. Despite acting like he wasn't a great student, he really was, when he applied himself. Still, he often pretended like he didn't care about school.

He noticed me, and surprisingly, he walked away from the girl to catch up with me.

"Hey, Dr. J.!" he exclaimed, patting me on the shoulder. "Can I call you that?"

Shrugging him off, I shook my head. "No."

"Why not?"

"Because it sounds like Dr. Dre," I stated, rolling my eyes. "I'm a professor, not a rapper."

He laughed. "True."

We walked out of the building and onto Washington Square toward the park. I zipped up my coat, and Trey pulled a beanie over his head. The sidewalks were packed with snow now, the chilly air cut through us, but the city bustled nonetheless like it always did. Christmas decorations lined every inch of the city too, with the holiday quickly approaching in just two weeks. I'd already gotten Tessa's Christmas present, but I was having a hell of a time trying to keep it out of her sight in the apartment.

The struggles of living with a girlfriend.

"So, I think I did pretty well on the final," Trey stated, rubbing his hands together for warmth. "I actually took the time to study for this one. I'm feeling really good about it."

"You should feel good about it," I said, nodding appreciatively. "We've only spent the last five months studying the material."

"Yeah, yeah," he quipped nonchalantly. "So, what'd you get Tessa for Christmas? I still can't figure out what to get her."

"I'm not telling you."

"What?" he exclaimed, stopping in his tracks. "Why not? It's not like I'm going to tell her. I need some ideas. She's so hard to buy for because she doesn't want anything. Trust me, I've asked. She's all, 'Save your money for expenses and rent.' It's fucking Christmas! I know she got me something, so I have to get her something. That's how this sibling thing works."

I laughed. "Is that so?"

He fell back in step with me as we headed into Washington Square Park. Carter and I had made plans to meet up in the park before heading to Elly's office for lunch since he was also giving a final in one of the nearby buildings.

"You really won't help a brother out? What kind of boyfriend are you? I'd help you out if the situation were reversed. Which reminds me, you should tell me what you got her so I can approve it. She might not like your gift."

"She'll like it," I replied, mainly to reassure myself. I'd been worrying about her reaction ever since I bought it. "I mean, she might not at first, but she will. I think."

"Please tell me you didn't get her a dog, or even worse, a cat! The last thing Tessa wants is to shovel shit out of a litter box for the next ten years."

"Actually, the average lifespan of a domesticated cat is fifteen years."

"Excuse me, Dr. Know-It-All. The next fifteen years," he said, sarcastically correcting himself. "So, what'd you get her? You didn't get her sex stuff, did you? Because that's something I'd rather not know."

"No sex stuff." I sighed, turning to face him. Suddenly I heard a woman scream and my body went on high alert. "What the—"

A series of gunshots stopped me mid-sentence as all hell broke loose in the park. Around us, people screamed and scrambled to take cover, and more shots were fired. I couldn't tell where they were coming from, but I grabbed Trey and dragged him down to the ground with me. "GET DOWN!"

"Holy fucking shit!" His eyes were wide with fear, quickly moving back and forth, taking in our surroundings. "Where the hell is the shooter?"

"I-I don't . . ." A piercing pain traveled down my arm, the agony unlike anything I'd ever felt as it hemorrhaged through my system at a damaging pace. On my stomach, I took in the scene before me. A few people were lying on the ground in Washington Square Park while others were running away from the scene. Campus security swarmed the area with their guns drawn, cautiously pointing them at a kid in a black coat.

I closed my eyes and rolled to my left, holding my shoulder with my hand as I settled onto my back, silently cursing the discomfort in my arm.

Two more shots were fired, and then all I heard were the sounds of people's cries and sirens wailing in the distance.

"They got him," Trey said discreetly, concern still quivering in his voice. "The one they were closing in on. They shot him."

"That's . . . a relief." Smelling the scent of blood, I opened my eyes. *Fuck.*

Trey crawled to his knees and ripped off his beanie, and then he noticed the blood. "Justin, you're bleeding!"

"I got hit but . . ." I reached into my pocket and grabbed my phone. "I need you to call Carter Jennings. His number is in there. I was supposed to meet him here to go to lunch. I need you to make sure he's okay."

"I will in a minute. We need to stop the bleeding. At least until help arrives." He quickly shrugged out of his coat, not giving one damn about how cold it was, then slipped off his button-down and began tying it around my shoulder and upper arm. Turning me on my side for a minute, he studied my back. "It wasn't through and through. At least I don't see an exit."

"With this much blood, it must've hit an artery."

Hovering above me, he kept peering back at the bloodstained snow around my body. He tightened the shirt around my arm one last time to make a tourniquet. Then he grabbed my phone and dialed Carter. While he waited for an answer, his face turned almost as white as the snow. He covered my right side with his coat as if it was a blanket. "I'm sorry. I can't handle the sight of blood."

"It's okay," I offered, understandingly. Lying there, I recalled what Tessa had said about the night she was stabbed, how scared he was then. So, I tried my best to stay extra calm for his sake. "I'm going to be all right, Trey."

"You fucking better be." He tore the phone away from his ear and shook his head. "He's not answering. Who should I call? 9-1-1?"

Worry crept into my mind. "No, try him again."

He tapped the screen, but then my phone started ringing so he answered. "Carter, this is Trey, Tessa's brother. Yeah, I'm with him. Are you okay?"

He nodded and then held the phone up to my ear so I could talk to him. "Carter."

"Where the hell are you guys? It's fucking chaos around here."

"We're on the . . ." I swallowed the sting down and caught my breath before continuing, "We're on the northeast side of the park. We'd just left the Psych building before walking into the park."

"Okay, I'm headed your way."

"Carter, bring an EMT with you."

"You were hit?" he asked in disbelief.

"I think it nicked an artery because I've lost a lot of blood all ready."

"Fuck!" His breathing picked up over the line, and I could tell he was full on sprinting now. "Okay, just hang in there. I'll be there as soon as I can flag down an ambulance."

***

Tessa

It was noon when the phone at the clinic rang. We were usually closed over the lunch hour, but since Justin and Carter hadn't arrived yet, I answered the call, thinking it might be a patient needing to reschedule an appointment.

Grabbing the phone, I answered in my normal cheerful voice. "Dr. Ellyson's office, this is Tessa speaking, how may I help you?"

"Tessa."

"Carter?" His voice was so wary. The way he said my name, along with the sounds of sirens howling in the background, immediately sent my body into a panic. "You never call the clinic. You usually text one of our phones. What's going on?"

He took a deep breath and exhaled it. "There was a shooting on campus today. Washington Square Park to be exact."

"Trey." My eyes immediately filled with tears. His words were like a swift kick in the gut, sucking the air right out of my lungs as I covered my mouth to stifle a sob. "Do you know if Trey's okay?"

"He's fine."

I wiped a tear away, and then I asked, "And Justin? Is he okay?"

He paused for a second, and that one-second pause told me all I needed to know.

He's not okay.

"He was shot," Carter finally said. "He's lost some blood, so we're headed to the hospital now. Trey's riding with us, too."

I covered the receiver of the phone with both hands, and finally let a sob escape from my chest. Elly walked into the lobby, and I did my best to compose myself as I explained what had happened.

She put the call on speaker.

"Carter, what hospital are you guys headed to?"

"I don't know, babe," he replied. "When we get there, I'll text you so you know where to go."

"Okay," she said, grabbing my purse and coat. "We'll get there as soon as we can. I love you."

"I love you too, Elly."

"Wait," I interjected, before Elly hung up. "Can I talk to them? I need to talk to Trey and Justin."

"Of course."

I heard some shuffling on the other end, and then Trey's voice greeted me. "Hey, Tess."

"Hey," I said softly, my eyes refilling with tears. I ached to physically touch him and make sure he was okay. It didn't matter that he was an adult now and could take care of himself. I'd always see him as the little brother I raised. "You're all right?"

"Yeah, I'm good. Although this ambulance could have more comfortable seating."

I smiled at his sarcasm, and then thought about the reason they were in the ambulance. "Is he all right?"

"Why don't you ask him yourself?" More shuffling ensued on the other end, and then I heard Justin's breathing and started crying all over again.

"Don't cry, panion. I'm going to be okay."

"God, I hope so," I said, my voice shaking with snivels. "I can't lose you."

"You're not going to lose me."

Taking a deep breath, I exhaled slowly in an attempt to calm myself down for him. His voice was deep and languid on the other end of the phone, which only worried me more. "Promise me?"

He laughed weakly. "I promise."

"You can't go into any lights or go through any pearly gates, okay?"

"Okay."

"I love you." We hadn't said those words to each other yet, and I hated myself for waiting until now to say them to him. "I hate that I'm telling you that for the first time over the phone while you're in an ambulance."

"Then meet me at the hospital and tell me them in person after I get out of surgery," he quipped, allowing me to hear the smile in his voice.

"It's a date."

"I won't stand you up."

"I know you won't."

"Tessa?"

I smiled, loving the sound of my name. "Yeah, panion?"

He cleared his throat, and in a tone slightly more upbeat than before, he replied, "I love you."

"Okay, okay," Trey griped, taking the phone away from him. "You guys love each other. We get it. Just meet us at Langone. We just arrived, and they need to get him in there."

"We're on our way. Keep me updated with texts until we get there."

"Will do."

Chapter Seventeen

Tessa

By the time Elly and I arrived at Langone, Justin was already in surgery, and the surgical waiting room was filled with people waiting to hear about their loved ones. Carter had called all of our friends, and Fletcher picked up Bayler and Mrs. J. on his way to the hospital. Everyone was here for him, but the only person I wanted to see besides Justin right now was Trey.

I rushed over to him, relieved to see him with my own two eyes, and tightly wrapped my arms around his waist.

He sighed. "Tessa, I'm fine."

"I know." I pulled away and studied him closely. "But you could've been seriously hurt." I noticed the sweatshirt he had on wasn't his, but relaxed when I didn't see any blood on him or any signs of injury.

"The sweatshirt is Carter's," he said, looking down at the black material. "I used my button-down to stop the bleeding."

My heart ached for him because it'd happened to him again. All the blood. The fear of the unknown. The panic of trying to save a life. Those were Trey's nightmares, even if he didn't physically have them. I knew without asking that today brought all those memories back for him. Except instead of trying to save me, he'd saved the man I love.

Rubbing my hand up and down his arm, I leaned into him and rested my head on his shoulder. "Thank you for helping him. I know it wasn't easy for you."

"It was the right thing to do," he muttered, looking away from me. "He was hit in the shoulder, but it was still a lot of blood. The EMTs said they'd seen worse, thought he'd make a full recovery, but shit, Tessa, you see shows all the time where they go in stable and still don't make it."

"Those are just shows, Trey." I moved into his line of sight and made him look at me. I could still see the thirteen-year-old boy who'd been scared I wouldn't survive a stab wound. "You have to think positive. What you went through today was awful. I can't imagine the things you saw or the things you heard, but I need—no, *we* need—you to be optimistic. Can you do that? For me?"

"Yeah." He nodded solemnly.

"Thank you."

"I'm going to take a walk," he said, smiling down at me weakly. "Will you let me know if you hear any updates on him?"

"Of course."

He pushed off the wall and started down the corridor, running a hand through his short, brown hair. Exhaustion exuded from every one of his features. His normal, confident swagger was hindered, and worry lingered in his gray eyes.

It was early afternoon, but it felt like midnight. We'd all gone from thinking about lunch to hoping one of our own was going to be all right. And I needed to believe he'd be all right.

"You going to take your own advice?" Carter asked, grabbing me by the shoulders. He turned me to face him, and allowed a smile to spread across his face.

"He's my brother. I have to be strong for him."

"Then it's a good thing you have us here." He pulled me in for a hug, and I tightly clung to his back. "Justin's going to be okay."

Inhaling a deep breath, I mentally demanded my tears to stay away as I exhaled. "He has to be."

He ushered me over to the chairs where our friends sat, and planted me in the seat between Elly and Mrs. J. I felt a hand cover mine, and I looked down to see Mrs. J.'s bony fingers wrapping around mine.

"All we can do for him right now is pray," she said, relaxing back into her seat.

I'd never prayed in my life. Not about real, worrisome things, anyway. Leaning my head back against the wall, I turned toward her and whispered, "I'm in love with him."

"I know." She smiled sweetly, her bright blue eyes the same as Justin's gazing back at me. Her grip tightened on my hand as she closed her eyes. "But don't let your love for him make you worried sick over him. He wouldn't want that, and you know it. He'd want you to be proud of him because if he hadn't taken that bullet today, someone else would have, and they might not be as strong as Justin."

***

An hour later—maybe more—I wasn't sure, I was still impatiently waiting for an update on Justin. I'd lost all sense of time while restlessly milling around. Even Mitzi and Burg had shown up at the hospital to see Justin. All of us were growing more anxious the longer we waited. Trey had come back to the waiting room and fiddled with his camera to pass the time. Maverick and Harper called Mav's mom to check up on Seghen. Paige made a few calls for work. Carter massaged Elly's swollen feet. The rest of us stared at the doors, willing any sort of hospital personnel to walk through them with news.

When I saw Whitley push through the doors wearing her nursing scrubs, I jumped up from my seat and rushed over to her. "Please tell me you know something."

She smiled softly and glanced around at all of us. "He's doing well."

Thank God. I allowed the knots in my stomach to loosen slightly.

"They did encounter a minor complication, but—"

"What kind of complication?" Elly asked, brows furrowed.

Whitley kept her calm demeanor as she explained. "Justin's right lung collapsed shortly after surgery began, but that's very common among surgical patients who undergo anesthesia. The anesthesia changes a person's breathing pattern, which can sometimes cause a collapsed lung. So, like I said, just a minor complication that they easily corrected, and then they moved on to fixing the damage caused by the bullet."

"So, he's okay?" Trey asked timidly.

At this point, Whitley was surrounded by all of us, eager to know more about him.

"Yes," she said more cheerfully. "He should be back in his room now."

A warm sensation spread through my chest as happy tears threatened my eyes. "When will we be able to see him?"

"Well," she giggled, gazing at each of us. "I don't think you'll all fit in his room at once, so we might have you go in groups. But let's let the anesthesia wear off and check him over once more before any visitors go back."

Just like that, she'd given us the news we needed to relax. The gang dispersed around the waiting room. Some went to get drinks. Some were already on the phone ordering in food. Mrs. J. could finally go use the restroom. But I just stood there, smiling at Whitley.

"Thank you," I said, wrapping my arms around her.

"Janice called me right after I got called in to work," she replied, hugging me back. "I promised her I'd check on him as often as I could."

I nodded. "I should probably let you get back to work."

"The emergency room is completely full," she stated, as she redid her ponytail. "So many people have come in just from injuring themselves trying to get out of the park with the snow and ice. Then there are the patients who were actually shot. But they're all doing well so far, no fatalities. So, that's good."

"Yeah, it is."

"I'll come back out and get you when he's awake and ready for you, okay?"

"Okay," I said, grinning wider. "Thanks again, Whitley. I really appreciate you looking out for him."

"Anytime!"

When I walked back over to my seat in the waiting room, Paige sat down beside me and smiled. "How are you doing?"

"Better," I answered, relief washing away some of my anxiety. "Knowing he's going to be all right helps."

She nodded.

"I was just so scared he wasn't going to make it, that he was going to be taken from me," I confessed, shaking my head. I hadn't really voiced those feelings or allowed myself to listen to those thoughts, but they were in the back of my mind taking root this entire time. "I know that's selfish of me to think, but we just started dating, and then this happens. I feel so stupid for not telling him how I felt sooner. For worrying about such minuscule crap instead of pursuing a love I've always wanted. Now, I have him, and today, I could've easily lost him. Have you ever experienced a love like that, Paige?"

She was quiet for a moment before she nodded. "Yeah, I have."

I craned my neck, shooting her an incredulous stare. "What happened? How come you've never talked about it?"

She swallowed hard and a jaded smile curled at her lips. "It's been more than a decade, and it's still too hard to talk about. Even thinking about him still hurts."

The sadness in her voice made my heart break as I reached for her hand and covered it with mine.

"But that's how first great loves are supposed to be," she concluded with a shrug. "They're supposed to make you hurt. There's nothing selfish about loving someone so much you're afraid to lose them."

***

Justin

I woke up with a huge bandage over my right shoulder. The room was empty, but I heard the sound of machines and the hospital buzzing outside my room. A nurse peeked in and smiled at me, and then called for someone over her shoulder.

"Your nurse will be right in, Dr. Jameson."

I nodded carefully and relaxed back into the pillow. I tried moving my right arm, but a slice of pain shot through it, so I settled for keeping it stable. The rest of my body felt fine. Sure, I was a little tired, but I figured it was the drugs still lingering in my system.

"You're awake!"

Whitley's upbeat voice grabbed my attention and I smiled at her. "How long have I been out?"

"Not long actually," she laughed, as she went about checking my vitals. "You have quite the fan club out there waiting to come visit you though."

I appreciated all of them being here for me, but the one person I was most concerned about was Tessa. I remembered the discussion we had over the phone prior to arriving at the hospital. She was a mess when I talked to her, but she'd told me she loved me. "How's she doing? Is she upset and crying, or under control and concerned?"

The smile on Whit's face grew. "The latter. Tessa's a strong girl."

"Yeah, she is. And Grandma?"

"She's lived through wars; she can handle her grandson being shot."

I laughed weakly. "Now, you're starting to sound like her."

"She's a wise old bird."

Nodding, I closed my eyes for a second and allowed the hit of the pain medicine to take me while Whit went through her routine. I could still hear the cries and the shots being fired in the park. The sirens racing to the scene. An image of Trey's distraught face as he tried to stop the bleeding crept into my vision, but I blinked it away. It felt like the shooting had happened days ago, but I knew it had been only hours.

"Whit?"

"Yeah?"

"How many people were shot?"

"Eight, including the shooter."

"How are they doing?"

She placed her hand on my arm and smiled. "They're all alive and doing fine."

"Good," I said, nodding. "That's good to hear."

"Yes, it is." She looked through my chart, and then back at me. "Are you ready for some company or would you like to rest?"

"That depends . . ." I stated in my most charming tone, smiling to show off my dimples as I grabbed the remote and adjusted the bed so I could sit up. "Will you let Tessa stay with me?"

"You know I can't say no to your dimples," she said, shaking her head. "Of course, she can stay as long as she wants."

"Then bring them on back."

Minutes later, I could hear Grandma's voice carrying down the hall. Then she appeared in the doorway with Tessa and Trey close behind her as the three of them led in our friends.

"I tried to get them to come in groups," Whitley said, rolling her eyes. "Obviously, that didn't work."

I laughed. "It's fine."

"Justin . . ." Grandma said with a smile, shaking her head. She patted me on the cheek and gave me a kiss on the forehead. "I knew you'd be okay. You're not allowed to go on the menu before me."

"I know," I stated, appreciating her teasing nature. "That's exactly what I told the doctors before they took me in to surgery."

"Oh, I'm sure you did!" she laughed, and then studied my shoulder. "But you're doing okay?"

"Good as new," I said, catching Tessa's gaze. She was huddled off to the side, gazing back at me like she wanted me all to herself.

The feeling was mutual. After all, I had a date to uphold.

But I'd entertain our friends until then.

Trey stepped up to my bed and took my left hand in his. "I'm glad you're doing good, man."

"Thank you," I said, tightening my grip, "for not letting me bleed to death in a park."

He laughed lightly and then shrugged. "It was nothing."

"It was *something*," I reiterated, glancing back at Tessa who was attempting to hide the fact that she was wiping a tear from her eye.

Then my friends surrounded the bed, eager to know every little detail about how it all happened, so Trey and I told them. Carter filled in the spots from how he experienced it, and told them about the ride to the hospital.

"Did they get the bullet out of you?" Cash asked curiously. "It'd be pretty badass if they didn't. You can walk around with a bullet for the rest of your life, right?"

"Yes, but I won't because they did get it."

"Really?" Fletcher asked amused. "Where is it?"

Maverick smacked him. "Why do you want to see it?"

"I don't know," he replied with a shrug.

Carter shook his head as he wrapped his arm around Elly's shoulders. "If it were me, I would've told them to get rid of it. That's not a keepsake I'd want."

"Same here," Maverick said.

Agreed, I thought. I had no desire to see the bullet.

"Have you at least gotten to see your scar?" Cash asked.

I watched Tessa closely as she paced near the head of my bed. I could tell she was becoming more anxious with the way she kept twisting her hair around her finger, which in turn overwhelmed me, having the room full of people when all I wanted was alone time with her. I just wanted to feel her and hold her tight so she knew I was okay, calming her down with just my touch. "No, they haven't changed the dressing yet."

Cash opened his mouth to speak, but before he could get another word out, I stopped him by holding my left hand up.

"Guys," I stated, glancing around at their surprised faces. "I really appreciate you all being here for me, and waiting around so long to make sure I'd make it out okay, but . . . I really need to be alone with Tessa right now. I'm sorry. I don't want to be the asshole who kicks his friends out of his hospital room, but—"

"You don't need to explain," Maverick said, reaching for Harper's hand. "You're not an asshole for wanting to be with your girl. I've been there."

"Yeah," Elly agreed, smiling back at me. "We can come back later."

The gang filtered out after wishing me well, and Grandma made me promise to call her in the morning. Trey insisted on staying at the hospital with his sister, but he left my room with his camera in hand to give us some privacy.

Tessa moved to the left side of my bed and smiled weakly, like it was taking everything in her to keep it together. She kissed my cheek and then studied my features, grazing her fingertips over my facial hair as she examined me with her beautifully sad eyes. She was combing over every aspect of me to make sure I was all right, and I let her, knowing she needed it. But the more she studied me, the longer the silence grew between us, and then she broke like a dam giving way to a flood of tears as her body shuddered with sobs.

"Tessa," I sighed earnestly. With my one good arm, I moved over slightly and pulled her onto the bed with me, running my hand down her back to soothe her. "I'm okay. I'm going to be all right."

"I k-know," she stuttered hoarsely. She reached up and cupped my face before gently taking my lips. Her mouth felt familiar, warm and soft yet eager and enticing at the same time, like she thought she might never get to kiss me again. So, I sank into her, devouring her to the best of my abilities, twisting my tongue around hers and sucking until I elicited a sexy little moan out of her. Every kiss should've been executed in this slow, sensual manner, cherished until neither one of us could breathe.

I wanted to spend the rest of my life kissing her like this, and if today taught me anything, it was that my time here on Earth should be cherished.

With her.

When she broke away panting, she wiped away another fallen tear and said, "I love you, Justin. I love you so much."

Hearing and seeing her say those words for the first time triggered an unbreakable grin to spread across my face. "I love you, Tessa."

"I was so scared when I heard you'd been shot," she said, drying her face with her hand.

"I know." I pulled her closer and continued rubbing her back. "How's Trey doing?"

"He's okay," she grimaced. "I'm not really sure how he's handling it all. He shuts me out in times like these."

I nodded understandingly. "He had a moment in the park, when he was tying his shirt around my arm. His face went pale, and then he covered me up with his coat because he said he didn't like the sight of blood. I think . . . he might have had a flashback to the night you were stabbed."

She sighed audibly. "He was nervous when I got here, thinking you might not make it. It reminded me of when I was in the hospital after the stabbing."

"Has he ever talked to anyone about that night?"

"No," she replied, shaking her head. "But now, I'm thinking it wouldn't be a bad idea to suggest some sessions with Elly."

"Probably not," I stated. "But if you don't want him discussing that night with your friend, I can recommend a therapist just as good as Elly."

She was quiet for a moment, but then she shook her head again, determined. "No, I want it to be Elly. Someone he's comfortable with. And I don't care if anyone finds out about what happened that night. I've spent so much of my life worrying about crap. Now, it just seems ridiculous. Like with you. If I would've just told you how I felt about you, instead of worrying that you wouldn't want things to change between us or worrying that I wasn't good enough for you, we'd probably have gotten together sooner."

Entwining our hands together, I kissed her temple. "That's the thing about life though: no amount of regrets can change the past and no amount of anxiety can change the future. But if you really think about it, we've always been together. We started out as friends who danced with each other whenever we didn't have dates. Then we became roommates who accepted each other's habits. Now, we're panions who are completely in love with each other. It might have taken us a while to get here, but I don't regret a single minute of it because I got to know you, the real you, and I continue to fall in love with you every day."

She leaned up on her elbow so she could look at me, all the anguish in her features gone as a lively grin lingered on her lips. Her perfect gray eyes shined bright again, and they were smiling back at me. "You always manage to say all the right words to make me feel better, even when you're the one who's hurt."

Languidly, I brushed the hair out of her face and latched onto the nape of her neck, feeling the side effects of the pain meds. "Tessa, with you by my side, I'll never hurt."

A dreamy sigh escaped from her as she lay her head back on my pillow. "See, there you go again. I feel like I'm not contributing enough to this panionship. What am I supposed to do?"

I laughed faintly, but it quickly turned into a yawn. "Just lay here with me."

"Okay," she whispered softly as she kissed my cheek and let my eyes fall shut.

My body surrendered to the medication without a fight, but the last thing I heard before I slipped into sleep was her lovely voice.

"I love you, Justin Jameson. I'll lay with you forever."

That's all I needed from her.

Chapter Eighteen

Two Weeks Later

Justin

When I arrived home from the gym, I found Tessa in the kitchen baking. She was hunched over the countertop with a tube of frosting in her hand, decorating. The smell of freshly baked cookies hit me as I shrugged out of my coat and shut the door behind me. Today was Christmas Eve, and we had plans to go to church with Grandma tonight and eat dinner at her place afterward. In typical Tessa fashion, she'd spent most of the day in the kitchen preparing too much food.

I'd spent most of my afternoon at the gym with Maverick going through my physical therapy stretches since it was the holiday and the PT office I normally visited was closed. My arm was healing well. I already felt restless since I couldn't work out on a regular basis, but I was slowly getting back to my routine. Tessa had mastered redressing my wound early on, but thankfully I didn't need the dressing anymore. There was a scar now, and whenever I looked at it, I thought about what I told Tessa about her own scar: it was proof that I survived.

And I planned on taking advantage of my survival. Since the shooting, Tessa and I had grown closer. She still had the occasional night terror, more so after my hospital stay, but she and Trey had started therapy sessions, together and apart, to work through everything they'd been through. Sometimes, she even wanted me to attend her sessions with her. I willingly went, supporting her one hundred percent.

We laughed more often and enjoyed the ordinary things in life, like watching the snow fall while wrapped in each other's arms. We catered to our needs in stimulating, intense measures that took sex to a whole new level. We simply appreciated every moment like it might be our last, turning the ordinary into extraordinary every chance we got.

Walking into the kitchen, I stole an unfrosted cookie from the tray and smiled at Tessa. "How's it going, panion?"

"All I have left to do is frost these snowman sugar cookies," she said, wrapping her arms around my waist. She leaned into me and gave me a kiss, and then took a bite of the cookie in my hand. "I can't remember the last time I made sugar cookies."

I took a bite and nodded in approval. "They're good."

She smacked me in the stomach and scoffed. "The frosted ones are better!"

Laughing, I took in the rows of snowmen smothered in white frosting. I grabbed her hand and led her into our living room. "You don't skimp on the frosting. I like that in a woman."

"Good to know," she smirked.

We sat down on the couch together, and admired the Christmas tree lit up beside the TV. It wasn't a normal green

Christmas tree. Tessa insisted on having a white one because she thought they were prettier. So, we'd bought a fake white tree for our living room. It was the first Christmas decoration to ever grace my apartment, and I had to agree, it looked great in here. We'd decorated it with brightly colored ornaments and silver garland, strung white lights around it, and placed a white star on top. The tree, in its enormity, lit the living room in a romantic setting that needed no other lights. I think that's what I loved most about it; Tessa and I could spend hours in here with our tree.

But I couldn't forget the gifts underneath it. There were three packages neatly wrapped in their holiday-themed paper, just begging for us to rip them open. The minute I noticed a gift for me under the tree, I'd started nagging her to let me open it.

"It's Christmas Eve," I declared, nudging her arm.

She rolled her eyes. "You can't wait until tomorrow?"

"You can't tell me you're not curious about what I got you. I know you want to open your gift, too! Let's open them! Grandma always let us open gifts on Christmas Eve. It's tradition."

"Then what'd you do on Christmas morning?" she asked, completely serious. "I thought that's when everyone opened gifts."

Sometimes I forgot that Tessa didn't grow up celebrating holidays like most people. She never had Christmas Eves or Christmas mornings, and she never opened gifts, even on her birthday. She didn't have her own family traditions to uphold, so I was determined to teach her mine or create new ones with her.

"On Christmas morning, we'd sleep in and Grandma would make an awesome breakfast. Then we'd spend the day watching Christmas movies and eating leftovers from Christmas Eve."

Tessa sighed, pressing her lips together playfully. "Fine. We can open gifts now."

I jumped up from the couch. "Seriously?"

"Yes," she laughed. "But you have to open yours first."

"Okay." I grabbed her gift from me and handed it over to her, and then I set mine from her on the coffee table. Reaching for the last gift under the tree, I glanced over my shoulder at her. "Who's this from?"

"Trey said it's for both of us, that we're supposed to open it together," she said with a shrug. "He told me not to open it until after I opened yours. I figured you guys went in on something. You didn't?"

"No." Sitting back on my heels, I admired his wrap job, thoroughly impressed that the kid could wrap pretty damn well, even if he did use newspapers instead of actual wrapping paper. Glancing down at his present reminded me of the day of the shooting, when he was nagging me about Tessa's gift.

"What?"

I smiled nostalgically and shook my head. "The day of the shooting, he was begging me to tell him what I'd got you for Christmas. He didn't know what to get you. I was about to tell him, but then the shots were fired."

"Did you ever tell him?" she asked, in a hopeful tone.

I nodded. "Yeah, I told him in the hospital."

"Well, you must've helped him figure out what to get me . . . Or I should say us because it's to both of us, not just me."

"Yeah." I moved back over to the couch, placing Trey's present on the coffee table. Taking a seat next to her, I grabbed the box from her and smiled. "I love opening presents."

"Speaking of gifts, are you sure Mrs. J. is going to like what we got her?" she asked doubtfully. "I feel like just a gift card is impersonal. Maybe we should've gotten her something else, too."

"Tessa," I deadpanned. "We've been over this. Grandma is all about gift cards. She hates shopping, so she wouldn't want anyone wasting time on it just to find her something she might hate. Her theory on gifts: here's a gift card so you can buy whatever you want. She's going to love the hundred-dollar gift card we got her to Amazon. She loves Amazon; it has everything."

"Okay, fine," she grumbled, smiling weakly. "I'll let it go."

"Can I open my gift now?" I asked playfully.

"Yes, open it!"

Ripping the red and white candy cane paper off, I leaned over the box and peeled the tape off the lid. When it opened up, a mass of white tissue paper greeted me, and the smell of new leather permeated the air. I dug the tissue paper out to see a brand new brown leather messenger bag sitting in the box. I took it out, immediately admiring the silver personalized engraving on the front that said JAMESON. It was beautiful, and I was in need of a new bag for work. My old one had holes in it and was starting to fray on the edges. This one was perfect though. It had all the pockets, if not more than, my old one had, and it was slightly bigger than mine, which meant I'd be able to carry more.

"Tessa, this is just what I needed," I declared excitedly, giving her a quick peck on the lips. "Thank you."

"You're welcome," she giggled, moving closer to my side. "There's more though. Open the bag."

Eagerly, I unlatched the top and peered inside. She had the damn thing stuffed with more presents already unwrapped for me. The first item I pulled out was a timepiece. It was a Komono analog watch with a brown leather strap, stainless steel casing, and a navy face.

"If you don't like it, you can exchange it," she said shyly. "I just saw it, and thought it'd look good on you."

"No way am I exchanging this," I said, smiling at her. "I really do like it. I'll wear it tonight."

She leaned her head against my shoulder, pleased with herself. "There are a few more things."

I set the watch to the side and reached back into the bag. I pulled out a book, but when I realized it was a cookbook, the smile on my face fell. "A cookbook?"

"It's a man's cookbook!" she exclaimed, through a fit of laughter. "The recipes are super easy, and I thought you might enjoy it because it was written in a straightforward way. It even states it'll elevate your kitchen game."

"You think I don't have kitchen game?" I asked, playfully tickling her sides. "I assure you there are many things I can do in the kitchen. Specifically with you."

"Ha! I know, but cooking is not one of them, panion," she laughed, wrapping her arms around my neck. She pulled me in for a kiss, and pressed her forehead against mine. "Open the book."

I pulled away and opened it, smiling when I saw gift cards to my favorite take-out restaurants taped to the inside cover. She even wrote me a note: *When all else fails, use one of these and order take-out! Love, Tessa.*

"Perfect," I laughed, kissing her forehead. "Thank you."

She cupped my face in her soft hands and drew me in for a kiss. "There's one more item in there."

I grabbed the last gift and smiled. It was a game of Scrabble for the fridge, with the letters in magnetic tiles.

"You're always kicking everyone's ass in that Words With Friends game."

"And you thought this would improve my game?" I asked jokingly. "I don't think that's even possible."

"That's exactly why I got it!" she exclaimed. "So, you could teach me your ways while I teach you how to cook."

"Some teacher-student role-playing in the kitchen? Count me in," I teased, nodding to my gift in her lap. "You're turn."

She let go of me and turned her attention to her Christmas present, shaking it in an attempt to hear the gift rattle inside. "It's pretty light. What could it be?" The smile on her face widened as she ripped through the paper almost as fast as I did. She quickly undid the lid by sliding her finger under the tape.

Digging into the box, she pulled out her gift card to Amazon and laughed as she read what I'd written on the cardholder: *For the books you want me to read to you.*

CHERISHED BY YOU

The next gift card she grabbed was an iTunes card, and her face turned a shade of red as she read aloud: *For the music you can dance to naked.*

Then she peered inside and grabbed the last item sitting at the bottom of the box. A Leo Ingwer ring box.

"Justin . . ." She popped the box open slightly and peeked inside before shutting it abruptly. "There's a ring in there!"

I laughed, taking the box out of her shaking hand. "I know. I bought it."

As I moved to kneel down on one knee in front of her, I explained. "Lying in that hospital bed, I realized that our days here are numbered, that every single day we have left should be cherished."

Tears glistened in her eyes.

Opening the box, I grabbed the round two-carat diamond ring with its antique shank and smiled. "I bought this before the shooting, and I want you to know that because I need you to know this wasn't some impulse decision from getting shot. You know I'm not impulsive. I've thought this through, and even though we haven't been together very long, I know in my heart that I want to spend the rest of my days cherishing them with you. That is if you'll have me." Taking her hand in mine, I took a deep, nervous breath and exhaled it. "Will you marry me?"

"Yes!" she exclaimed, nodding enthusiastically. "Of course, I'll marry you!"

I quickly slid the ring onto her left hand and covered her mouth with mine, sealing the moment with a slow, satisfying kiss.

She broke away first and admired her hand. "Justin, it's gorgeous."

"I'm glad you like it," I said, running my finger along the length of hers. "It took me forever to find the one that reminded me of you."

"I love it," she said, wrapping her hands around my neck. "I love you so much."

"I love you too, panion," I wrapped my arms around her waist and drew her closer to the edge of the couch as I devoured her mouth.

"We still have one more gift to open," she mumbled against my lips. "Trey's."

I pulled her down into my lap on the floor, and grabbed his gift from the coffee table. It was rectangular-shaped and kind of heavy. Tessa ripped the newspaper wrapping off, and when she got down to the large package, I opened the slit at the top and grabbed the item inside. From the feel of the large frame in my hand, I guessed it was a Trey Wilder photograph.

Sliding it out of the package, I heard Tessa gasp and looked down to see what he'd captured.

It was a picture of us.

In my hospital bed, lying together.

On the black, elegant frame, Trey had a small silver plaque engraved with the title, *Bulletproof Love*.

"I can't believe he took such a beautiful picture of us," Tessa said, smiling proudly. "During such a difficult time."

It was really beautiful. The lighting centered around us and our loving embrace, with my arm holding her tightly to my side and her blessing me with one of her easy smiles. The hospital room looked forgotten in the picture, despite us lying in one of the beds. The bandage on my shoulder was hardly noticeable. The only thing I saw when I looked at the photograph was my fiancée.

"There's a note on the back," Tessa stated, reaching around to the backside of the frame. She opened the envelope and smiled as she read aloud, "Tessa and Justin, may this photograph always remind you that no matter what happens, your love for one another is bulletproof; together you can withstand anything."

I brushed a fallen tear from her eye and marveled at the photograph. Out of all his photographs we had hanging in the apartment, this one of us was officially my favorite. "Well, that explains why he wanted us to open it after you opened mine. He knew I was proposing. I actually asked him for permission."

"You did?" she asked incredulously.

"He thought I was either getting you a cat or sex stuff for Christmas." I smiled as I gazed back at her, memorizing the joy splashed across her face. "So, I had to clear that up."

She laughed loudly as she grabbed my face and kissed me hard. "Where are we going to hang his picture?"

"I was thinking the bedroom. For our eyes only."

"Good idea," she agreed, straddling her legs over my hips. "But whose room, yours or mine?"

A thought came to mind. "What about ours?"

Her brows furrowed. "We don't have a room here that's *ours*, though we do sleep in my bed more often than yours."

"We could get a place that's ours," I started, trailing my lips up her neck. "You know, one with spare bedrooms for kids and a big patio for fresh air. A master bedroom where we could hang our photograph and a large office with enough space for both our desks. You'll need a desk for your event planning."

"Somewhere we can make lots of memories and grow old together."

"A place we can cherish for the rest of our lives," I concluded, skimming my hands up and down her sides. "What do you say?"

She angled my head up to her, and right before she kissed me, she said, "Ours sounds perfect."

The End

Extra

Surprised By You

(Love in the City, #3.5)

Tessa

Walking in to Judge's, the excitement radiated off all of us. Newlyweds, Carter and Ellyson Jennings, couldn't keep their hands off each other, while the rest of our gang found bar stools and ordered drinks to celebrate.

We'd just left the hospital after witnessing two of our best friends welcome their beautiful little girl into the world. Maverick Jones and Harper Jennings had started dating at the beginning of the year. The two met while Carter and Elly were planning their wedding; Carter's older sister designed Elly's wedding dress, and Elly introduced the two when Harper volunteered as a mentor at the health clinic in Maverick's gym. Just three months into their relationship, Harper found out she was pregnant, and we couldn't have been happier for them. Fatherhood looked great on Mav, and Harper had always dreamed of becoming a mom.

Now, we had Carter and Elly following in their footsteps as Carter announced earlier that he couldn't wait to meet Baby Jones' cousin.

Our group was expanding, giving us more reason to celebrate, even though we probably would've ended up here regardless of tonight's events. Judge's Bar was owned by another member of our group, Fletcher Haney. He'd inherited it after his grandfather passed away, and we'd made it our regular hangout for years now. Fletcher also had a number of clubs sprinkled throughout the city, which we also frequented, but for the important moments, we favored the laid-back, homey atmosphere Judge's provided.

As usual, Cash sat at the end of the bar so that he could help fill drinks whenever the bartender got busy. He rented the apartment above the bar, so he worked here part-time whenever Fletcher ran short on staff. Next to him sat Justin and Paige, who'd been awfully quiet ever since the baby was born. Justin was an introvert and quiet in general. Paige had a fear of babies and pregnancy, so she likely wanted nothing more than to get the hell out of here. Elly and Carter sat between us, and to my right was Bayler Jennings, Carter's younger sister, and Fletcher.

"I still can't believe you kept Elly's pregnancy a secret for four months!" Bayler stated, shaking her head at Carter.

He smiled and shrugged his shoulders. "She made me, or else I probably would've called the minute the test turned positive."

His excitement was infectious, and I couldn't help smiling, too. Carter had made it perfectly clear after Elly's cancer scare last winter that he wanted to have children with her someday. She'd had one of her ovaries removed after her doctor found a mass, and luckily, the results came back benign. During that time, they'd promised to live life to the fullest, no matter what.

They'd just tied the knot four months ago.

But it was still a surprise that they were able to keep such a huge secret from our group for this long, especially since I worked for Elly as her receptionist at her psych clinic. Thinking back on the last few weeks of work, I recalled her wearing looser clothes, which explained why I never noticed the adorable bump protruding from her belly now.

"I didn't even know you guys were trying!" I said, smiling at Elly.

"Well," she laughed, blushing slightly, "leaving my birth control pills at home was my wedding gift to Carter for the honeymoon."

"We really didn't expect it to happen to fast," he added, linking his fingers through Elly's.

"You still could've told us!" Bayler said, biting the straw to her cocktail.

Elly and Carter exchanged a solemn look, and then she said, "I just wanted to make sure the baby stayed healthy before telling everyone. Now, that I'm further along, I feel better about sharing the news."

"So, when are you due?" Bayler asked.

"February 23rd."

"Are you guys going to find out the sex?" I asked, eagerly. A fun idea for a gender reveal party here at the bar was already brewing inside my head.

"Ugh!" Bayler groaned, rolling her eyes. "I swear to God, if you guys pull a Harper and Mav, and don't tell us the baby's name once you decide, I'm just going to call it whatever I want!"

"Babe," Fletcher laughed, wrapping his arms around her waist. "We all know that won't happen."

"Speaking of secrets . . ." I alluded, eyeing Bayler. "You and Fletcher spent most of this past summer keeping your sexcapades a secret from all of us!"

With that, she buried her head in Fletcher's shoulder and laughed. After their cover was blown, Bayler's commitment issues tore them apart, but tonight, they'd showed up at the hospital hand-in-hand, happier than I'd ever seen them.

"You Jennings are just great secret keepers!" I stated, causing Elly to nearly spit out her water in hysterics.

"Are you kidding me?!" Elly exclaimed, rolling her eyes. She dabbed the corner of her mouth with a napkin, and then pointed at Carter. "Do you know how many times I had to use sex to shut him up so he wouldn't run out and tell the world we'd made a baby?"

Laughing, I looked over at Carter, whose smile had turned into a sly smirk with his wife's confession. "It wasn't that bad of a deal."

"Not for you, but when I was bloated and dealing with morning sickness, it was," she continued, shaking her head.

Bayler held her hand up in object. "Okay, spare us the barfy details, please!"

I swiveled slightly on my stool and nudged Elly's arm. "So, you never answered my question about the sex?"

"It was amazing!" Carter interjected in a playful manner. "A secluded beach, my beautiful, new wife completely naked under the sta—"

"My ears!" Bayler shrieked, slapping her hands over her ears and glaring at her brother. "She didn't mean *that* kind of sex, you idiot!"

"It *was* amazing," Elly said, smiling blissfully at Carter, "but let's keep that to ourselves."

"Whatever!" I scoffed, waving for Carter to continue. "Some of us have to live vicariously."

"That's my brother," Bayler said with a cringe.

"So, you can tell us about your latest romp with Fletcher after he's done."

Carter groaned, wrinkling his nose. "No, thank you."

I loved teasing them.

"Okay, fine!" I laughed. "But just tell me, do I get to throw a gender reveal party or not?"

"Ooh." Elly perked up in her seat and the smile on her face widened. "A gender reveal party? That sounds like more fun than a baby shower."

"Yeah, I thought we could have it right here at Judge's. We could invite all your friends and family, and make an evening out of it. I already have the perfect idea for revealing the gender to everyone."

"That sounds perfect!" she exclaimed, wrapping her arms around me in a hug. "Thank you so much!"

"You're welcome!" I replied, breaking away from her. "Congratulations, again! You're going to be a great mom."

Picking up my margarita, I lifted it up in the air for a toast and smiled at each one of my friends. "To having babies!"

"To having babies!" they cheered.

***

When last call finally came, the eight of us finished our drinks and prepared to leave. Walking outside, I twisted the belt of my coat around my waist and pulled it tight. It was a little after two o'clock in the morning, and we had just shut down Fletcher's bar. The October air was chilly, and the wind sliced through us like a knife, making our breaths more conspicuous in the night.

Feeling tipsy and numb from the cold, I stared off into space, while Elly and Carter hailed a cab with Paige, and Fletcher and Bayler piled into his car to head back to his place. I rubbed my hands together for warmth, regretting the fact that I'd left my gloves at home.

"Tessa?" I heard, turning my head toward the sound of my name.

To my right stood my biggest crush, Justin Jameson, and he was smiling at me. He didn't know how I felt about him, of course, because he was the most unobservant man on the planet. No matter how sexy I looked in my pink fit and flare dress that fashioned curves I didn't have, dressing to impress him was completely useless. I could've been standing here naked on the sidewalk, and he probably would've looked away and handed me a coat to cover up.

He was a gentleman like that, and that was just one of his many traits I admired.

"Yeah?" I asked, mirroring his smile.

"Would you like to share a cab?" he asked chivalrously, gesturing to the back door of the cab idling at the curb.

Could I really trust myself to sit in a cab with him for thirty minutes and not make a stupid move?

Probably not.

"Thanks," I said, politely waving him off. "But I think I'll just take the train home."

His brows furrowed, and the dimples disappeared from his face. "The train? You can't take the train at this hour; it's not safe."

Even though growing up in Grand Concourse taught me how to survive a late night train ride, he was probably right. Thankfully, I didn't live in such a neighborhood anymore.

"It's not that late," I insisted, rolling my eyes at him.

Scoffing at my response, he opened the back door of the cab, and then took my hand in his and pulled me toward him. "Get in the cab."

"Okay, okay," I teased drunkenly, plopping down into the backseat and sliding across the leather bench. "I'm in."

"Much better." He climbed in beside me, and proceeded to rattle off my address for the driver as he steered the car back into traffic.

"We can go to your place first," I offered in a serious tone. "I know it's closer."

"I don't care whose place is closest," he said, shooting me his undeniably gorgeous smirk that made my insides tingle. "The lady comes first."

If all men thought that way, the world would be a happier place.

"All right." Relaxing back against the seat, I continued admiring him from the passenger side. Years ago, when I first became friends with Elly and everyone, I remembered meeting Justin and thinking he was the most gorgeous creature put on this planet. Now, after hanging around him numerous times at the beach, I knew underneath the leather jacket, sweater and jeans he currently wore, he looked like a man who just ran in from the ocean, carrying his surfboard under his arm, the lean muscles of his abs and the brawn of his arms and legs flexing with each step. He looked like summertime with his naturally tanned skin and his sandy hair kept long all year round, giving him the option to rock the man bun whenever he desired. Tonight, he had it down, parted neatly in the middle, allowing the strands to frame his chiseled face and further daring my idle hands to take a swim through it. His warm, hazel-blue eyes looked like a body of water some days, and glowed like a golden halo set ablaze by blue flames, but right now, the heat from them boring into mine ignited a carnal need from within that had me pressing my thighs together for relief.

"What?" he asked playfully.

"You're pretty."

Did I just say that out loud? How drunk am I?

He laughed. "Thanks?"

I joined him in laughter, trying my best to cover up my flushed, embarrassed cheeks.

Dear driver, please go faster so I don't use my drunkenness as an excuse to make a move on a friend. Amen.

Amen? I thought, giggling aloud.

Never attended church in my entire life, and here I was trying to pray.

To the cab driver.

"What's so funny?" Justin pried.

"Nothing." Resting my head against the window, I turned my attention to the buildings passing by us outside. At this time of night, it was a little easier to get around the city, but not much. Traffic still piled up downtown in the city that never slept, making it difficult to get to where we needed to go. Although, it would've taken longer on the train with all of its stops, which only reminded me of why I was in the cab and with whom.

With my hands sitting in my lap, I tried to mentally simmer the raw, sexual desire racing through my body, but it'd been so long since I last had sex, my hymen probably grew back together.

Is that even possible?

No, it can't be.

"Tessa," Justin said, interrupting my thoughts. "We're here."

"Really?" I asked incredulously, looking over his shoulder, as if he were lying.

Sure enough. Home sweet home.

Grabbing my purse, I started to dig around for money to pay the driver, but when Justin's hand covered mine, I stopped. I couldn't move with him touching me, even if it was just the simplest gesture of his hand over mine. I wanted more. I wanted to thread my fingers through his and lead him up to my room.

"It's on me," he offered, smiling. He handed the driver a few bills, leaving him a generous tip given the late hour, and then crawled out of the cab with me. "Come on, let's get you upstairs."

"Wait," I said, halting my steps. "You're coming up?"

He looked at me like I was crazy for questioning him, and maybe I was, but if he came upstairs, there was a very good chance I wouldn't be able to stop myself from doing something . . . like kissing him.

"Of course," he said, placing his hand on my lower back. "I want to make sure you get inside safe."

"O-okay," I stuttered, leading us up the steps, keys in hand.

Jiggling the first key into the metal slot, I turned it and unlocked the door to my building. Habitually, I reached for the second key on my ring and headed toward the elevator.

"I'm on the fifth floor," I stated, pressing the silver button on the wall.

Justin nodded wordlessly and dropped his hand from my back, putting some distance between us.

My building had the slowest elevator, but it was better than taking the stairs in four-inch heels. When we finally reached my floor, I stepped out in a hurry to get away from the awkward silence that had settled between us. I was the one making this awkward with my pent-up feelings. Justin looked cool as ice, sauntering along behind me without a care in the world. He had no idea how much I loved his relaxed swagger and the scent of his spicy, crisp cologne lingering around me. I could ignore my feelings for him when we were around the rest of our friends, but when I was alone with him, my body and mind became hypersensitive to him.

"This is it." I nodded to my door with a weak smile lining my lips. "I made it here safe."

With my back to him, I unlocked the apartment, stepped inside, and flipped on the lights. I tossed my keys back inside my purse, and then my nervous hands went to my coat and attempted to untie the sash, until I heard him clear his throat behind me.

I looked over my shoulder and found him leaning against the door jam, his hands stuffed inside the front pockets of his jeans. In the light of my apartment, his bloodshot eyes and the alcohol-induced glaze swimming in them made his intoxication more obvious. I couldn't remember the last time I'd see Justin this drunk. He was usually more reserved when we all went out, the one who always kept himself in control and took care of those of us who didn't. But tonight, he was standing in my doorway, and all I could think about was walking up to him and kissing him.

And that was the last thing I should have been thinking about, given his uninhibited state.

"Are you going to invite me in?" he asked, his lips curling up into his signature, adorable smirk.

I could play this two ways. One, I could invite him in and make up the couch for him so he could sleep off the booze, or two, I could invite him in and act out every scenario I've ever imagined doing with him and blame it on the alcohol come morning.

If I was more sober and my libido wasn't such a demanding bitch, I probably would've gone with one, but I didn't.

"Maybe," I replied.

Sliding my coat off my shoulders, I tossed it over a chair and walked back over to him. I gazed up and found dark, hooded eyes peering back at me.

Does he want me back?

There was only one way to find out.

Lifting my hands, I brushed his hair out of his face and said in a soft voice, "I want to try something."

And then I covered his lips with mine, and the kiss that ensued was electrifying, sending every nerve in my body into a perpetual state of want. I hoisted my arms around his shoulders as his hands anxiously grabbed at my waist and hauled me up against him.

Without breaking the kiss, I walked us back into my apartment, and he kicked the door shut behind him. He led us over to the nearest countertop in the kitchen, and then lifted me up and moved to stand between my legs as he wrapped mine around his lean waist. Dragging his tongue along the seam of my lips, he silently begged me to open, and I willingly complied, eager for more. He stroked inside me and moaned as I slowly tangled around him and sucked.

"Tessa," he pleaded in a soft tone.

I ignored him and attempted to deepen the kiss, but he broke away and leaned his forehead against mine on a groan.

"Tessa, Tessa, Tessa." He shook his head, as if he was trying to erase the kiss from his mind. "We shouldn't do this. We're both drunk."

Cupping his face in my hands, I pressed a chaste kiss to his lips and calmly encouraged him not to deny us this moment. "I don't care. I want you."

He ran his hands down my sides, and his eyes traced the movement until they settled on my waist. Gripping my hips tight, he buried his head into my neck and breathed me in. "You have no idea how many times I've wanted to do this with you. Drunk is not how I pictured it."

"So, we'll sober up," I promised, tilting my head to the right.

Laughing, his teeth grazed the flesh of my neck and bit at me. "And how do you propose we do that?"

"Preferably naked in the bedroom," I replied.

His laughter deepened, and the sound of it trembled through my body straight down to my love box. I kicked off my heels and then took his hands in mine. He peered down at me smiling and helped me off the counter. Standing with my back to his front, he moved my long brown hair over my shoulder and kissed the back of my neck. "Lead the way."

Once we were in my room, he shucked his jacket and took a seat on the edge of my bed, eyeing my short, pink dress.

"Come here," he said, in a serious tone.

I walked over to him and his legs widened for me to stand in between them. He pulled me close by the backs of my thighs. With my hands resting on his shoulders, he proceeded to run his hands up my legs and under my dress, dragging it away from my body the further he went. When he had it up to my shoulders, I lifted my arms in the air and he gracefully discarded the dress from my body. Standing in only my pink, lace thong, insecurity settled in my stomach as his gaze landed on my bare chest.

"No bra tonight?" he mused, appreciatively.

"There was one built in to the dress," I explained, looking down at my B-cups. "It's not like I would've needed one anyway."

Running his hands from my waist to my chest, he palmed my breasts. "You're perfect the way you are."

Blushing slightly, I reached for the bottom of his sweater. "And you're still fully clothed."

He pressed a kiss to my sternum, and then grabbed the back of his sweater and pulled it over his head. A white t-shirt followed his sweater as I worked on unbuckling his belt. Once he was naked from the waist up, he flicked open the button on his jeans, pushed them off over his hips and then kicked them off along with his shoes and socks.

"Commando tonight?" I asked, eyeing the size and length of him. He was just how I imagined he would be: long and thick. One look at the size of his hands and feet made a woman speculate the size of his cock, and I'd been right.

"There were boxers built in to the jeans," he mocked, trying his best to hold back laughter.

"Oh, you're a funny man now, huh?" I countered, pushing him back on the bed before jumping him.

He caught me and settled me on top of him, my legs straddling his thighs, and I leaned down to kiss him. As our kisses deepened and tongues tangoed, our hands ran rampant, touching every inch of each other, until my hand settled around his rigid cock and began stroking him.

The smile dropped from his face as he tilted his head back and allowed need to take over.

"Who's laughing now?" I asked, in a soft, teasing tone.

His hips rocked up into me, but then he grabbed my wrist roughly mid stroke. "If you keep doing that, I'm not going to last."

That caught my attention. The teasing had to stop because I didn't want this to be over within seconds. I wanted a whole night with him, even if it was just one night; I'd take it.

"Okay," I murmured, setting my hand on his chest.

"But you can," he remarked, before flipping me onto my back.

Dazed and slightly confused, I smiled up at him. "What?"

"You can last all night," he explained, kneeling between my legs. He kissed my neck and then trailed kisses down my body as he continued, "It's really not fair that women can have multiple orgasms."

Goosebumps broke out across my skin with the feel of his stubble and warm breath brushing up against my skin. "Is that so?"

"Mhmm," he said, grabbing the waistband of my panties and tugging. "Are you particularly fond of these?"

"Of course not, I could always go—"

The lady in the box interrupted this train of thought to bask in the wonderful feel of my panties being torn off.

Whoa.

Pleasure trembled through me so hard and quick, I nearly orgasmed right then and there.

"Commando?" he questioned with a smirk, tossing the pink material over his shoulder and finishing my sentence for me.

"Yes," I sighed, resting my head back against a pillow. All he'd done so far was kiss me, touch me and rip ten-dollar panties off my body, and I was already out of breath.

Justin positioned my legs over his shoulders, and then continued his onslaught of kisses by pressing his lips to the inside of my thighs and sucking on the tender flesh. He ran his fingers along my clit, playfully tugging and teasing me until I moaned an incoherent whisper about how good it felt, and then he moved southward to my opening and pushed two digits inside, causing my back to bow in a torturous ache for more. He moved with such ease and finesse around my body, it was as if he had me memorized. And maybe he did. If he had thought about this before, like I had, he already knew everything he wanted to do to me. Every touch, every kiss, every move he made was completely thought out with the sole purpose of pleasuring me. Even drunken foreplay with him was better than any sex I'd had thus far in my life.

"You're gorgeous," he muttered, pumping his fingers inside of me.

"Oh, God," I cried, closing my eyes. Rocking hard against his hand, I felt my release spiral out of control as he beckoned me closer and closer to the irresistible chaos.

"Tell me what you need."

"More," I whimpered, running my fingers through his hair and latching on tight.

"More what?" he asked, his mouth just centimeters from where I wanted it.

My muscles tightened around him, so I begged. "Justin!"

In a flash, he removed his fingers and replaced them with his mouth, kissing me in a whole other way than he had all night. His tongue licked inside me, matching the fury of pleasure his fingers delivered to my clit. The build up was unlike anything I'd ever experienced before as I cried and writhed against him until my orgasm broke from the inside out, like a rubber band stretched too far, sending me into outer space with the snap of its release, where I reveled in the glory of an euphoric lack of gravity.

When I entered the atmosphere of my bedroom again, I found Justin rolling on a condom, and I felt like crying at the beautiful sight of his strong body hovering over mine, so determined and protective. How this night went from physical to utterly intimate was a mystery to me, but I blinked back the tears and kissed him hard in an attempt to get my emotions in check.

Threading his fingers through mine, he pressed me into the mattress and brought his mouth to my chest where he continued paying my body the attention it so desperately craved from him. He lapped and teased the swells of my breasts with his tongue, using his teeth to bite and graze and his lips to suck my nipples into hard, swollen tips. Then he blew on them, and sensation flooded my system once again, causing a moan to slip from my lips.

Wrapping my legs around his hips, I rocked up into him, just enough so that the tip of his cock dipped through my wetness.

"Tessa," he warned, looking up at me.

"I want you with me," I said innocently, reaching for his cock. I positioned him at my opening, and then caressed his face with my other hand. "Please."

With that, he gripped my hips and thrust all the way inside, and then leaned his head against mine before covering my lips with his.

"You feel too good," he moaned, pulling out slowly and pushing back in the same torturous manner.

"Faster," I said, linking my ankles together behind his back. At my request, he made his movements even slower, and playfully yawned.

"Like this?" he asked, with his cock almost out of me.

"Seriously!" I whined, wiggling my hips closer to him.

He laughed and then without another word, he slammed into me hard and fast, eliciting a deep moan from me as I reveled in the feel of his smooth shaft hitting that lucky spot.

"Too. Fucking. Good," he repeated, enunciating each word with a hard thrust.

"God, I know." My hips went to work, meeting each one of his strokes that grew rougher than the last, and before I knew it, I was digging my nails into his shoulders and readying myself for another out-of-body experience.

"Justin," I begged, as my insides gripped him like a glove. "I'm almost—"

"I know." He reached down and started rubbing circles against my swollen clit.

"That's it!" I yelped, arching into him as my body started to quake with tremors. My orgasm erupted from me so hard and fast, it felt like my bones were shaking as I rocketed back to the heavenly place he took me before. "Oh, God. Justin!"

Then my name fell from his lips, and he joined me, pumping into me not once, twice, but three more times before his orgasm overtook him, and he came violently, with his muscles flexed above me, appearing more handsome than I'd ever seen him before.

He slumped against me and buried his head in my neck; the smell of sex lingered. Our bodies were slick with perspiration, our lungs still supplicating for air, but I'd never felt better in my entire life. I wished I could freeze this moment of peaceful satisfaction, so that we never had to leave it in the past.

Justin rolled to my side and gazed over at me. His tired eyes looked like the ocean now, beautiful and blue, and right now, they were looking at me with contentment. Justin was so introverted most of the time, but tonight, I'd seen an array of emotions from him. I wondered if it was from the sex with me, or the alcohol.

He rested a hand on my hip, and smiled. "What are you thinking about?"

"Nothing," I lied, shaking my head. If he knew how often I thought about him, he'd probably run from my bedroom.

"Liar," he said, pulling me closer to him. "We just had sex. You can tell me anything, and I know you're thinking about something; no one ever thinks about nothing."

"Yeah," I said softly, resting my head on his shoulder. Emotion knotted in my throat as tears threatened my eyes again. Despite my feelings for him, I knew there couldn't be more between us. He was my friend, and as introverted as he was, I knew he hated change. Tonight, we could blame the alcohol, and tomorrow, we could pretend none of this ever happened.

"Tessa?" he asked, turning my face toward him. He noticed the tears and caressed my cheek. "Talk to me."

"This felt like more than sex," I confessed, eyeing him cautiously.

He sighed, nodding. "I know."

"You felt it, too?" I asked in disbelief.

"No," he replied solemnly, shaking his head this time. "Because this isn't—"

"What do you mean, no? You just said you knew."

Cupping my face in his hands, sadness clouded his eyes as he pressed a chaste kiss to my lips, and then whispered, "This isn't real, Tessa."

"What?" I asked angrily, confused by his words. He opened his mouth to speak, but I continued, "This is too real. What I feel for you is real! The sex we just had, the orgasms you gave me, the drinks we had earlier with our friends; it's all real!"

"If you'd just wake up, you'd realize that this was all just a—"

CHERISHED BY YOU

Opening my eyes, I jolted up in bed gasping for air. I could hear the sound of my heart racing in my ears as the quiet darkness of my room greeted me. The sheet was gathered around my waist, and the bed was empty on either side of me. A film of sweat covered my skin.

Justin wasn't here.

It really *was* just a dream.

But it felt so real.

How is that even possible?

Pushing the covers further down with my feet, I studied myself. My pajama shorts and cami top covered my body, which made me feel a little better knowing I wasn't completely naked. My hair still sat in a messy bun on top of my head, only slightly looser now. My fair skin was still flushed.

I lay back down and allowed my breathing to even out and my body to cool off. I couldn't get past the fact that the dream—specifically the sex—had felt so *incredibly* real. I could still feel the touch of his hands, the softness of his lips, and the weight of his body against mine. Staring up at the ceiling, I thought about the orgasms and wondered . . . *Did those really happen? Could a woman really come in her sleep? Twice?*

Reaching a hand inside my shorts to investigate, my eyes widened in shock as I found the cotton material of my thong totally soaked from my arousal.

Well, that's never happened before!

The best sex of my life, and it was only a dream!

Checking the time on my alarm clock, I realized I only had thirty more minutes until I needed to get up for work, so I stayed awake and thought about Justin Jameson.

Surprise, surprise.

Acknowledgements

I cherish each and every one of the following people for helping me share the Love in the City stories with the world. You have all impacted my writing in so many ways, and I'm truly grateful for all the hard work and encouragement you continuously throw my way.

Beth Suit at BB Books: You're seriously the best editor, but you're so much more than an editor to me, and I cannot thank you enough for everything you do. Not only do you take the time to truly understand my characters and their stories, but you also believe in them as much as I do. Your encouragement and friendship means the world to me, and I thank God every day that I get to work with an editor as awesome as you.

Aprilla the Hun aka April Faulkner: Thank you for always making the copyediting process so stress-free! Copyediting a book isn't a job to you. It's an opportunity to experience a story before anyone else and make it the best it can be, and I love that you seize that opportunity with every story I write. Thank you for always giving me your best, and for shaping my work into tip-top condition!

Brenda Wright at Formatting Done Wright: Your efficiency in formatting a book to perfection is topnotch! I thank you for being so reliable, and for always turning my stories into beautiful masterpieces.

Michelle Preast at IndieBookCovers: This cover is my favorite out of all the Love in the City covers. I know the teal was hard to work with, especially since we didn't want the couple looking like the Hulk, but being the talented graphic designer you are, you took the time to get it just right, and I appreciate that. You're simply a dream to work with, and I thank you for always making my book cover dreams come true!

Nuss' Navy: You're truly the best fans! Thank you for all the encouragement you always give while I'm writing. Having a place where I can go and talk about my characters with others who enjoy them is so much fun; I hope you enjoy the group as much as I do. Thank you for always being eager for more from my Love in the City gang. I promise we have so much more to share with you! When I write a sexy, cute, or hilarious line, I immediately want to share it with you guys. Thank you for always respecting my work and my mission in Nuss' Navy to never put down anyone in this industry whether it be the writer, the publisher or your fellow readers. You're the best group of sailors a girl could ask for, and I thank you for anchoring your hearts to my books.

Book Bloggers: To all of you who have helped spread the word about my books, thank you, thank you, thank you! I know it's hard to run a blog, and it still blows my mind that most of you do it for free. You should probably be making thousands by now. But seriously, thank you for generously sharing your love of reading with others. Your posts, your reviews, your awesome teaser graphics do not go unnoticed, and I appreciate all your hard work and everything you do to support the writing industry. I know that type of passion as an avid reader myself, and I thank you for channeling it through your book blogs to share with the world. You're an imperative part of this industry, whether you're a big or small blog, all of you make an impact. We writers need you as much as you need our next book; may we never forget that!

My family, friends, Gunner, and Stag: Thank you for always understanding when the characters and the story come before anything else. I know it may sound ridiculous to you, but I can't shut my brain off from the stories it wants to tell and the characters it wants to create. Thank you for always supporting my creative passion, even when you say or do things that could end up in a book. I love you.

To you, the reader, thank you for taking a chance on Justin and Tessa's story. I hope you enjoyed it! My writing may be new to you, or it may be material you already love reading, but I truly appreciate you branching out to try new authors. Stay tuned for Paige's story in the next installment of the Love in the City series!

About the Author

Steph Nuss was born and raised in rural Kansas, where she currently resides with her black Labrador son named Gunner. She grew up with a passion for reading and writing. When she's not immersed into the land of fiction, she enjoys listening to music that came before her time, watching movies and reruns of her favorite shows, and hanging out with her family and friends. She also has a bachelor's degree in psychology that she'll never use…unless she's profiling her characters of course.

Follow Steph
www.stephnuss.com
Nuss' Navy
Facebook
Twitter
Goodreads

Made in the USA
Middletown, DE
15 April 2017